Dead
Aim

Dead Aim

Iris Johansen

BANTAM BOOKS
New York Toronto London Sydney Auckland

DEAD AIM

A Bantam Book

Published by Bantam Dell
A Division of Random House, Inc.
New York, New York

Book design by Virginia Norey

ISBN 0-553-80246-1

Manufactured in the United States of America

Dead
Aim

1

Arapahoe Junction, Colorado
October 15

"I know I'm late, dammit." Alex Graham's hand clenched on her cell phone. "I'll get those pictures to you as soon as I can."

"You'd get them to me sooner if you'd stop working in the rubble and start taking pictures of those rescue workers whose job it is to do it," Jim Karak said sarcastically. "Old news is no news, Alex. That dam broke almost a week ago and the magazine goes to press in two days."

"They're still digging survivors from the landslide caused by the dam break."

"Then you should be taking warm, heroic pictures instead of manning a shovel. You're breaking one of the cardinal rules. You're becoming part of the story."

"There may be people alive beneath that—" It was no use. Karak had one priority and that was the story. "You'll get the pictures." She hung up and leaned back against the wall and rubbed her temple. God, she was tired. She'd be lucky if Karak didn't call her back and tell her to find another magazine to publish her work. She wasn't being fair and certainly not professional. If she hadn't had a decent track record before this, Karak would have dumped her days ago.

"Problems?" Sarah Logan and her dog, Monty, were standing in the doorway of the trailer.

"A few." Alex grimaced as she rose to her feet. "It seems I'm not doing my job. I'm not focusing on what's important."

"You could have fooled me." Sarah filled Monty's bowl with water and sat down on the floor beside him while he drank. "We found a baby alive in that hellhole this morning. I'd say that was pretty important."

"Me too." Alex smiled. "Screw Karak."

Sarah didn't return her smile. "I don't want you to lose your job, Alex. I know how much your work means to you. There are other volunteers out there helping to dig."

Alex lifted her brows. "Oh, then you have too much help?"

"You know there's no such thing in a disaster like this. We have to work fast or— Okay, we need you. I just don't want you to be hurt. God knows there's enough pain in this world."

And Sarah Logan witnessed a good deal of it, Alex thought. She and her golden retriever, Monty, were in a canine search-and-rescue team, and Alex had run across her on half a dozen disaster sites during the last five years. In the horror of natural and man-made tragedies, a strong bond of friendship had been forged. "I'll be okay."

"Your editor is right. This isn't your job." She shook her head. "Look at you. You're covered in dirt from head to toe. Your hands are bleeding from that shovel and you haven't slept in twenty-four hours."

"Have you?"

Sarah ignored the question. "And it's more than your hands that are bleeding. Take a step back, Alex. It will break you if you get too close to it. Believe me, I know."

"It's not as though I haven't been to other disaster sites."

"But then you weren't as involved. You were taking photographs and helping in the first-aid tent. You weren't uncovering the bodies of people you hoped would be alive."

She didn't want to think of those bodies. There had been

too many in the last few days. "Yet you do it all the time. You could stay home and live soft, and yet every time there's a call, you and Monty are off and running. I'm surprised your husband doesn't raise hell."

"He doesn't like it, but he understands." Sarah frowned. "But we're not talking about me. I've watched you work and there's no one more dedicated. You love what you do and you've told me a dozen times that your job is to tell the story. Don't get sidetracked."

"I'm not sidetracked. I'll get it done." She bent down and stroked Monty's soft fur. "I just can't— I'll get it done."

Sarah stared at her, troubled. "I don't think you should accept assignments like this anymore. I've seen it coming since Ground Zero, but it's getting worse. You've . . . changed."

Steel and concrete and that stinging smoke that seemed to cover the world like a shroud.

"Ground Zero changed all of us."

Sarah and Monty crawling among the ruins while Alex watched helplessly.

Sarah and Alex holding desperately to each other while the tears poured down their faces.

Sarah nodded. "But I had someone to go home to while I healed. I should have made you come with me."

"Life had to go on. I had to go on." She shrugged. "And if I took some baggage with me, then that's the way it had to be. I'm usually okay. This one is rough. It's brought back too many memories."

"But it's not the same," Sarah said gently. "We've found survivors here, Alex. Seventy-two so far."

"That's not enough," she whispered. "It's never enough. I can't stand by and let—" She cleared her throat and changed the subject. "Is it your rest time?"

Sarah shook her head. "I just had to get Monty some water. My canteen was empty. We still have a few hours to work until dark. It's less dangerous for Monty if he can see clearly what's out there." She paused. "But we've just had two bits of good news. The President is coming here next week."

"It's about time. Vice President Shepard was here the day after the dam break."

"Yeah, I was impressed. But it's when the President shows up that FEMA and all the aid organizations get a boost."

"That's good." She made a face. "Maybe I can convince Karak I was only waiting for Andreas to show up so that I could give him a really big story." She shook her head. "Nah, I'm no good at lying. Besides, security is so tight around the President right now that I wouldn't get within a mile of him."

"I'm surprised he's coming at all. There was a bombing at the embassy in Mexico City last night."

"The same terrorist group?"

Sarah nodded. "Matanza claimed it. And an effigy of Andreas was left burning on the lawn."

"Bastards." It was the third embassy attack by the Guatemalan terrorist group in the last six months. If it wasn't the Middle East, it was Guatemala or Venezuela. Juan Cordoba and his Matanza group had always been rabid revolutionaries in their own country, but now—fueled by drug money and Al Qaeda support—they had grown powerful enough to take aim at Andreas and the administration that was trying to stabilize the party in power. It seemed impossible to Alex that there had ever been a time when her country hadn't been surrounded by terror and ugliness and threats. Yet she could remember a childhood filled with trust and innocence and the belief that nothing really bad could come knocking on her door. The memory filled her with frustration and anger and immense sadness. "I hope your second bit of good news is better than your first."

"Hey, you have to take the bitter with the sweet. At least Andreas isn't letting anyone scare him into ignoring people who need him. He should be safe enough visiting this site. All the evidence points to a natural disaster here." She smiled.

"And the preliminary report on the ground on the other side of the dam says it appears to be fairly stable. They're sending some teams up there tomorrow morning to do a final check. When the landslide buried this area, they were afraid the ground on the other side might be compromised."

"Jesus. That's all these poor people need. Another landslide."

"They tried to evacuate everyone from that area just for safety's sake. But it looks like they can go back home." Sarah stroked Monty's head. "Time to go back to work, boy." She stood up and headed for the door. "And it's a good time for you to take some photographs."

"How bossy can you get?" Alex followed her and stood in the doorway, gazing out at the disaster site. Every time she looked at the devastation it made her sick. The Arapahoe Dam had broken five days earlier and the water had rushed down into the valley below, killing over a hundred and twenty people. But the series of landslides caused by the explosive force of the water on either side of the valley was the horror they were dealing with now. The rock slides had buried the homes and businesses of Arapahoe Junction under tons of rock, and the area was still so unstable the rescue had to be done painstakingly by hand, not machine. Her glance shifted across the jagged wreck of the dam to the hills on the other side. The rocky terrain looked blessedly sturdy in a shaky world.

Christ, she was glad there wasn't going to be another horror piled on top of this one.

"Stop looking at it," Sarah called back to her. "Take those photos."

Sure, take the pictures. Ignore the fact that there might be more people alive under those rocks.

"Promise me," Sarah said.

"I promise. I'll take the damn photos. I'll get them and send them out today." She grabbed her shovel, which was leaning against the trailer. As Sarah had said, there was still light and the job on this side of the gorge was monumental. "But not now. I can't do it now. . . ."

It was late afternoon when Alex stopped working and went back to the trailer to get her camera.

She'd cut it close and she'd have to work fast to get the photos before dark. Well, if she didn't get all she needed she'd improvise.

A helicopter was descending at the first-aid tent a few hundred yards away from the trailer and she waved at Ken Nader, the pilot, as he got out of the aircraft.

He waved back and called, "I brought you that special lens to replace the one you said you damaged."

"Thanks. I don't need it right now. I'll be over later to get it." She turned and started up the hill.

The hillside was still crawling with men and women carefully picking away at the rocks. She'd gotten to know a few of them this week as they'd worked side by side. Janet Delsey was a resident of the town that had been buried beneath the landslide. She'd been in Denver when the tragedy happened. She worked in the local library, and her parents had not been found yet.

Alex focused and took the picture.

Bill Adams was a truck driver who had been passing through when he'd heard about the dam. He'd parked his rig and volunteered to help.

She snapped the picture.

Carey Melway was a college student, full of idealism and hope, who had come down from Salt Lake City. Alex had watched him change from a kid to an adult in these last few days.

She took the picture.

Dead Aim

She took four rolls of film in the next hour. The volunteers, the canine rescue teams, the flooded gorge.

"You left it a little late." Sarah was carefully making her way down the side of the mountain, followed by Monty. "Are you going to have enough material?"

"Too much." She looked at Janet Delsey again. "Do you think she has any chance of finding her parents alive?"

"A chance, if we can get to them in time. At least this isn't a mud slide. There are pockets of air beneath those rocks." She motioned for Monty. "I have to get down and feed him his dinner and vitamins. Are you almost finished?"

Alex shook her head. "I've got most of the human-interest shots, but I need a photograph that tells the big story, the scope of the rescue operation."

She waved her hand. "Good luck. You'll need it."

Sarah was right. It was difficult to encompass the full depth of a tragedy when you were on top of it.

On top of it.

Her gaze flew across the gorge. The terrain was higher there and it probably afforded a view of both the flooded valley and the workers laboring on the landslide. Sarah had said they were ninety percent sure the ground over there was safe.

If she could get across the gorge.

She couldn't walk across it or swim across it. Which left only one other means of transportation.

She turned and hurried down the slope toward the first-aid tent.

The helicopter circled and then dipped closer to the trees. "If that ground looks even a little wobbly, I'm not leaving you here," Ken Nader told Alex grimly. "You got the aerial shots. That should be enough for you. I don't know why I let you talk me into this."

"Because you're a good guy and you knew I had to have

these pictures. And you can see it's safe here. The worst that can happen to me is if I fall down that slope into the floodwaters." She grinned as she stowed her camera in her backpack. "And if I'm that clumsy, then I deserve to drown. Just go back to the first-aid tent in case they have an emergency and pick me up in an hour."

"You'd better be here." He set down in a glade in the trees. "I don't like this, Alex."

"It will be fine. I'm not stupid. I don't take chances." She jumped out of the helicopter. "Thanks, Ken." She adjusted her backpack with her equipment, waved, and turned away. "One hour . . ."

It took her fifteen minutes before she could get out of the forest and start climbing the hill toward the huge red rock on the pinnacle she'd seen from the other side of the gorge.

The sun was going down and twilight was hovering.

Hurry. Get up there before it's dark.

She was quickly loading and adjusting her camera in the last few minutes before she reached the pinnacle.

Now, if she had enough light . . .

Oh, my God.

The entire valley was spread before her. The tops of houses drowned in the floodwaters below. Moving lanterns and floodlights dotted the site of the landslide. Men and women looking small and helpless as ants trying to stop the death and destruction.

She drew a deep, shaky breath, raised the camera, and took the picture.

Then she took another and another.

She didn't stop until it was fully dark and she could see only the lanterns and floodlights.

How long had she been here? she wondered as she repacked her equipment and started down the hill. Probably too long, but she hadn't heard Ken's helicopter, so she still had time to get to the glade. He'd wait anyway. In spite of his threat, he wouldn't leave her there.

Her pace quickened when she heard the rotors of the helicopter. Strange, she hadn't seen the aircraft lights when she'd been looking out over the gorge. She supposed it could have been circling and come in from the east, but she couldn't—

"There's Powers. Hurry up, for God's sake." A man's voice, harsh, rough, coming from around the turn on the trail ahead.

She stopped in surprise. What the hell? It couldn't be a camper in this time of crisis, but it could be one of the engineers or scientists who had been examining the remains of the dam. She slowly moved closer.

"That's it. Let's go." Another voice, deeper, guttural.

"Keep your flashlight on to guide him in."

The helicopter was louder, descending, almost overhead. Still no lights.

Something was definitely not as it should be.

She edged into the trees as she rounded the bend. Two men were standing in the clearing where Ken had dropped her, their flashlights held shoulder-high. A helicopter was now hovering close to the ground.

As it landed, a bright light pierced the darkness. Her gaze flew to the sky. Ken's helicopter. The other helicopter had been so close she hadn't noticed the sound of Ken's approach.

But she saw it now. Ken's lights beamed down on the helicopter and the men on the ground, lighting the glade with daylight clarity. It illuminated not only the men's features but the rage and the fear in their expressions.

One man was shouting at the pilot. She couldn't hear the words, but she saw the pilot lift a rifle.

My God, he was pointing—

A fiery explosion lit the sky as the bullet hit Ken's helicopter's gas tank.

Iris Johansen

"No!" She didn't know she screamed the word until the taller man whirled to face the trees where she was standing.

She ran.

She heard an oath and then a crashing in the bushes behind her.

She zigzagged through the trees.

Don't go up the trail. She'd be trapped on the pinnacle.

Down the slope toward the flooded valley.

A bullet whistled by her ear.

They were closer.

Her chest was heaving as she struggled for breath.

The slope was steep here, and she lost her footing and slid ten feet down the incline.

"We don't have the time. Powers wants us out of here. Get back to the helicopter and let it bury the bitch."

She risked a look over her shoulder as she got to her feet. The men had turned and were climbing back up the slope. Then they were out of sight.

She couldn't believe that they'd just abandoned the hunt and gone back up the slope. She had to get to the bottom of the hill and try to get across the flooded valley.

But why had they left? Why had they run out of time?

Let it bury the bitch.

Bury.

Let it bury— Jesus.

The ground rumbled and then moved beneath her feet. She glanced up at the top of the hill. Huge rocks were tumbling toward her down the hill.

Landslide.

It would be on her in seconds. No time to get out of the way.

Bury the bitch.

Bury the bitch.

She'd be *damned* if she'd let those bastards bury her. Screw them.

Dead Aim

She tore off her backpack and dropped it to the ground. She ran to the edge of the slope and jumped the thirty feet into the floodwaters below.

St. Joseph's Hospital
Denver, Colorado

She knew where she was the moment she opened her eyes.

Lord, she hated hospitals. They reminded her of that night when her father—

"Hey, it's about time you woke up." Sarah Logan smiled down at her. "How do you feel?"

How did she feel? She hurt all over and she was seeing Sarah through a haze. "Dizzy."

"You should be. You got clunked by some debris that washed up on that roof you were clinging to and got a dandy concussion. You've been unconscious for almost twenty-four hours."

"Water?"

"You don't remember?"

She tried to concentrate through the pain. Swimming. She had been swimming. Dirty water. She had tried to climb to the top branches of a tree jutting out of the flood, but the branch had broken. She vaguely remembered managing to clamber to the roof of one of the housetops. "Some of it. I don't remember being hit on the head. Is that all that's wrong with me?"

"Bruises everywhere. Exposure. You must have been in that water for hours before they spotted you on the roof. You're a mess." She took Alex's hand. "And you're going to have to explain to the authorities how you got that way. Ken Nader's helicopter blew up and crashed in a glade across the dam. Do you know anything about it?"

A rifle lifting, aiming at Ken's helicopter. A fiery explosion that lit the sky.

"They shot him."

Sarah stiffened. "What? Who shot him?"

"There were three men. I think . . . it was the pilot who shot him. They did it. . . . I couldn't believe it." She closed her eyes. *Running. Slipping and sliding down the slope.*

Bury the bitch.

Her lids flew open. "Landslide. There was a landslide, wasn't there? Was anyone else hurt?"

Sarah shook her head. "But the entire area is buried under a mountain of rock."

"They wanted it buried. They did something. . . ."

"What?"

"I don't know. Dynamite? No, it wasn't an explosion. I heard a low rumble and then the rocks— I don't know what they did."

"No one heard an explosion. Not after the helicopter crashed."

"They did it. I know they did it."

"I'm not saying they didn't. I'm saying no one heard it."

"You believe me?"

"I'm scared to believe you. I hope you'll go back to sleep and when you wake up you'll tell me this was a bad dream. If you don't, then, yes, I'll believe you." She patted Alex's hand. "I've got to go back to the site. It's time for my shift. You get some rest. After this is over, I want you to come home with me and recuperate. You'll like our place. It's on the ocean and it's very peaceful."

"How's the rescue operation going?"

"Okay. Three more canine rescue teams arrived yesterday, and they're a big help." She paused. "We found Janet Delsey's parents. They're both dead."

"Damn." She felt the tears sting her eyes. "God, I'm sorry."

"We all are."

Dead Aim

She swallowed hard to ease the tightness of her throat. "I need to get back. When can I get out of here?"

"A day or two. You'll have to talk to the police first. They want to make out a report on the helicopter crash."

"Murder. It was murder."

"Then tell them that." She leaned forward and brushed a kiss on Alex's forehead. "I'm glad you're still in one piece. You scared me."

"I want to see the police now."

"I'll call them when I leave. Though I think you should give it a few hours."

"It's been too long already." Her lips tightened. "Ken would be alive now if I hadn't asked him to take me over that gorge and pick me up. I want those bastards caught. I can't let them—" She inhaled sharply as a thought occurred to her. "If they set off that landslide, couldn't they have started the other one that buried the entire town?"

Sarah nodded grimly. "A very nasty possibility. But no one's found traces of any sabotage. I hope to hell you're wrong."

"I do too. Why would anyone . . ." She shook her head. "I can't think. Nothing makes sense."

"Rest. You're still pretty woozy. Just tell the police what happened and let them put the pieces together."

She didn't know if she could do anything else, Alex thought wearily. Her head was pounding and all she could see was Ken's helicopter exploding. . . . "Thanks for coming, Sarah."

"Hey, we're friends. You'd have been here for me. May I do anything else for you?"

"Camera . . . Lost my camera . . . Could you get me a replacement and special lenses until I'm able to choose one for myself?"

"Sure. I know what you use. And I may do such a good job of choosing one for you that you'll decide to keep it." Sarah moved toward the door. "Now I've got to go collect Monty from the security guard in the gift shop downstairs before he's spoiled rotten. Everyone in the gift shop was giving him belly rubs." She glanced back over her shoulder. "I'll be back tomorrow morning. If you need me, call me on my cell phone."

"I know what kind of pressure you're under. You don't have to come back here."

Sarah grinned. "I don't have to do anything. I'll see you tomorrow."

"It's quite a story," Detective Dan Leopold said. "Is that all, Ms. Graham?"

"Isn't it enough?" The detective had been polite but totally noncommittal as Alex told him what had happened at the dam. "For God's sake, they murdered Ken Nader. They may have been responsible for that landslide that buried the town. Don't you believe me?"

"Easy. I didn't mean to upset you." He added earnestly, "And I think there's every chance there's substance to your story. You're a photojournalist who's been in some rough spots, and you're used to accurately reporting what you see. It's just that we'll have a few problems verifying."

"What problems?"

"First, no one saw a second helicopter in the area."

"I told you, there were no lights."

"Two, Nader's helicopter crashed in the glade, and if there was any evidence of a second helicopter being there, the resulting fire must have destroyed it. Three, we haven't found a conclusive cause for the explosion." He paused. "No bullet was found."

"Were you looking for one?"

"No, good point. But our forensic team isn't stupid. They look for everything. Naturally, I'll tell them to go back and see if they can find anything that would corroborate what you've told me."

"Dammit, I *saw* it."

He nodded. "You also thought the same perpetrators started the landslides. Why would they do that?"

"How the hell do I know?"

"We've been told by the experts that the slide was probably caused by an aftershock to an area that was already unstable."

"What? They just issued a report that there was a ninety percent chance the area was stable."

"But not a hundred percent chance. They said they could have been wrong. We found no trace of explosive devices."

"Look again. And look at Arapahoe Junction."

"We will. I'm just telling you how it is." His lips tightened grimly. "There's no way we wouldn't delve as deep as we can when it concerns a tragedy of that magnitude. Since the World Trade Center catastrophe, everyone is being damn careful. But there have been FBI, politicians, engineers, and scientists by the carload all over that site, trying to find out what happened to cause that dam break and the ensuing landslide. No one found any signs of sabotage. There were readings on the seismograph machines in San Francisco indicating a possible four-point-two earthquake in this area the night the dam broke."

"It happened," she said through her teeth. "I don't know about the dam or Arapahoe Junction, but I know that second landslide was caused by the same men who killed Ken Nader."

"Then I'm sure we'll find some evidence to prove it. You said they called the pilot Powers? We'll try to trace him. I'll check out everything you've told me." He stood up. "I'll do my best. I'd like you to come to the precinct tomorrow and look through the mug books and databases of suspected terrorists. Will you do that?"

"You bet I will."

"Don't get your hopes up. You'll have to get lucky to find them."

"I have to try." She met his gaze. "You have to try too. You can't let them get away with it. You're not even sure I'm telling the truth, are you?"

"I'm sure you think you are." He wearily shook his head. "Look at it from my point of view. You've been in the hospital for two days suffering from concussion. Isn't it possible that you might not remember things exactly as they occurred? It's happened before with head-injury victims."

"No, it's not possible."

He smiled. "Okay. It wouldn't have made any difference anyway. I'd still do my job. Come on, Jerry, let's get out of here."

The lanky young sergeant in the corner, who'd been silent throughout the interview, rose to his feet. "Good night, Ms. Graham, I hope you feel better."

"Thank you."

"I'll see you tomorrow at the precinct," Detective Leopold said.

"Oh, I'll be there."

"Pretty crazy stuff," Jerry Tedworth said to Leopold as soon as they'd left the hospital room. "Do you believe her?"

"She makes it hard for me not to. She's smart and she's strong and she absolutely believes what she's telling us."

"Like you said, she's had a bad knock on the head."

"Wishful thinking. I hope to hell she didn't get it right."

"Why not?"

"Because if Arapahoe Junction and the dam were also targets, that would mean mass murder. Who commits mass murder? It takes a special kind of criminal. Nuts. Sociopaths. Terrorists. We don't want to have to deal with a case like that." He punched the button at the elevator. "We'd better hope she's just having hallucinations."

Breathe deep. Calm down.

Her head was pounding and Alex forced herself to unclench her fists. All this emotion wasn't going to help anything. Leopold hadn't been out of line in suspecting she might not have all her marbles at present. At least he had listened and promised he'd check into everything she'd told him. But it didn't stop the anger and frustration she was feeling.

Anger and frustration and this haunting antiseptic smell of a hospital room.

Dad . . .

She quickly blocked the memory. Don't think about her father. Jesus, she had to get out of here. She didn't need that wound ripped open. Well, tomorrow she'd go to the police station and see if she could identify any pictures in the mug books.

If they were there, she'd know them. Every feature of those faces was engraved permanently on her memory.

"She's being discharged tomorrow," Lester said as soon as Powers answered the phone. "Two police detectives were there to see her tonight."

Powers muttered an oath. "You should have gotten to her while she was unconscious."

"I told you, her room's right next to the nurses' station. I couldn't do it without being noticed. I'll find a way to put her down tomorrow."

"You'd better. If you'd been on time, I wouldn't have had to take down that helicopter. And, dammit, she can recognize me."

He didn't care that the woman could also recognize both

him and Decker, Lester thought. "Maybe you shouldn't have come along."

"And trust the two of you to do the job right? I had to be sure. It's too important. I'm the one who has to report to Betworth."

Bastard. "Well, you can trust me to do this one. I'll let you know when she's no longer a problem." He hung up.

He leaned back against the brick wall and looked up at the seventh floor of St. Joseph's Hospital. Too bad he hadn't been able to reach Graham before she talked to the police.

Oh, well, he was used to doing damage control.

Sarah was waiting for Alex when she came out of the police station late the next afternoon. She was still wearing her work clothes and had obviously come straight from the site. "Any luck?"

Alex wearily shook her head. "It seemed as if there were thousands of faces. . . . They were all blurring together. But I'll be coming back."

"I know you will." Sarah unlocked her car door and motioned for Monty to get in the backseat. "That's a given. When?"

"Tomorrow." She got into the passenger seat. "I'll need to pick up my rental car at Arapahoe Junction so that I'll be mobile. May I go back with you?"

Sarah nodded. "That's why I'm here. I thought you'd want to go back." She pulled away from the curb. "Why don't you try to nap on the way up there? You probably shouldn't even be out of the hospital yet."

"You're the one who should be sleeping." Alex glanced back at the golden retriever, who was stretched out on the backseat. "Like Monty."

"He needs it. Monty's the one who does the work. I just go along for the ride."

"Yeah, sure." Alex stared unseeingly out the window. "Leopold isn't sure that I'm not imagining everything. He says there's no proof. Do you believe me, Sarah?"

"Damn straight I do. I called John after I left you last night. He's going to try to light a fire under the FBI team who's doing the investigation at the dam."

If anyone could do that, it was Sarah's husband, John Logan, Alex thought. He was a billionaire whose influence stretched from the political elite of Washington to Wall Street. "Good. Though I don't know what the hell they're going to find at the dam that they didn't before. They went over that entire area with a fine-tooth comb." She rubbed her temple. "But maybe they'll be able to find the helicopter and pilot."

"That's possible." Sarah gave her a sideways glance. "Now stop thinking and close your eyes, dammit."

"What else did Logan say?"

"Quite a bit." She made a face. "He said for me to go home. He said it was bad enough that he had to worry about me on disaster sites, but he wasn't about to let me run around with scumbags blowing up dams."

"And you said?"

"Nothing. He didn't expect me to cave. I told him I'd be home when the job was done." Her expression became shadowed. "Which may be pretty soon. I think they're going to change the status at Arapahoe from rescue to recovery tomorrow. They say there's not much chance of there being anyone left alive."

"Shit."

"Right." She drew a deep breath. "But even if the job is done, I'm not leaving you alone here. If you won't come home with me, I'm staying with you."

"No, I can't blame your husband for being worried. He's right. You have enough on your plate without worrying about me."

"Shut up," Sarah said. "We've discussed this before."

"I'm not your responsibility."

Sarah didn't answer.

God, she was stubborn.

Stubborn, loyal, and brave, and the best friend a woman could have. All good reasons to get her to go home to her husband and leave Alex to solve her own problems. But Alex couldn't argue with her right now. She was so exhausted she could barely put two sentences together. She leaned her head back against the seat rest. "We'll talk later."

Sarah chuckled. "That's what John said, and in exactly that tone." She switched on the headlights as the sun disappeared behind the mountains. "And I'll tell you what I told him. Don't mess with me or I'll sic my dog on you."

Alex found herself smiling as she repeated, "We'll talk later."

"Go to sleep. It's going to be another hour or so before we get to the site."

Alex doubted she could sleep, but she fell silent, gazing out at the rolling foothills through which they were driving. This was wonderful country. Purple shadows, white peaks in the distance, such a beautiful place. Terrible things shouldn't happen in beautiful places like this. . . .

2

She woke with a start to full darkness.

Monty was barking, jumping back and forth on the back-seat, trying to climb up to the back window.

She shook her head to clear it. "What's wrong with him?"

"I don't know." Sarah was looking at her rearview mirror. "Maybe he doesn't like that asshole tailgating me."

Alex glanced behind her at the two brilliant headlights glaring from the car behind them. "Monty's smart, but I doubt if he's aware of traffic violations, Sarah."

"You never know." She frowned. "It's not like him to—" Her expression cleared. "The idiot's passing me, thank God. I'm going to let him do it. I don't know what his hurry is; I'm doing the speed limit. You'd think that—" Monty lunged over to the side window, and his barking became frantically shrill as the car pulled almost even with them. "Easy, boy. It's okay."

But it wasn't okay. Alex caught a glint of metal in the hand of the shadowy figure driving the other car. Oh, God, a gun. "Duck!" She reached over and pushed Sarah down and against the door.

The glass shattered.

Sarah gasped as the bullet struck her. Blood stained the shoulder of her sweater as she slumped forward.

The jeep skidded across the tarmac, the headlights spearing the valley hundreds of feet below.

Alex grabbed the steering wheel, her foot reaching over to stomp on the brake as the jeep plunged off the mountain road.

Death.

They were going to die.

The jeep plunged down the steep, rocky slope toward the waiting darkness.

The jeep stopped abruptly. Alex realized dazedly that it had hit a tree.

Monty was crawling over the back of the front seat, trying desperately to get to Sarah.

Sarah.

Blood was still running down Sarah's arm and she was slumped against the door.

"Sarah . . ." She had to get Sarah out of the car and try to stop the bleeding.

She opened the passenger door and started to get out.

Nothing was beneath her feet.

She looked down and swallowed hard as shock ran through her. The jeep was balanced on a jutting outcrop of the mountain, hundreds of feet above the valley. The vehicle had only been stopped from catapulting over the ledge by a scrawny pine tree balanced precariously at the edge of the slope. There was no way they could get out the passenger door. She reached over Sarah and pushed at her door. It opened a crack and then stuck. She opened the window. "Out, boy."

He didn't move.

"Dammit, out! I have to get her out of here!"

Monty looked at her a moment and then jumped out the window.

Alex crawled over Sarah. Monty was sitting quietly beside the car and whined when she wriggled out the window.

"I know. We'll get her out." She pulled the door, trying to get leverage to open it. It moved only a few inches. She pulled again, using all her strength. The door opened another foot. It would have to do.

She grabbed Sarah under the armpits and tugged. Awkward. So damn awkward. She tugged again. What if she was causing Sarah to bleed more? Don't think about it. What else could she do? If that tree gave way, the jeep might topple over at any minute.

So get her out of the car. Get her against the cliff wall.

It took her another few minutes to pull Sarah out of the car and drag her across the ledge to comparative safety under the outcropping of the cliff wall.

Monty sat down beside Sarah and looked pleadingly at Alex.

"I know. I'll try to help her." She opened Sarah's sweater and then her blouse. The wound was high and the bleeding wasn't as bad as she'd feared, she realized with relief. "Stay with her, Monty."

She went back to the jeep, grabbed Sarah's handbag, and pulled out her cell phone.

Call 911. Tell them to come.

Tell them they had to come and save Sarah.

The 911 operator was quick and efficient, and it was frustrating how little information Alex could give her. "I don't know where I am. Somewhere on Highway 30 between Denver and Arapahoe Junction. I told you, I woke up and—"

Someone was shining a flashlight down at them from the road above.

A man was silhouetted against the headlights of the car behind him.

Monty growled.

Her heart jumped. Keep calm. Don't panic. He would have a difficult time reaching them even if he tried to descend the steep slope. And an accurate shot would be nearly impossible from that almost vertical angle.

"I'll keep my cell line open," she said to the 911 operator. "See if you can trace it. Maybe you can at least zero in on the closest tower." She drew Monty closer to the cliff wall next to Sarah and hopefully out of range of that bastard above.

What if he did try to come down? She had no weapon. She'd left her gun behind in the trailer. God, she felt helpless. Like a sitting duck.

She wasn't helpless, dammit. She would hear that bastard on the rock and she would fight. If nothing else, she'd tackle him or push him off the damn mountain. She ran to the jeep, got the first-aid kit and blanket out of the back. A weapon. What could she use as a weapon? The small shovel Sarah always kept in her vehicles. She grabbed the shovel and ran back to Sarah.

She dressed Sarah's wound and covered her. Sweet Jesus, why didn't she regain consciousness? Alex drew her protectively closer.

But her other hand tightened on the shovel.

Arapahoe Junction

A tall, muscular man straightened away from the door to Sarah's hospital room as Alex came down the hall. "Ms. Graham? I'm John Logan."

She recognized him immediately from the photos Sarah had shown her. But the photographs couldn't capture the sheer dominant presence of the man. He had been frantic when Alex phoned him when they'd gotten to the hospital a few hours ago. Now he was fully in control and chilly, very chilly. How could she blame him, she thought wearily. He probably thought she was at fault for Sarah's injury, and he was right. "The doctors say that Sarah will be fine. She'll be out of here in a few days, but it will take another couple months to fully recuperate."

"I know all that." His words were curt. "What I don't know is how I'm supposed to make sure she has the time to recuperate."

"I don't know what you mean."

"Sarah tells me you're a good friend. Then you should know that her life is rescue. She needs to help people." His lips tightened. "And it seems you're the current project."

"I told her I didn't want her involved."

"And did she listen? No, of course not. You're not only in trouble, you're her friend." His tone became harsher. "Well, be a friend and get the hell out of her life for a while."

Alex nodded. "I'll talk to her again."

"Haven't you been listening to me? That won't do the job. You've got to be tucked away safe somewhere so that she can get well without worrying about you. Have you got that?"

She shook her head. "No, I don't know what the devil you're talking about."

"I'm saying that I can't have you running around with people shooting at you."

She grimaced. "I assure you that I'd like to avoid that too."

"Good. Then here's what we're going to do. I'm going to talk to the FBI and arrange for them to put you in a safe house while they investigate both the helicopter crash and the attempt on your and Sarah's lives. You'll be comfortable and secure and it will solve—" He stopped as he saw her shaking her head. "Why the hell not?"

"I have a job to do too. I can't hide. I'll be careful and I'll accept FBI surveillance, but I won't crawl in a hole and let those bastards intimidate me."

"You think that damn story is worth the risk?"

"I think finding the people who hurt my friend is worth

the risk. And if they also caused that landslide and dam break, there's no question. I don't think you'd let yourself be hidden away, would you?"

"I'd do anything I had to do to save Sarah." He stared her directly in the eye. "Under other circumstances I might admire your attitude, but I can't have you getting in the way. I love my wife and I won't have her hurt again."

"She won't be hurt. I promise. I won't let her near me."

"That's not good enough." He muttered an oath. "Don't you think I'm going to go after the bastards who shot Sarah? But I can't do it now. I have to get her well first. Leave it to me."

She shook her head.

He drew a deep breath. "Think about it. Reconsider. I'm taking Sarah to our place by the ocean. When she gets well enough to ask questions, I want to be able to tell her you're absolutely safe."

"I'm sorry. There's no use talking anymore. I can't do it."

A multitude of expressions flitted over his face as he watched her open the door. "Believe me, I'm sorry too."

He turned and strode toward the policeman standing guard down the hall.

That had almost sounded like a threat, Alex thought. Logan clearly liked his own way and was terribly concerned about Sarah. Well, so was she. She had been terrified all the way to the hospital until she'd gotten the word that Sarah was going to be all right.

Sarah's eyes were closed as Alex approached the bed. But she must have sensed a presence, for her lids lifted. "Hi."

"How do you feel?"

"Blurry. They've got me doped up." Her voice was slurred. "I think . . . Was John here?"

"Yes."

"Good. Always wanted you to meet him."

"I'd rather it not have been like this."

"Where's Monty?"

"He's curled up beside your bed. I raised hell until they let him stay. It helped that they knew you were one of the search-and-rescue teams. You and the other rescue workers are their heroes."

"Bull. But thanks for Monty. . . ." She yawned. "Sleepy."

"I'll get out of here. I just wanted to see— I wanted to make sure you were okay."

"Fine . . ." Her eyes were closing. Then she suddenly came awake. "Who was it? Who tried to hurt you?"

She shook her head. "I don't know. He was gone by the time the fire department came."

"Tell John. You could be . . . Might happen again."

"Hey, I'm fine. Leopold called in the FBI and I'm going to be positively surrounded." She brushed the hair from Sarah's face. "And you were the one who got shot."

"Bad aim?"

"He probably aimed for you because he wanted the car to go off the cliff and explode. There wouldn't have been much evidence left." She leaned forward and kissed her cheek. "Now stop worrying and go to sleep. Everything will be fine. I'm going to go now. Leopold wants me to talk to Bob Jurgens, some FBI agent."

"Good. But tell John." She was dozing off again. "He'll fix it. He's good at fixing things."

Alex had a sudden memory of Logan's grim expression when she'd told him that she wasn't going to do what he wanted. "I'm sure he is," she murmured as she headed for the door. "And I imagine he's pretty good at breaking things too."

Sarah was sleeping.

Logan sat down in the visitor's chair and covered her hand with his own. God, she looked fragile.

Don't panic. The doctor said she was going to be fine.

He'd better be right. Logan wouldn't be able to stand it if Sarah was taken from—

Stop it. She was going to get well.

Monty whimpered, got up, and put his chin on Logan's knee.

"Shh." He stroked the dog's head. "We've got to let her sleep. We have to take care of her, boy."

And he would take care of her. This wasn't going to happen again. He couldn't take any chance of Sarah being hurt. He would stay here beside her for a little while, holding her hand and celebrating the fact that she was alive and still with him.

And then he would phone Galen.

The White House
3:35 A.M.

"Could I speak to you for a moment, Mr. President?"

Andreas leaned back in his chair and rubbed his eyes. God, he was tired. He must be getting old. "As long as you're not here to tell me there's been another bombing, Keller. I'm not up to that right now."

The Secret Service man smiled faintly as he shook his head. "I beg to disagree. I've known you too long, sir. In an emergency you bounce right back."

"Your confidence is gratifying," Andreas said dryly. "If totally misplaced. Why are you here, Keller?"

"It's the trip to Arapahoe Junction, sir. There have been some developments that make me uneasy. I want to cancel your visit."

Andreas stiffened. "What developments?"

"I told you about the recent landslide. It's not safe."

"Bullshit." His gaze narrowed on Keller's face. "You told me that the dam disaster was probably caused by an earthquake. This second landslide seems to indicate an aftershock. Has anything changed?"

"No, it's the most likely explanation. There doesn't appear to be anything suspicious."

"Well, I want to go there and see for myself."

"Sir, we weren't compromised."

"*Compromised?* What a nice clean word when you're talking about the death of over a hundred people." He met Keller's gaze. "I'll accept the possibility that natural disasters happen. I won't accept the possibility that we may not be exploring every avenue to determine that's what it really was."

"The CIA assures me that there's absolutely no sign there was terrorist involvement at Arapahoe Dam. Ben Danley says Cordoba and his Matanza group were too busy staging the bombing in Mexico City. They may be widespread, but it would take enormous resources to attack us on our own turf. That hasn't been their modus operandi in the past."

"That doesn't mean they can't change. Maybe they're graduating to the big leagues."

"Mexico City was fairly big league, sir," Keller said quietly. "Two of our embassy workers were killed. I know it pales in comparison to Arapahoe Junction, but I'd say Matanza was stepping up to the—"

"I know," Andreas said. "I wasn't thinking." He was so tired it was difficult to focus. "So tell me the real reason you don't want me to go to Arapahoe Dam."

Keller hesitated. "It's not just this trip. I believe you should stick close to the White House for the next few months. I've proved I can keep you safe here. We've managed to foil two attempts on your life since the last election."

"And I'm duly grateful." He grimaced. "I'm particularly grateful you managed to keep the attempts from Chelsea."

"I don't want gratitude for doing my job. I'm only saying that the Matanza threats against you are becoming increasingly frequent and pointed. There'll come a time when Cordoba and his group will have to put up or shut up and lose face among their fellow terrorists. I think that time is very near."

"So do I."

"Then don't go. The Vice President can make the trip. You know he's offered to go wherever we think there may be a threat to you."

"And I let Shepard stand in for me at two hot spots I'd rather have handled myself."

"But it would be perfectly logical to let him go to Arapahoe. He's already visited there once with Homeland Security, right after the break. This would just be a follow-up. You could empower him to do anything you would do."

"We don't even know that there is a threat at Arapahoe. And I'm not going to let just the possibility that it might have been Matanza change my schedule. I've cooperated, I've given in to your restrictions more than I like, Keller. Since you have no proof, I'm going to Arapahoe Dam as planned." He smiled as he bent over his desk. "It's your baby. Protect me. I guarantee my wife will have your head if I lose mine."

He sighed. "I don't have the slightest doubt of that, Mr. President."

Ben Danley got to his feet as Keller came out of Andreas's office. "No luck?"

Keller shook his head. "He's going." He grimaced. "I might have had a leg to stand on if you and your CIA buddies hadn't sworn that Matanza had nothing to do with the dam break. Want to change your mind?"

Danley shook his head. "I have to call them the way I see them. Unless new evidence surfaces, I have to stand by my intelligence reports."

"Well, your intelligence reports could have been a little timelier about the Mexico City bombing."

"I don't have to take that from you, Keller," he said coldly. "You have no idea the problems we're facing."

"If I did, then I'd be better able to make judgment calls. Under Homeland Security we're supposed to be one big happy family." He waved his hand as Danley opened his mouth to reply. "I don't give a damn about anything the CIA does as long as you don't get in my way." He jerked his thumb at the door to Andreas's office. "I like that stubborn son of a bitch. I'm going to make sure he stays alive."

"How do you expect to do that if you can't even keep him from wandering all over the country?" Danley didn't wait for a reply as he headed for the door. "If there's any change in the situation, I'll let you know."

Danley waited until he was driving down Pennsylvania Avenue before he placed the call to Betworth. "He's going to Arapahoc. Since there's no proof of sabotage, Keller couldn't talk him out of it."

"I didn't think he'd be able to do it," Betworth said. "Naturally Andreas would be suspicious. I thought the seismograph report might allay some of it, but evidently . . ." He was silent a moment, thinking. "And this Alex Graham business is troubling. I believe we'll have to do some adjusting to our plans. I'll let you know." He hung up.

Stockton, Maine

The muscles of Judd Morgan's spine tightened as he felt eyes watching him from outside the open window.

Runne?

He bent over the canvas, listening.

No, not Runne.

There wasn't enough purple in the shadow of the man's cloak. He added the smallest brush stroke before he called, "What the hell are you doing here, Galen?"

"How did you know it was me?"

He turned to face the window. "I know your footsteps."

Galen chuckled. "And that's why you left all those fallen leaves spread on the ground in front of the window." He hoisted himself onto the windowsill and swung his legs over. "Snap, crackle, pop. Did I crunch loud enough for you?"

"You know you did." Sean Galen could be as quiet and lethal as a panther when he made the effort. "You sounded like a hippopotamus."

"I thought it wise to let you know I was coming. I've seen you react to the unexpected, and Elena wants me to come back in one piece."

"How is Elena?"

"Fine. Strong. Beautiful."

"Lethal."

"Only when she's betrayed. You're lucky she didn't follow you and cut your throat."

Judd shrugged. "I did what I had to do. I tried to make sure no one was hurt."

"And that you got away with thirty million in drug money."

"I needed it." He set his brush down. "Is that why you're here? You want to save Elena the trouble of getting even?"

Galen shook his head. "She wouldn't thank me for doing that. You'll be glad to know she's looking forward, not back, these days."

"I am glad." He smiled. "And relieved. I like Elena." His smile faded. "And I like you, Galen. I'm sorry I had to disappoint you. You know why I had to have the money."

"You needed bribe money to get the CIA's hit men to take the sanction off you. Dammit, I was trying to pull strings to get you clear. Why couldn't you wait?"

"It was taking too long. Another three months and they would have found me. They needed a scapegoat very badly, and dead meat is absolutely required in these situations."

"Well, evidently the money hasn't helped, or you wouldn't be hiding out here in the woods."

"I'm getting there. The cover-up went to the top on that North Korean sanction, and politicians have to be careful with a sudden influx of cash."

"If they don't find you before you get out from under." Galen paused. "Like I did."

Judd smiled faintly. "But you're extraordinarily qualified in that area."

"You didn't make it easy. You've moved four times in the last month."

"How did you find me?"

"Your new obsession." Galen's gaze went to the painting on the easel. "You lived at my ranch for months. I knew you'd need paints and canvas and you particularly like the quality of the paints from that dealer in Nova Scotia."

Judd nodded approvingly. "Very good. And the next question is, why have you found me?"

"I have a job for you."

Judd went still. "I take it you're not hiring me to paint Elena's portrait."

"No way."

"Then I have to refuse. I'm out of the business."

"The wages are very high."

"I don't need money, Galen."

"I don't imagine you do, after the money you took from Chavez. But you need that sanction taken off you and I know a man who can do it."

"For a price?" His lips twisted. "Who does he want taken down?"

Galen shook his head. "He wants someone kept alive." Galen dropped into a chair and stretched out his legs. "Could I have a cup of coffee from the pot on that table? It was a damn cold walk from the road."

"No one invited you to make it." Judd crossed the room,

poured him a cup, and took it to him. "If your man wants to pay me to keep someone alive, then he must think it's going to be difficult to do it."

"Not easy."

"Who?"

"Alex Graham."

"Never heard of him."

"Her. She's a photojournalist covering the dam break at Arapahoe Junction."

He went still. "Arapahoe Junction?"

"Even if you've been on the move you must have heard about the break."

"Oh, yes. I've heard about it. And?"

"She claims she saw someone cause a landslide on the other side of the dam."

"I thought the dam break was supposed to be an accident."

"They can't find any evidence to the contrary, but the FBI isn't taking any chances. An attempt was made on Graham's life two nights ago. Her friend, Sarah Logan, was shot instead."

His brows lifted. "Logan?"

Galen nodded. "John Logan's wife. She's going to be fine, but he's a tad upset. So upset he wants to make sure Alex Graham is nowhere near his wife until this mess is cleared up."

"The woman is a target because she's a witness? Then why don't the police or the FBI put her in a safe house?"

"She won't have it. Logan tried to persuade her, but she balked."

"Then how am I supposed to keep her safe if she insists on staying in the open?"

Galen smiled. "I've never known you to quibble when an obstacle gets in your way. You'll do whatever is necessary. I told you, Logan wants to make sure."

"And Logan is going to get this sanction taken off me?" He

shook his head. "He tried to pull strings before, but he struck out."

"You didn't give him enough time. He's had the President's ear since he's been involved in Homeland Security. All you have to do is make sure Alex Graham remains safe and sound until the FBI finds out what the hell happened at Arapahoe Dam."

"And I assume I don't get my payoff until the woman is considered out of danger?"

"That's right."

"Bullshit. If I make myself visible, I could get taken out while I'm playing bodyguard."

"Maybe you could find a way to work around it. The payoff is worth it."

Freedom. Yes, that would be worth almost any risk. He thought about it. It was tempting. Logan was an honest man and would keep his word. Judd wouldn't admit it to Galen, but his own efforts to bribe his way to safety had come to a dead end lately. But he could see any number of possible pitfalls looming in a situation that involved working in the shadow of the FBI.

Arapahoe Junction . . .

He shook his head. "It's not my scene. I'll work out my problems my own way."

"Look, this job's important to me. Logan is my friend. Actually, he called me and asked me to do it."

"Then why don't you?"

"I promised I'd stay close to home, and I don't want to worry Elena." He paused and a smile lit his face. "She's pregnant."

"Congratulations."

"We're pretty happy about it." His smile faded. "So I'm calling in debts. You could have gotten eliminated if I hadn't given you a place to hide when they put out word of the sanction. You owe me, Judd."

"What makes you think that means anything to me?"

"Like I said, I know you."

Judd shook his head. "No, you don't."

"Elena said that you once threatened to take her out if she got me into trouble."

"Threats are easy."

"And you didn't mean it?"

Yes, he'd meant it. He didn't permit himself to become close to many people, but Galen had barged into his life and made himself his friend. "Maybe."

"That was hard to say, wasn't it?"

Judd smiled faintly. "You've always insisted on thinking the best of me. Why? Do you hate to admit you're wrong?"

"Probably. It would be a great blow to my self-esteem. You should be glad I don't believe you're the bastard Elena thinks you are. I don't think you'd have sold us out for the money."

"But I did sell you out."

"Not really." He paused. "If you had, I'd have made sure that you didn't survive to paint any more pretty pictures." Galen finished his coffee and stood up. He pulled a large manila envelope from his jacket pocket and dropped it on the coffee table. "A dossier on Alex Graham. I thought you might want to look it over. Now I'll get out of here and leave you to think about the proposition."

"I've already turned it down."

"But that was before I appealed to your gentler side." He started for the door and then stopped and gazed at the painting on the easel. It was of a slim, bearded man in Renaissance dress stepping out from behind a curtain. "That's really very good. His expression is . . . exceptional. It's mocking yet . . ." He thought about it. "Haunted."

"But then, we're all haunted by something, aren't we?"

"And there's a tension. . . . He looks lethal. Who is he supposed to be?"

Judd shrugged. "No one in particular. I just woke up one morning and started to paint him."

Galen was still studying it and suddenly snapped his fingers. "He's an assassin, a Renaissance assassin."

"Is he?"

"Isn't he?"

"I suppose he could be." He smiled faintly. "But I assure you I had no intention of creating a self-portrait."

"Remarkable . . ." Galen headed for the door. "Call me."

Judd picked up his paintbrush as the door closed behind Galen. He wouldn't call him. Even if Arapahoe Junction weren't involved, getting mixed up with a job like this would be a mistake. He was no bodyguard, and the last thing he wanted to do was try to protect this woman. He was having enough trouble protecting himself. There was no way he'd let himself be persuaded by sentiment.

Besides, he wanted to finish this painting. It had been driving him since he'd first started it last week. He didn't need any interruptions.

He bent over the easel.

More shadow in the cloak.

More richness in the velvet of the doublet.

More torment in the face of the assassin.

Galen waited until he had crossed the state line into Massachusetts before he dialed Logan.

"I've found Morgan and made the offer," he said as soon as he reached Logan. "It's a possible."

"You're sure he's the right man? He may be more dangerous than our shooter."

"Almost certainly. That's why you need him."

"He's a loose cannon." Logan paused. "I never questioned you before when you told me he'd had a raw deal. But I'm questioning you now. There's a hell of a lot at stake. The word is that he disobeyed orders and almost caused a diplomatic incident. That the sanction on that North Korean general was canceled and he went ahead and did it anyway."

"It wasn't canceled. Just deemed a mistake after the fact."

"So he claimed."

"And I believe him. He did what he was ordered to do, what the United States government trained him to do." He added wearily, "My God, I'm sick to death of all this hypocrisy. They can't have it both ways. The military picks up kids with potential and gives them a bunch of brainwashing about patriotism and duty and then sends them out to kill. If they have a good eye and steady nerves, they may even put them in the Airborne Rangers like they did Morgan. They taught him how to kill and blow up everything in sight and praised him for it. When he proved to be exceptional, they upped the ante and sent him alone behind enemy lines in the Middle East to take out the enemy. Do you know how many terrorists he's killed in these last years? But exceptional also means expendable. He became a little hot, so the CIA picked him up for their dirty tricks and the cycle began again."

Logan didn't speak for a moment. "You like him."

"Yes, I've always liked him. God knows why. And I wouldn't have recommended him to you if I didn't think he could do the job. He has great qualifications. He knows how to run, how to hide, and how to get rid of anyone in his way."

There was a pause on the other end of the line before Logan said, "I've always been puzzled about the difficulty I ran into when I was trying to pull strings to get the heat off Morgan."

"Puzzled?"

"It should have been easier. I'm no amateur when it comes to getting my own way with politicians and bureaucrats, but I ran into a stone wall when I mentioned his name."

"They were trying to protect their asses."

"Maybe. Or maybe not."

"Look, do you want to use him or not?"

Another silence. "If you really think he's the best man for the job. When will I know if he consents to do it?"

"When I do."

"And you think he'll go for it?"

"It's hard to tell. Judd's always been hard to read. I've got a hunch he'll— I don't know. I have to let him mull it over. I'll call you." He hung up the phone. He wasn't about to commit himself to Logan. Even though Galen's instincts were telling him he'd made an impact, Judd might still turn him down.

It had to be instinct. Judd's face had all the expression of a slab of granite, and he sure as hell wasn't predictable. Elena would testify to that fact. She'd probably never forgive him for the Chavez deal.

Elena. At the thought of her, his foot pressed harder on the accelerator. Forget about Judd and Alex Graham and everyone else. If he could get a quick flight out of Boston, he might be home with Elena tonight.

It was done.

God, he was tired. Judd rubbed his eyes as he propped his feet on the coffee table. It must be close to three in the morning, and he'd been working on the painting since Galen left hours ago.

Was it good? How the hell did he know? He supposed it was the best he could do at this particular stage. It was certainly better than he'd been able to do a year ago. He'd been sketching faces for years, but when he'd fled the Company and started to dedicate himself to painting, he'd been unable to do anything but landscapes and still lifes. It was only recently he'd begun to bring people back into the mix, and now portraiture was becoming an obsession. It was fascinating to delve deep, to tear through the layers and find what lay beneath. Not many people were at all what they seemed on the surface, and painting them was like exploring a new territory. His gaze met the eyes of the assassin in the picture. He'd denied to Galen that this particular painting was a form of therapy, but perhaps he'd lied. He lifted his coffee cup in a toast and murmured, "Hello, brother."

He took a drink of coffee and then grimaced. Cold and bitter. He should have made a fresh pot. He set the cup on the coffee table beside the envelope Galen had tossed there.

Arapahoe Dam.

Ignore the envelope. He had to look out for his own neck.

Arapahoe Junction.

What the devil did he care if the woman was idiot enough to think she could tilt at windmills? He'd already made a decision that there was no way he was going to open that Pandora's box. He was in enough trouble.

What had she seen at Arapahoe Dam?

Oh, what the hell. He opened the envelope and drew out the dossier and three photos. He wouldn't look at the photos. He had found as long as he didn't look at the faces he could keep himself remote and unemotional.

He scanned the opening paragraphs, which described the events that had led to Logan's offer, and then the dossier itself.

Alex Graham, age twenty-nine. Born and raised in Westacre, New Jersey, of middle-class parents who divorced when she was thirteen. Her mother, Ellen, was a computer information-systems specialist with IBM and her father, Michael, a fireman with the Newark fire department. A civil enough divorce. Though her mother retained custody, she'd spent every other weekend with her father. She won a photo contest sponsored by *National Geographic* at sixteen and was awarded a journalism scholarship to Columbia University when she graduated from high school. She'd quit college in her junior year and gone to photograph the horrendous earthquake in Tibet. The resulting photos had earned her acclaim

Dead Aim

and a place on the staff of *Newsweek*. From that point on it had been a steady climb upward in her chosen profession. She was now a freelance photojournalist and contributed principally to *World Life*.

Her mother had died of emphysema three years after Alex left school, and her father was killed at the World Trade Center a few years later. She had been engaged once but never married.

All cut and dried, Judd thought. It read like an obituary. Which it might turn out to be if Alex Graham wasn't very careful.

Not his problem. He tossed the dossier back on the table. Let Galen get someone else for the job.

But Galen hadn't said that when Judd was in trouble. He had stepped in and yanked him out from under the threat and kept him safe for months.

Forget it. This was the last job he should get near. They could very well be waiting for him. He couldn't afford to be soft when it might put everything he valued in jeopardy. He picked up the photos and started to jam them back into the envelope. He wouldn't look at them. He wouldn't let Alex Graham become a real person to him. Judd wasn't Galen, and he wouldn't be a quixotic ass and pretend that he was anything but what life had made him. He would do what was best for himself and screw—

Oh, shit.

The photo of Alex Graham was faceup, staring at him.

My God, what a remarkable face. She was not a beautiful woman, unless you considered strength beauty. Her short brown hair was clean and shining, pushed back and styled simply. Her high cheekbones were clean cut and her mouth wide and sensitive. Deep-set brown eyes sparkled with vitality and intensity. The snapshot had been taken somewhere in the mountains, and she was gazing out of the picture with a touch of defiance.

Why?

He glanced at the other photos. One was obviously a passport photo, but the other one was at a disaster site and she looked exhausted and heartsick. Yet her eyes . . . Defiance and wariness. What was behind those barriers she was putting up?

It was just a face. Don't let curiosity influence cool judgment. Don't let her become a person to you. It was always a mistake to—

Dammit, it was already too late.

Okay, she was alive for him. Then bend the situation to suit yourself. He knew how to make himself invisible. He could do the job and no one, not even Alex Graham, would be aware he was around. He could still stay apart and in full control.

His phone rang. "Hello."

"Galen. Have you finished the painting?"

"Yes. Is that why you're calling me at four in the morning?"

"Not exactly. But I didn't want you to have any distractions getting in the way of the job."

"I told you I wasn't—"

"I thought you might have second thoughts."

Judd stared down at the photograph of Alex Graham.

"Judd?"

"Maybe."

Galen was silent for a moment. "How do I turn the maybe into a yes?"

"You and Logan let me do anything I have to do. If I have to take the gloves off, I don't want anyone getting in my way. You see that I have a clear playing field."

"He's not going to agree to get the sanction taken off you yet."

"I'm not talking about the past, only the present."

"What are you thinking about?"

"You don't want to know. It might jar you out of that cozy

little cocoon you're sharing with Elena. Just be ready to jump in case I need you."

"Okay. I'll call Logan. If there's any problem, I'll let you know."

"Tonight. If I'm going to do this, it's got to be right away. If this is a professional job, Graham is on borrowed time. I don't want to waste any planning on a dead woman."

"She's not dead yet. If you don't hear from me in an hour, it's a go." He hung up.

Jesus, he should have his head examined, Judd thought wearily. Why had he committed himself? Alex Graham meant nothing to him.

Because he was tired and angry and sick of being a target? Because lately he'd been tempted to just stay and wait for Runne to find him?

Judd leaned his head back on the couch, his gaze returning to the mocking face of the assassin in the painting. "Okay, so it's not the brightest decision I've ever made. . . ."

3

"None of them is here." Alex wearily leaned back in the chair and gazed at Leopold across the desk. "Do you have any more mug shots?"

"None that meet your description. That's why we have databases. You'd have been sitting in that chair for the next year if we'd let you do a random check."

"They've got to have records. People who do things like this don't go through life without stumbling over the law."

"I agree. That's why I've set up an appointment for you at the local FBI field office tomorrow morning. They have a much more extensive database." Leopold poured a cup of coffee and handed it to her. "If you're up to it."

"I'm up to it." She took a sip of coffee. "I've got to be up to it. They can't get away with this."

"Then we'll find them. If the databases don't pan out, we'll call in a police artist and you can give us a description to work with."

"Jesus, why didn't I take their damn pictures that night? I didn't even think of it. I saw Ken blow up and I—" She drew a shaky breath. "I screamed. Isn't that pathetic? Instead of doing something useful. I screamed."

– 44 –

"Even if you'd taken their pictures, your equipment is buried beneath that landslide."

She made a face. "I can't see you letting that stop you if you were convinced the dam was sabotaged. You'd bring in the cranes and every federal security organization in the country. Right?"

"Right." Leopold smiled. "But you didn't take their pictures, and all the experts are still saying there was no sabotage. We've never found proof that Nader's helicopter was brought down. So all we have is an attempt on your life." He held up his hand. "I don't want to minimize the seriousness of that, you understand."

"I know." Leopold was a good guy and he had been as sympathetic and helpful as he could during the last few days. "The proof's got to be there."

"Then maybe the FBI can find it." The phone rang and he answered it. A moment later he handed the phone to her. "Speak of the devil. Bob Jurgens. He wants to talk to you. Remember him? I introduced you to him at the hospital."

"Why shouldn't I remember him? I wasn't that banged up." She remembered Jurgens very well. Smooth, polite, and very disapproving.

Jurgens's voice was just as disapproving when she took the phone from Leopold. "I understand you're not having much luck with identifying the men who attacked you. I think you'd better reconsider our offer to put you in protective custody. A safe house is the obvious solution. I have just the place that—"

"*No*. Not only no, but hell, no." Her hand tightened on the phone. Why wouldn't he leave her alone? "Maybe I didn't make myself clear. Arapahoe Junction isn't that much different than what happened at WTC. You give in to people like this and let them change your life and they win. I won't let them win."

"I'm sorry to hear you say that. I hope Leopold can persuade you to change your mind. I'll be in touch."

She handed the phone back to Leopold. "He wants to put me in some safe house and let me twiddle my thumbs while he completes his investigation."

"So I understand. Personally, I don't care much for those by-the-book FBI agents, but he appears to be very thorough and he's got a team out there scouring the entire crash area."

"He said he hoped you could convince me to let him tuck me away. Does he have you in his pocket?"

Leopold shook his head. "We try to work together, but we run our own show. I admit he did call and suggest I try to influence you. The safe house isn't a bad idea."

"It's a very bad idea." She stood up. "And it probably originated with John Logan." She shook her head as she translated a flicker of expression on Leopold's face. "You too?"

"He talked to me. I didn't think you'd go along with it. I told him we had your security well in hand."

"So you're responsible for that blue unmarked Toyota that's been following me since I left the hotel this morning?"

He grinned. "Busted. But how do you know it's not someone more sinister than my humble self?"

"That's why I'm telling you about it. Is it a Toyota?"

He nodded as he picked up the phone and dialed a number. "What color and model car are we using for the surveillance on Alex Graham?" He listened. "And the license number?" He jotted the number down on his pad. "Thanks." He handed Alex the slip of paper. "This one is ours. If you suspect anyone else is following you, then get on the phone and call me right away."

"Don't worry." She tucked the note in her purse. "I'll yell if I even get a glimmer I'm in danger. I believe in letting the police earn those tax dollars. Particularly when it means keeping my neck intact." She moved toward the door. "Thanks for everything, Detective."

Dead Aim

"Thank you." Leopold walked her out of the office and down the steps. "I'll just see you to your car. Wouldn't want you to be cheated out of those tax dollars."

Alex glanced in the rearview mirror as she turned the corner and approached the Golden Nugget Hotel.

The blue Toyota was still behind her, keeping a discreet one-block distance.

She turned left, went down the underground parking ramp, and parked beside the elevator doors. She glanced quickly around before getting out and punching the button for the elevator.

She tensed.

Another car was coming down the ramp.

The elevator doors opened and she quickly stepped inside and pushed the button for the seventh floor.

No response.

She pushed the button again.

The car was closer, coming down the last curve in the ramp.

Her hand reached inside her bag for her .38 revolver. Dammit, why didn't the doors of the elevator—

She stabbed the button again.

The car on the ramp came into view.

It was the blue Toyota.

She breathed a sigh of relief and released the grasp on her gun to wave at the driver behind the wheel.

He waved back. He parked in a space a short distance away as she punched the elevator button one more time.

At last the elevator doors slid shut.

Lester muttered a curse as he threw the radio-control device on the seat beside him. What the hell had happened? Decker had promised him the elevator doors would jam if he pressed the damn switch. He should have known better than to trust anyone but himself. Fucking screwup. Now he'd have to find a way to get into Graham's hotel room.

He got out of the blue Toyota and strode toward the bank of elevators. He had to move fast. He pressed the button for the elevator. He didn't know how much time he had left before—

The doors of the elevator opened.

"Pardon me."

He whirled to see a man coming down the emergency stairs.

"I do hate to spoil your plans," the man said softly. "But I really can't let you get in that elevator."

Shit. Cop?

Lester's hand dove into his jacket for his holstered Glock.

"Too late." Morgan shot him in the head.

Alex was just picking the phone up to call Sarah when the fire alarms in the hall started wailing.

She stiffened. A little too convenient? A fire was a great way to get someone out of a hotel room. She dialed the front desk. Busy.

She dialed Leopold at the precinct. "There's a fire alarm going off at my hotel. Will you check and see if it's legitimate?"

"I'm on it." He hung up.

Well, if the alarm was legitimate she wasn't going to stay here and burn up. She'd already gotten her handbag and camera equipment from the bedroom when the phone rang.

"The fire department is on the way. The hotel called and reported a fire in a car in the underground lot," Leopold said when she picked up. "It reached the gas tank and exploded. The smoke has entered the ventilating system. They're afraid there will be other explosions down there, so they're evacuating the hotel."

She headed for the door. "Then I'm out of here."

"Good idea. I'll have an officer meet you in the lobby."

The hall was only a little smoky, but it was filled with people heading for the emergency stairs at the end of the corridor.

"This way." A teenage boy was motioning her forward. "Don't be scared. It's only seven stories. We'll get out."

She smiled and nodded. "I'm sure we will." She started down the concrete steps. "You go on. I'll be fine."

"No, I'll stay with you."

"Joseph." A middle-aged woman was motioning him to come. "We don't want to get separated."

The teenager frowned. "She's alone, Mom. She might need help."

Sweet kid. "Go on," Alex said. "I'm coming. I promise I won't panic."

"Joseph." The boy's mother's voice was shrill. She was being pushed against the wall as more people flooded the steps from the exits on the other floors.

"Okay. Okay." Joseph suddenly grabbed Alex's arm and pulled her down the stairs. "Come on. You gotta come with us."

"Really, I'll be fine. You don't—" She stopped arguing. The important thing was for all of them to get out of there.

Fifth floor.

The smoke was getting worse.

Fourth floor.

She could barely move in the shuffling crowd.

Third floor.

"Stand to one side, please. We have to get up the stairs." It was a fireman pushing his way up the stairwell. "There's been another fire reported on the fourth floor."

She moved to huddle against the wall with the rest of the people on the stairs.

The fireman was below her, then beside her. He started to go past her and then stopped abruptly. The firefighter had cool blue eyes and a hard face, but his gaze was concerned as it searched her face. "You okay, ma'am? Are your lungs burning? You look like the smoke has gotten to you."

"I scarcely—"

He reached out and took her wrist.

Warmth. Strength. Safety.

His fingers moved to the inside of her wrist. "Your pulse is going crazy. Do you have asthma or any respiratory problems?"

"No, nothing like—"

Christ, she was dizzy. Her knees were buckling. . . .

But he was catching her. "Don't you worry, ma'am. I'll take good care of you."

Cool blue eyes.

No, cold blue eyes, icy blue eyes . . .

Music.

Ravel, she recognized dimly. She liked Ravel. Dad had liked it too. He hadn't cared for many classical selections, but he'd said Ravel was full of thunder. . . .

Like her head. Damn, it was pounding.

"Open your eyes. I've got something that will make you feel better."

She slowly opened her eyes.

Blue eyes. The fireman with blue eyes.

"It's only aspirin." He was holding a glass of water and two pills. "It will take care of the headache."

"I'll vote for that." She swallowed the aspirins and water and handed the glass back to him. He wasn't dressed in the fireman's uniform anymore. He wore a red flannel shirt and jeans, but he still had that air of complete confidence that had impressed her on the stairs.

Stairs. She came abruptly wide awake. She wasn't in the stairwell any longer. She was lying on a couch. She looked beyond him to see a fire leaping briskly in a huge stone fireplace that climbed to a rough-hewn beamed ceiling.

Definitely not a hotel room.

"Where am I?"

He set the glass down on the end table. "At a lodge in the mountains."

"What?"

"The situation was heating up. It was necessary that I get you out of sight for a while."

She sat up on the couch. "Who the hell are you?"

"Judd Morgan. Don't worry, I'm no threat to you."

And she was supposed to believe him? Even when she'd been only half conscious she was aware of—what? Coldness, confidence, an overpowering presence.

He nodded as he saw her expression. "Considering the company you've been keeping lately, I don't wonder you're suspicious. But if I'd meant you any harm, I'd have had every opportunity to put you down while you were sleeping."

"And why was I sleeping? I felt perfectly normal. I shouldn't have fallen—"

"Just a harmless sedative, but it kept you out for the length of time I needed it to. I had to get you out of there and in a safe environment, and that was the most efficient way to do it."

"A sedative? You knocked me out?"

He shrugged. "Like I said, the most innocuous way of accomplishing an end. Even the headache will be gone soon."

"Why would you do that?" A phrase suddenly sank home. "Safe environment?" Anger was quickly replacing the shock. "My God, are you with the police or FBI? I told them I wouldn't go along with—" He was shaking his head. "Then why the devil would you do something like this?"

"John Logan made me an offer I couldn't refuse."

She looked at him incredulously. "He *paid* you to do this?"

"Well, he didn't tell me to snatch you. Only to make sure you were safe and his wife would know that." He smiled. "Unfortunately, I couldn't do one without the other."

"You bastard. Kidnapping is a federal offense."

He nodded. "So I've heard." He moved across the room toward the kitchenette. "I've got a stew on the stove. It should be ready in fifteen minutes if you want to wash up."

"I don't want to wash up. I'm getting out of here."

He shook his head. "Sorry, not possible. You don't know where you are, and I have the keys to the Land Rover outside. You could try to walk, but it's started to snow and you'd probably not make it to anywhere near civilization before you got hypothermia." He glanced at her handbag lying on the coffee table. "Oh, and I took the gun and telephone out of your bag. I didn't think photographers carried deadly weapons as a rule, but I guess your work has taken you into some hot spots." He moved over to the stove. "Fifteen minutes."

She stared at Morgan in rage and frustration. She wanted to murder him. "They'll be looking for you. Leopold was sending an officer to meet me in the lobby."

He nodded.

"I'm not going to put up with this. I won't be kept a prisoner so some son of a bitch like you can earn a few bucks."

He didn't answer.

She had another thought. "Jesus, you set that hotel on fire, didn't you?"

"Just your rental car in the parking garage. I parked it far enough away from the other cars so that it wouldn't cause more than a minor problem."

"Just? Minor problem?" She was working her way through the scenario. "You had it all planned. You were probably the one who called the fire department. You even had a fireman's uniform ready. Why?"

He didn't look up from the stew he was stirring. "I always believe in being prepared. Your father was a fireman. I knew you'd be suspicious of anyone else, but you'd instinctively trust anyone who wore the uniform."

She felt a chill go through her as she remembered how safe she'd felt when he touched her wrist in that stairwell. He had thought it all out and come up with a plan that had caught her at her most vulnerable.

She shook her head. "I still can't believe Logan would authorize a kidnapping."

"I told you, he didn't exactly authorize it. I just made it part of the deal that he'd cover any action I thought necessary to protect you." He shrugged. "There was an outside chance that you might not even have had to know I was around. But when I saw the way the situation was shaping up, I knew I had to get you away."

"I don't need you. I'm being protected by the police."

He shook his head.

"Call Detective Leopold. He'll tell you. Hell, they've been following me for two days."

"I know. Blue Toyota. Two officers."

She nodded. "One even followed me back to the hotel tonight."

He shook his head. "They were taken out in the parking lot across from the precinct while you were inside this afternoon. The Toyota was driven out of the parking lot fifteen minutes after you went into the precinct, but not by the same men who drove it in. They went to the hotel and the driver left his partner there to do some fine-tuning to the elevator, then went back to the parking lot and waited for you to come out."

"What?"

"They were both very good, very professional. I was impressed."

She stared at him in disbelief. "You're saying that they killed the officers who were following me and took their place?"

He nodded. "There wasn't time or opportunity to get rid of the bodies, so I imagine they're in the trunk of the Toyota."

She shook her head. "I don't believe you."

"You will. It will just take a little while. Why should I lie?"

"I don't know. Any more than I know why you should tell me the truth."

He looked down at the stew. "Ten minutes," he said quietly. "Your bedroom is down the hall to the left. I don't have any clothes for you, so I put some of my stuff in your bureau drawer. You'll have to make do. I'm afraid I was a little unprepared. I didn't want it to come to this."

She slowly rose to her feet. "I'm going to make your life hell. This isn't going to be worth your while."

"You may be right. You've already caused me more problems than you know."

"Good." She grabbed her purse and camera bag, strode down the hall, and slammed the door of the bedroom. A moment later she was splashing water on her face in the adjoining bathroom. She wiped her face on the guest towel and then went into the bedroom and stared out at the heavily falling snow. Between the darkness and the snow she could barely see the mountains.

She doubted if the cold water was going to make her any sharper or more able to cope. She was still feeling fuzzy from that blasted sedative. What the devil had he given her?

Okay, try to think. This entire episode was like something from a bad movie. She went to the bed and checked her purse. No gun, no phone. Nothing that even resembled a weapon, unless you counted a ballpoint pen.

But there were probably knives in the kitchen.

She'd always hated the thought of knife wounds. She

might not have to use a weapon. It was clear Morgan was intelligent enough to respect a threat. Play the situation by ear.

Logan. He was the one who'd hired Morgan. He could fire him. That was another path she could explore.

Well, she couldn't accomplish anything by hiding here in the bedroom. She would face him, learn as much as she could from him, and then find a way to get out of here.

Decker watched the two morgue attendants slide Lester's body into the hearse.

What the hell had happened?

A cold chill went through him. It didn't matter what had happened. The woman was gone. Lester was dead and the police would probably ID him within hours. Powers would be furious.

Okay, think fast. Damage control. Find a hook and wriggle out from beneath the censure and punishment to come. He had to cover his ass.

Find the hook.

He hurried back into the hotel.

"Sit down." Morgan put a bowl of steaming stew down on a place mat at the kitchen table. "You must be hungry. I didn't give you much time to eat dinner before I called in the alarm."

"That was totally irresponsible. Someone could have been hurt."

"It was a judgment call. There was a bigger chance of you being hurt if I didn't get you out of there." He sat down across the table from her. "So I got you out. Eat your stew."

"How do I know you didn't put something in it?"

He smiled. "You don't."

But it wasn't likely. As he'd said before, he could have

killed her at any time while she was lying there helpless. She picked up her spoon and dipped it into the stew. "How long was I unconscious?"

"Not too long." He offered her a bowl of rolls. "I'm not going to tell you how long because you'd immediately start trying to figure out how close we are to Denver. The less you know, the better for me."

"I will get away from here." She smiled through bared teeth. "And then I'll make sure you and Logan are punished."

"Logan too? But won't that hurt your friend Sarah?"

"He had no right to—" But there was no way she could hurt Sarah. She drew a deep breath. She'd think about Logan later. "I'm not even sure Logan did hire you."

"I know. That's why I'm going to let you talk to him after dinner."

"What?"

"This situation is going to be difficult enough. It will make it easier for both of us if you believe I'm here to protect, not hurt, you." He took a bite of stew. "Anger is okay, but I don't want you to be afraid of me. Fear sucks."

"I'm not afraid of you."

"Yes, you are." He gave her a steady glance. "Not all the time. It comes and goes, but it's there."

"And who are you to analyze—" She stopped as she met his gaze. "I'd be stupid not to be wary of someone who's just kidnapped me."

"Be wary. Wary is smart." He smiled slightly. "And you're very smart."

"How do you know?" She remembered the remark about her fireman father. "You've managed to get a dossier on me."

He nodded. "And it was very interesting reading."

"I'm glad I could entertain you."

"*Entertain* isn't quite the word. Your career has led you into some pretty rough scrapes. It's a wonder you were able to wriggle out of some of them." He got up from the table to bring a pot of coffee from the counter. "For instance, when you shot that terrorist in Iran, I'd have bet against your chances of getting out of the country alive. You did all the wrong things to preserve your neck."

"Like what?"

"You trusted someone in the Embassy to arrange to smuggle you out. The Embassy is always too visible. You waited two days to head for the border. It should have given the terrorist group time to find you. They must have had extremely poor intelligence and leadership." He poured coffee into her cup. "And you didn't kill your target."

"I'm not a murderer. I was there to get a story. I shot Al Habim in self-defense."

"And because you didn't kill him, he came after you again in Cairo. If the CIA hadn't had you under surveillance, you could have been history."

"Why do you think they had me under surveillance? Do you think I'm stupid? I knew Al Habim would come looking for me. I was hoping the CIA would catch him and be able to extract information."

"Excellent." He smiled. "But evidently the Company had reasons to want him dead. So you might as well have done it yourself and saved everyone the trouble."

"Is that what you would have done?"

"Every case is different, but I tend to lean toward keeping myself alive and in one piece. The CIA is always a wild card. There are too many politicians with too many agendas whirling around them."

"You talk as if you know."

"I have a certain familiarity with them." He lifted his cup to his lips. "I have a great admiration for many of their agents, but I've found that no one but me has quite the same desire to maintain my health and well-being."

"I can see why," she said through her teeth.

"My, what bitterness. Are you only tolerant when it concerns terrorists?"

"I'm not tolerant of anyone who interferes with my life or freedom." She pushed back her chair. "And now I want to talk to John Logan. Call him."

"Whatever you say. I'm surprised you waited this long." He pulled out his cell phone and dialed a number. "Logan? Judd Morgan. Alex Graham wants to talk to you." He handed her the phone, rose to his feet, and began stacking the dishes. "Give him hell. I shouldn't be the only one suffering."

She ignored him. "Logan?"

"Sorry, Alex. I didn't want to do this."

She recognized his voice. Until this moment she hadn't really believed what Morgan had said. "Bullshit. You tell this bastard to let me go."

"I can't do it. I told you where my priority lies. Sarah has to be safe, and if you won't be sensible, then you'll have to be—"

"Kidnapped?"

"Kept safe in spite of yourself."

"And you think I'll put up with it? I'm getting out of here, and when I do, I'm going to cause you so much trouble your head will spin."

"I'm sure you will. But hopefully the FBI will have removed any threat to Sarah by that time. I'm pulling every string I know to find out who those men at Arapahoe Junction were."

"And I'm supposed to sit here locked up with this asshole while you try to do something the FBI can't?"

"I have a chance. I have a friend who specializes in that kind of information."

"Another criminal like Morgan?"

"No, not like Morgan. I understand he has different talents."

"Kidnapping."

"It wasn't supposed to come down to that. Morgan tells me that the situation called for more drastic measures than he'd planned."

"But you agreed to it."

"After the fact." He paused. "He said it was the only way to keep you alive, and keeping you alive is the only way I can keep Sarah safe. That's the only thing that's important to me."

"My God. Who the hell do you think you are?"

"A man who loves Sarah." He paused. "As you do, Alex."

"I told you I wouldn't do anything to endanger her. What you've done is totally beyond the pale." She looked at Morgan across the kitchen. "And you turned this . . . thug loose on me."

Morgan raised his brows. "Thug?" he murmured. "Isn't that a rather antiquated term?"

"Tell him to let me go, Logan."

"I can't do that. Don't worry, I've been assured you're perfectly safe with him. He's no threat."

She would have laughed if she hadn't been so angry. She didn't know exactly who or what Judd Morgan was, but he was about as unthreatening as a coiled rattlesnake. "He'll be no danger when I'm a thousand miles away from him or he's behind bars."

"Believe me, if I'd had any doubts about your safety, I'd have never made a deal with him. Do you think I don't know I'd have to answer to Sarah if anything happened to you?"

"Sarah will be as furious as I am with you."

"Maybe. But she'll be alive." He paused. "And you'll be alive. The end justifies the means."

"The hell it does."

"We disagree. Is there anything else you'd like to say to me?"

"Let me go."

"Anything else?"

"No, dammit, I want you to—" It was no use. She drew a deep breath. "How is Sarah?"

"Wonderful. Champing at the bit to get up. Nagging me to try to find out where the FBI has you hidden so she can come and see you."

"Damn you." She hung up the phone and glared at Morgan across the room. "And damn you, Morgan."

"It must be very frustrating for you." He crossed the room and took the phone from her. "And I'm sure Logan didn't succeed in reassuring you that I'm Sir Lancelot and not Jack the Ripper."

"No."

"But you believe that Logan's deal with me didn't include any harm to you?"

"Maybe."

"And that Logan, being the powerhouse he is, would be very upset if I broke my end of the bargain?"

"Possibly."

"Then look at it this way. If I killed you and buried you in the snow, Logan would come after me with guns blazing. Doesn't that give you a sense of security?"

She gazed at him incredulously. "Should it?"

He sighed. "I guess not. I was reaching." He put the dishes in the dishwasher. "But I think you're not as uneasy as you were before you spoke to Logan. Want your coffee now?"

"No." She got to her feet. "I don't want anything you can give me but out."

"It's possible you might get what you want."

She stiffened. "What?"

"I have to think about it. Things aren't shaping up the way I intended. I was planning on staying in the background, but I blew it at the hotel."

"I agree."

"No, not by taking you. That was necessary. But there are video cameras all over that hotel. I took out the ones in the garage, but I didn't have time to get to the cameras in the stairwell."

"Good. Then your face will be on every APB in the U.S."

"I was sure that would be your reaction. But it's not the police I'm concerned about at present."

"You don't want those scumbags to target you too? Well, it serves you right."

"Deserving or not, it doesn't alter the fact that I have a problem."

Her gaze narrowed on his face. "And you might betray Logan to solve it?"

"Let's say I might make adjustments to our agreement."

Hope flared. "Let me go and I'll forget I ever saw you."

He shook his head.

"I don't break my word."

He studied her and then smiled. "No, I don't think you do."

"Then let me go. You don't want the trouble and I'll be big-time trouble."

"A promise?"

Her smile was only a baring of her teeth. "Oh, yes."

He chuckled. "My God, I wish you could meet Elena. I think you and she might be soul mates."

"I'm not interested in meeting any of your friends."

"It's just as well. The last I heard, she wanted to cut my throat. I don't need more than one of you to contend with at any given time."

Her hands clenched into fists. "Are you going to let me go?"

His smile faded. "I have to consider the possibilities. I learned a long time ago that every action has a domino effect. I knew I should never have taken this job. Now if I let you go and you get killed, it will have a direct impact on me. One, Logan will be out for my head. Two, whoever is after you may think I'm part of the equation and target me. Three, the police may decide I'm involved in your demise and try to arrest me. Since I won't have Logan to run interference, it would put me in a very precarious position and that would not be—"

"Oh, for God's sake."

"No, for Judd Morgan's sake." He added, "That's what I'm trying to tell you. I always look out for number one."

"How surprising."

"Sorry, we all can't be heroes who run into burning buildings."

"I'd never make that mistake."

"You already did."

A smoke-filled stairwell. His hand grasping her wrist. Safety.

"You took me by surprise."

"Because you want to believe in heroes."

"They exist. I've known quite a few."

"Like your father."

"Like my father." She stared him in the eye. "And I'm not going to forgive you for dressing up and pretending you're anything like him."

"I didn't think you would. I knew it would probably be a cardinal sin in your eyes." He shrugged. "But there are sins and then there are sins. I've learned to view transgressions in perspective." He turned on the dishwasher. "For instance, it would be a really great sin to permit a man of my brilliance and talent to be taken down by those lowlifes who blew up Arapahoe Dam. I have to make sure such sacrilege doesn't happen."

"No matter who else gets hurt."

"Oh, I didn't say that." He smiled. "Never make assumptions, Alex. It's not a black-and-white world." He turned away. "Now, if you're sure you don't want anything else from me, I believe I'll go to the study and do a little work."

"Planning your next heist?"

"Could be. Or maybe I'm going to think about domino effects."

"Listen to me." Her voice vibrated with urgency. "I have to get out of here. Those men killed innocent people. I can't let them walk away. I won't let them walk away. I *saw* them. I may be the only person who can make sure they're punished."

"It's not your responsibility. Let the police and the FBI handle it."

"It *is* my responsibility. When something like that disaster happens, it's everyone's responsibility. You can't just stand on the sidelines and hope someone else—" She stopped and wearily shook her head. "Or maybe you can. You're so damn cold. I can see you standing in the background, afraid to come any closer because something might touch you."

"Do you want me to deny it? I'm very comfortable on the outside. It's where I intend to stay." He turned away. "All that emotion must have exhausted you. I'd suggest you go to your room and get some sleep. You probably still feel a little groggy from that sedative."

"Wait." She moistened her lips. "What are the chances of you changing your mind about your deal with Logan?"

He thought about it. "Probably not very high. But the possibility does exist."

She watched in helpless frustration as he disappeared through a doorway opening off the living room.

No, not helpless. She would *not* be helpless.

She crossed the kitchen and opened the cutlery drawer.

There was a scrawled note lying in the empty drawer.

Sorry.

Damn him.

4

"Here's the tape. I got it right before the police team started their search." Decker dropped the case on the desk in front of Powers. "Though I don't know how much good it will do. The camera only got a back shot of him going up the stairs, and that big-ass fireman's hat almost hid his face when he was carrying Graham out the second-floor exit."

"It better do us a hell of a lot of good," Powers said softly. "You screwed up. We lost Graham, and you left Lester's body for the FBI to find."

"I wasn't supposed to be there," Decker said defensively. "I did my job."

"Then somebody undid it. Which is just as bad." He picked up the tape. "I'll send this to Washington to have it examined. You'd better hope they can ID that fireman. He's the key to finding Graham." He flipped open his phone. "I'm going to get a hell of a lot of heat from Betworth about this, and you can bet I'm not going to take it alone."

Decker belligerently lifted his chin. "I'm not worried about Betworth."

"No?" Powers dialed Betworth's number. "And what about Runne?" He nodded as he saw the change of expression on

Decker's face. "Different story, isn't it? You're scared shitless of Runne."

"I'm not scared. He's just . . . weird."

"Well, Betworth might decide to turn him loose on you, so I wouldn't get too cocky." Betworth answered the phone, and Powers deliberately made his tone cheerful. "Good news, we're on our way to finding Graham."

Idiots!

Charles Betworth muttered a curse as he hung up the phone.

Arapahoe Dam had been a nightmare from the beginning. It had not accomplished its principal aim, and the cleanup was proving to be a complete debacle. Powers was supposed to be a competent professional, but Betworth had seen no sign of it during these last weeks. It was time he made the move that he'd wanted to avoid.

He quickly dialed Danley. "I need you to meet me tonight. We have to do something about that situation we discussed. I'm afraid we're going to have to escalate our time frame and go to Plan B."

"Is that wise?"

He smothered his irritation. Danley had been skittish for the last two weeks and Betworth had had to keep the bastard calm. "I don't believe we have a choice. Boldness sometimes carries the day. As long as you and Jurgens give the correct orders and make damn sure they're carried out, we'll be fine. We'll discuss it tonight." He hung up. Boldness would have to carry the day in this case. No reason why it wouldn't work. All the preparations had been made. Of course, he'd have to call Guatemala City and make sure Cordoba—

A discreet knock on the door before it opened. "I'm sorry to disturb you, sir."

Iris Johansen

He glanced up to see Hannah Carter, his secretary, standing tentatively in the doorway. "What is it?"

"You have an appointment at the White House in ten minutes. You're meeting with the Vice President and the Secretary of the Interior. I was afraid you'd forgot—"

"I did." He forced a smile as he rose to his feet. "But I can always count on you to save my ass, Hannah."

"I'll call the Vice President's secretary and tell her you were held up by the environmental people." Hannah smiled back at him. "He's been having real trouble for the past two months getting them to okay that bill approving massive shoring up of our infrastructure."

"Brilliant. You should be doing this job, not me. I'm on my way."

She flushed with pleasure, as he'd known she would. It was always worthwhile to devote a few minutes a day to making the people around you feel important. Spreading honey was the best way to maintain control. Hannah had been working for him for ten years, and he couldn't hope to have a more devoted employee. Honey usually worked with Danley too. He'd drawn him in with praise and compliments and then slammed the door once he committed himself.

But honey was not the method he'd use on Powers if he didn't stop making mistakes.

He might have to send Runne out there to do a little prodding. If he could locate the arrogant bastard. Runne hadn't answered his phone for two days, and even when he did deign to communicate it was questionable that he'd agree to do what Betworth ordered. If he weren't so useful, Betworth would tell Powers to get rid of him and get someone else for the job.

No, Runne was perfect. He'd chosen him for that very volatility and fanaticism. Betworth could handle him until the job was done. There was no need to dispose of him, as long as Runne remained obsessed with the hunt.

Dead Aim

The house appeared empty.

But Morgan was clever. It could be a trap.

Runne moved swiftly, silently over the autumn leaves spread on the ground before the window. He'd already disabled the alarm system, and it took only a moment to cut the glass of the window and unlock it.

Darkness.

Are you in there, Morgan?

He waited.

Silence. Emptiness.

Morgan was gone. He could *feel* it. Disappointment surged through him.

He swung over the windowsill into the room.

Paintings. Canvases. Morgan's studio. Like the studios in the other two houses where he'd just missed catching him.

Frustration and sorrow soared within him as he looked around.

Morgan hadn't bothered to pack up his canvases and take them with him, even though he'd known Runne would find this hiding place as he'd found the others. He knew Runne would not destroy them.

Destroy the man.

Destroy the soul.

Never destroy the beauty.

He would not turn on the lights. He would not look at the paintings. They would hurt too much.

But he knew the sketch would be somewhere in full view where he could find it. Morgan always took pains to make sure he wouldn't miss it.

There it was. By the window.

He didn't want to see it.

Yes, he did. At this moment he wanted nothing more in life than to see that sketch. He slowly walked toward it. As he drew closer, he saw that it wasn't just one sketch this time. There were several. He picked them up and held each one up to the moonlight streaming in the window.

Twisted. Haunted. Passionate.

It was Runne's face, sketched over and over. Each portrayal more revealing than the next. It made Runne feel naked and angry . . . and sad. He could feel the tears run down his cheeks.

Morgan, may you rot in hell.

It couldn't go on. Life was too unbearable. He couldn't keep hunting him down and then having him slip through his fingers.

He had to die.

Alex carefully opened her bedroom door.

It was after three A.M., and she could see the crack of light beneath the door of the study but no moving shadow on the other side. It was the fourth time she'd checked out the study and found it the same.

Hell, maybe Morgan had sat down in a chair or couch and fallen asleep.

Not likely.

He was probably listening, waiting for her to make a move.

Well, she was going to make one. What could she lose? Morgan didn't want her dead, so he wasn't going to shoot her if he caught her. She'd try the Land Rover first and see if she could hot-wire it. She'd spent the last few hours prying the brass trim off the marble fireplace in her bedroom to make a jimmy stick. If that didn't work, she'd hike down the mountain and see if she could see the lights of another house. For all she knew, Denver might be only a few miles away.

Dead Aim

What she did know was that she couldn't wait any longer. She had to *do* something.

She closed the door and went over to the window she'd opened a few minutes ago. It was snowing harder and there was already a little pile of snow dampening the carpet.

She pulled her jacket closer around her and swung over the windowsill.

She'd gotten the Land Rover started.

Judd smiled and put down his brush as he heard the roar of the engine.

Smart woman. He wondered how she'd managed to open the door.

He heard the vehicle's tires crunch in the snow as she peeled away from the lodge and down the mountain. He moved across the room to the closet and got out his jacket and gloves. A moment later he was trudging down the mountain, his gaze on the taillights on the road ahead of him.

He hadn't gone ten yards before he lost his footing and slipped. He recovered before he fell, but it wasn't the cold that sent a chill through him.

Ice.

Shit.

Dammit, the snow was so heavy she could barely see the road ahead of her.

Alex lifted her foot from the accelerator and braked lightly. Even the slight pressure caused the Land Rover to skid on the ice-covered road.

She frantically turned the wheel into the skid and then straightened the car.

God, that had been close. A foot more and she would have been off the road and plunging down the mountain.

Iris Johansen

She drew a deep, shaky breath to steady her nerves.

No big deal. She just had to drive more slowly. This Land Rover was a strong workhorse of a vehicle and meant for rough driving. She just wished she could see better. Once she got down this mountain she'd be—

Icy branches looming out of the darkness, blocking the road, reaching out . . .

"No!" She turned the wheel, but it was too late. A branch shattered the windshield as she skidded on the ice and into the tree.

"Jesus!"

Judd broke into a run as he came around the curve, sliding and falling and then getting to his feet again.

The headlights of the Land Rover were piercing the darkness, but the SUV had come to a stop, wheels still spinning as it rested on top of the fallen tree—and the big branch that had smashed through the windshield, splitting on impact to a dagger-thin splinter.

A splinter that had entered Alex's body and was pinning her to the seat.

"This is going to hurt."

What was he talking about? She already hurt, Alex thought dazedly.

"Do you hear me? I can't wait. I have to get you out of here. I've got to break this branch and get you free. I'll try to be quick, but you mustn't fight me or you'll tear more. Do you hear me, Alex?"

"I . . . hear you." She opened her eyes to see his face before her.

Icy blue eyes. Ice everywhere. The windshield lay shattered around her like glittering cubes.

Dead Aim

His hand was closing on the branch.

She stiffened as she realized what he intended to do. "No!"

"I have to do it. I have to get you back up to the lodge. I can't leave you to get help. You could die of hypothermia out here."

"Hurt . . ."

"I know." His hand gently stroked her hair. "It's going to hurt like hell. But only for an instant and then it won't hurt anymore. I'll take care of you."

Safety. Smoke. Dad . . .

No, this wasn't him. Her father was dead.

God, she missed him. . . .

"Alex, will you try not to jerk?" He held her gaze with his own. "I'll take care of you. I promise you'll be safe. I promise you'll live if you'll only help me."

"Dad . . ."

"It's not your father, Alex."

Yet her father was here. Acrid smoke, rescue dogs, and Sarah holding her. Life was important. She had to remember that, or her father would have died for nothing. She nodded and closed her eyes. "Do it."

Agony.

"I need a doctor up here, Galen," Morgan said as soon as Galen answered the phone. "Someone who's good and fast and will keep his mouth shut."

"Why?"

"There's been sort of an accident."

"I don't like the sound of this."

"Alex is hurt."

"Oh, shit. Tell me you didn't cause this 'accident.' "

"I can't do that. I think she's going to be okay, but I want to make sure there's no nerve damage. I don't want her crippled. I need a doctor to clean and stitch the wound. One that won't insist on her going to the hospital."

"What did you do to her?"

"Nothing that she won't get over . . . eventually."

"My God, Logan's going to murder you."

"He'll have to stand in line. So will you get me the doctor?"

"Give me fifteen minutes."

Morgan went back to the bedroom and checked Alex. She was pale, still unconscious, but her pulse was steady. He should probably take this waiting period to go back down to the scene of the accident to clear the road so that the doctor could get to the lodge.

Jesus, she was pale.

Screw what he should do. He wasn't going anywhere right now. He'd wait until he had to leave her.

Judd Morgan was sitting in a chair beside the bed.

She had seen him there before, she realized drowsily. How many times? Five? Six? She couldn't remember. But he'd been there, sketching in that pad as he was doing now.

"What . . . are you doing?"

He glanced up and put aside his pad. "You must be feeling better if curiosity is raising its head."

"Better than what?"

"You've had a fever for the last two days. The doctor said your body was fighting infection."

"Doctor?"

"You don't remember him? Dr. Kedrow. I dragged him up here to tend that extremely nasty wound in your shoulder."

Her right shoulder was swathed in bandages.

A razor-sharp branch stabbing through her flesh.

"Now you remember." His gaze was on her face. "You're okay. The branch went into your shoulder very high up. No permanent damage, but you might have to have plastic surgery if you want to get rid of the scar."

"It . . . hurt."

Dead Aim

"I'd say that's an understatement. You were very gutsy. I was impressed."

"Don't want you to be impressed. . . ." She was having trouble forming the words. They kept drifting away from her. "Want you to let me go."

"We'll talk about that later."

"I want to talk about it now."

"You're half asleep. Later." He picked up his pencil again. "Just go back to sleep. You're fine. You're safe. . . ."

I promise you'll be safe.

Dad.

Not Dad.

Judd Morgan, who was the last man she should believe or trust . . .

"What are you sketching?"

He looked up and smiled. "So you're with me again. How do you feel?"

She thought about it. "Better. Stronger."

"And mad as hell?"

"I'm sure that will come. I'm not up to it right now."

"Let me help you in that direction." He lowered his gaze to his sketch as his pencil moved over the pad. "I'm to blame for what happened to you."

"Of course you are. I wouldn't be here if you hadn't brought—" He was shaking his head. "More?"

"I cut that pine down to block the road."

Her eyes widened in shock. "What?"

"I thought it was likely you'd try to get down the mountain. From what I'd learned about you, I knew it wouldn't do any good to try to stop you. You had to discover it was impossible yourself."

"So you tried to kill me by causing me to crash into that damn tree."

He shook his head. "A miscalculation. I didn't expect you to crash into the pine. You should have had time to see the tree and stop. I didn't count on the ice."

"Miscalculation?"

"Now you're mad as hell."

It was an understatement. She was so angry she felt as if even the roots of her hair were on fire. "You bet I am. I'd be interested to know what you'd have done if I'd stopped the Land Rover in time and taken off on foot."

"Gone after you. I'm very good at tracking."

He was sitting perfectly relaxed, but she could suddenly envision him in the woods, swift, tense, predatory. It didn't defuse the rage she was feeling. "You'd have hunted me down like an animal?"

He didn't answer. "I'm sorry. I didn't mean to hurt you."

"Well, you did, damn you."

He nodded. "Which means I owe you. I find that position very uncomfortable, but it may work to your advantage."

"You bastard."

"I believe this is when I should make my exit. You need a little time to cool down." He rose to his feet. "I'll go get you something to eat."

"And I'll throw it at you."

"That's okay. I've gotten enough down you in the past couple days that missing a meal won't hurt."

She had a vague memory of him sitting beside her, spooning something hot and liquid into her mouth. "If I'd had my wits about me, I'd—"

"Shh. I know. You'd have spit in my eye." He moved toward the door. "And I'd deserve it. I don't usually make mistakes this big. But you should use it to get what you want."

"I want to push you off this mountain."

"That would only give you temporary satisfaction. I'm sure you can think of a more long-term goal." He glanced back at her as he opened the door. "It might help you to know that the dominoes are falling in your direction right now."

She stiffened. "What do you mean?"

"I mean I have to make reparations. I have very few codes I live by, but you stumbled onto one of them. It means I have to figure how to give you what you want and still keep you alive."

He was gone before she had a chance to question him. What was he up to? Did he expect her to believe he was having twinges of conscience because he was responsible for this wound? She would be an idiot to be that gullible. He was a kidnapper and a paid thug and she didn't know what else. He was ruthless and cold and without—

Yet she did believe him. She didn't know about the twinges of conscience, but he was a complicated man and his moral structure was probably also convoluted. Most strong people had to have some sort of rules to guide their lives. Maybe the fact that she'd been hurt had tapped into some humane reservoir beneath that cool surface.

Or maybe not. Maybe he was trying to find another way to control her.

There was only one way to find out. Challenge him. Test him.

Jesus, she didn't feel strong enough right now to challenge a Muppet.

So get over it. Move.

She slowly, carefully, sat up.

Her shoulder throbbed and her head swam with dizziness.

Get to the bathroom. Wash your face.

Yeah, sure.

She held on to the nightstand as she got to her feet.

Darkness.

It passed within a minute or two, but she still stood there waiting for her strength to come back. She took deep breaths and tried to focus on something besides the desire to fall back on the bed.

The sketch pad Morgan had tossed on the footstool when

he'd gotten to his feet. It was lying sideways on the hassock, but she could tell that it was a sketch of a face.

Vulnerable. Frail. Troubled.

It was Alex's face.

Was that how he saw her? Well, he had a few things to learn. She was neither weak nor vulnerable. She could feel the energy flow through her as the adrenaline kicked in. She let go of the nightstand and moved determinedly toward the bathroom.

She was back in bed and flipping through the pages of Morgan's sketchbook when he came into the room carrying a tray.

"Invasion of privacy." His tone was light as he set the tray down on the nightstand beside her. "I could sue."

"When all these sketches are of me? I don't think so." She looked up with a cool stare. "You must have been very bored."

"You weren't the most entertaining company. I had to keep myself occupied."

"This isn't me." She closed the sketchbook. "You've made me . . . weak."

He shook his head. "There's nothing weak about you. It's not uncommon for a subject to see what they fear in a portrait."

"I'm not afraid. I see what you've sketched."

He flipped open the pad to the first sketch. "You're ill; you're without defenses." He pointed to the line of her mouth. "But there's strength here. And do you see the tension in the jawline? Determination. You wouldn't let go even when you were feverish. You were a very interesting subject."

He was too close. He wasn't touching her, but she could feel the heat of his body and she instinctively tensed. "And you didn't feel in the least guilty for sketching me when I was helpless?"

He smiled. "You know what a ruthless bastard I am. I take what I'm given."

"And also what you're not given."

"True. But I never thought of you as helpless." He took the pad from her and handed her a small plate. "So stop brooding and eat your ham sandwich."

He'd taken a step back, and she breathed a sigh of relief. It was idiotic to be this physically aware of him. It must be because she had been hurt and his power and presence were in such sharp contrast.

He smiled. "I thought you'd prefer finger food to spilling soup down your chest in front of me."

She did prefer it. She was feeling clumsy and vulnerable enough without— She had a sudden thought. "I'm wearing your shirt. How did I get it on?"

"Me." He sat down in the chair and put his feet on the hassock. "It wasn't in the doctor's job description and I didn't want to offend him. I'm sorry if it upsets you."

"It doesn't upset me. That's the least of my worries." She bit into the sandwich. "I was just curious."

"I should have known better. A woman who can hot-wire a car wouldn't let a little thing like nudity bother her."

"There are too many ways a person can be naked besides the physical." She tapped the sketch pad. "This bothers me more. You . . . intruded."

"You have a very interesting face, but I promise I won't do it again without your permission."

She believed him. "You're very good—for a criminal."

He laughed. "That was a grudging compliment. I'm glad I didn't disappoint you."

"You couldn't disappoint me. I don't expect anything from you."

"Good. A clean slate." He made a face. "I wish."

"You're a fine artist. Which makes it even worse that you ignore your gift to do things that hurt other people." She shrugged. "Not that it makes any difference to me. Do what you want, be what you want."

"Thank you."

She ignored the irony in his tone. "As long as you give me the same privilege and let me go my own way." She stared him in the eye. "So prove you didn't lie to me. Let me go. Put up or shut up."

"It's not that easy. All the roadblocks I mentioned before are still in place." He held up his hand as she started to interrupt. "I didn't say I wasn't willing to find a way around them. I'm in a delicate situation. I made a deal with Logan and I don't want to break it."

"Are you afraid of him?"

"No," he said quietly. "I'm afraid of you. Because there's every chance you could get me killed."

"I don't want to get anyone killed. I just want to find the men who buried those men, women, and children at Arapahoe Junction."

"I know. And since you won't give up until you find them, you won't be safe until you do." He turned away. "And I promised you that I'd keep you safe. So I have no choice. I have to find and get rid of them."

"You expect me to believe you'll help me find them?"

"And dispose of them. After that I figure my debt is paid and you're on your own. Finish your sandwich and milk. We have work to do."

"What?"

"Recuperation time is over. I take it you didn't ID any of the men at the dam in the databases?"

She shook her head.

"Police artist?"

"That was going to be the next step."

"The next step is here. You give me features and I'll put them on paper. We'll get faces and then we'll get names."

She stared at him for a moment. "You mean it."

He sat down and flipped open the sketch pad. "You're damn right I do."

"Longer sideburns?" Morgan asked.

"No, but the forehead was broader, the hair receding."

Morgan's pencil moved quickly over the pad. "Any moles or scars?"

"I don't remember."

"That's not acceptable."

"I only saw him for a few seconds. I was paying attention to the men outside the helicopter."

"You remembered the other two faces."

"He was inside the helicopter. There was shadow. . . ."

Ken's helicopter exploding in a ball of flame.

"You don't want to remember."

"Screw you."

He ignored her, his gaze on the pad. "You said he was the one who fired the shot. Take it from the point where he lifted his hand and pointed the gun."

"I don't remember."

"What kind of gun was it?"

"I don't know."

"What size? A magnum? A thirty-eight?"

"A rifle . . ."

"Okay, he's lifting the rifle. Follow the line from barrel to stock. Do you see it?"

Metal gleaming blue in the lights of Ken's helicopter.

"Do you see it?"

"I see it."

"Then you have to be able to see his face. Lips?"

"Thin."

"Cheekbones?"

"High."

"How high?"

"His face is kind of . . . diamond shape."

"Good." His pencil was flying over the pad. "Eyebrows?"

Eyes squinting as he aimed the rifle.

"Bushy."

"Eye color?"

"I can't see them. Dark, I think."

"Nose?"

"Straight. Short. Slightly flared nostrils."

"Okay. We've got a start. Give me a minute and I'll let you see it and we'll make the changes." He bent over the pad.

That had been the procedure all afternoon. Morgan had probed and questioned and made her remember details she had forgotten. Working on the sketches of the first two men had not been easy, but it was on the last one that she had drawn a blank.

A blank Morgan had not let her maintain.

He was tireless and his concentration seemed, if anything, more intense while he was working on this last sketch.

"What about his neck? No double chin?"

"No. The line was firm, sharp, and he— What's wrong?"

He'd frozen, his pencil still, as he stared at the sketch.

"Nothing. Just making sure I got everything." His pencil began flying across the pad again.

A few minutes later he glanced up at her. "You did well."

"You forced me to do well."

"And you resent it."

"No. Well, maybe on one level. But it was necessary for me to remember. No matter how much it hurt. It was my job." She sat up and braced herself. "Are you ready to show me the sketch?"

"Are you ready to see it?" He smiled faintly. "Hell, yes, you are." He turned the pad around. "The shooter."

He'd sketched in the rifle pressed against the face of the man.

She flinched and then forced herself to concentrate on the face. "He looks too . . . smooth. The face was thin, but there were wrinkles around his eyes when he squinted."

Morgan turned the pad back and began to work. "Ears."

"Close to his head, I think. I didn't see. . . . The rifle was—"

Dead Aim

"Think about it." His tone was hard, incisive, demanding, as his pencil moved over the pad. "You remembered the sideburns. You have to remember the ears."

"I'll remember. Give me a minute."

"Just spit it out. You're on a roll."

"For God's sake, give me a break."

He glanced up at her. "Is that what you want from me?"

Hardness. Coolness. Without mercy.

No, she didn't want a break from him. She wanted exactly what she was being given. Intelligence. Dedication. Determination. "Hell, no."

"I didn't think so."

She closed her eyes, remembering. "He had small ears, close to his head, and his lobes were full, almost plump. . . ."

"I think we're as close as we're going to get." Morgan got to his feet. "We'll go over them again after you've taken a nap."

"I don't need a nap. I can look at the sketches now."

"You could look, but would you see them? It's been seven hours. You're getting woozy. I wasn't easy on you."

"No." Her gaze was fastened on the pad. "Those likenesses are really close, Morgan. Are we going to send them to Leopold?"

"Maybe."

"What?"

"Don't get edgy. We'll get an ID. There are other sources that may be faster." He moved toward the door. "Take a nap while I clean these up. We'll talk later."

"I want to talk now. I didn't work my ass off to get those sketches right to have them end up anywhere but in the hands of people who can find and ID these men."

"One's already been ID'd."

Her eyes widened. "What are you talking about?"

He held up the second sketch they'd worked on. "George

Lester. He was the man who was driving the blue Toyota and tried to put you down."

"How do you know who he is?"

"I called a friend, and he checked and found that the police had done a fingerprint and dental check on him. Definitely George Lester from Detroit. Very ugly customer but a loner. That's going to make it difficult for us."

"Dental check? You make it sound—" She stopped. "He's dead?"

He shrugged. "I didn't know we'd need him."

"You killed him?"

"He was going after you. It would have been only a matter of time before he got you. It seemed the reasonable thing to do."

"Killing is never reasonable."

"I beg to disagree. But this time it wasn't smart. I was only interested in getting him off your case, not finding his connections. Now we'll have to start at square one."

"Why didn't you tell me?"

"It would only have upset you. You have a soft heart. You didn't even kill Al Habim when he targeted you. It seemed the most efficient way to protect you."

So casual. So cool.

He glanced back over his shoulder as he opened the door. "That's right," he said, as if reading her mind. "One cold son of a bitch. But there are uses for men like me. You'll probably find a few before we're done."

She stared at the door after it had shut behind him.

She was filled with shock, confusion, and a sense of foreboding.

There are uses for men like me.

But she didn't know anyone who would dare to try to use Judd Morgan.

Okay. Rest. Think. Analyze the situation. Decide if she could place even a small amount of trust in a man who had killed a man because it was efficient.

5

"Shit!"

Powers snatched up the report off the fax machine, scanned it, and then dialed Betworth. "The report just came in from Quantico on the man in the stairwell, sir."

"Morgan?"

"How did you—" Sometimes he thought the bastard was psychic. "Yes, they had trouble with the video or we would have had the ID sooner. You expected him to turn up here?"

"It was always a possibility. We didn't think Morgan could make the connection, but we weren't certain. And according to his file, you never know how Morgan is going to jump. But I would have thought he'd show up right after the dam break. I had the CIA ready to gather him in if he decided to do a little snooping. I was a little worried about John Logan's connection with Graham."

"Logan?"

"He was pulling every string he could to have Graham put in a safe house after his wife was shot. And it was Logan who tried to get the sanction lifted on Morgan several months ago. He's got a lot of influence. I had a hell of a time blocking it."

"We've had Logan under surveillance since Graham disappeared. He's at his home in California and hasn't tried to make contact."

"Have you been able to monitor his phones?"

"No way. He's got a state-of-the-art security and communication system."

"Then I suggest you'd better figure a way to find out what we need. I understand he's very fond of his wife. Good-bye, Powers."

"I have sketches of the other two men Alex saw at Arapahoe Junction," Judd said as soon as Galen answered. "I need to know who they are."

"Alex gave you descriptions? You know how tricky memory can be. Can you rely on her?"

"Yes."

"No doubts?"

"No doubts."

"Can you fax them?"

"I think you'd better come and pick them up."

"You're halfway across the country. Why?"

"I may need you here. I have a bad feeling. . . . Have you told Logan about Alex's injury?"

"Not yet."

"It's just as well. I don't need Logan upset enough to get in my way. How soon can you get here?"

"I'm on my way." He hung up.

Morgan sat down at the kitchen table and pulled out the sketches. He threw the other two sketches aside to look at the one they'd worked on last—the shooter. He drew a deep breath and then slowly let it out. He'd almost blown it. Exhausted as Alex had been, she'd noticed his reaction. He had to be more careful.

Careful? The idea was laughable. He'd known that safety was out the window the minute he finished that sketch. Until then there had been a chance that the dam break didn't have anything to do with Z-3.

Okay, he could still back off and disappear. He could find another way to keep Alex safe.

Alex.

What the hell? He'd give it a little more time. He'd clean up these sketches while Alex was napping and get a final approval before giving them to Galen. It should be only a matter of hours before he arrived. Galen never wasted time when he went into motion.

"You shouldn't be up." Morgan got up from his chair and came toward her. "Why didn't you call me? I would have helped you."

"I'm fine." She brushed by him and went toward the fire. "A little cold."

"You need time to heal, and I pushed you hard today. You're tired and your body temperature probably dropped. You should try to get more sleep."

She held out her hands to the blaze. "I didn't mean to sleep at all." She had thought she was so disturbed she would lie there for hours, but she'd dropped off almost immediately. "What have you been doing?"

"Cleaning up the sketches. Waiting for Galen."

"Galen?"

"A friend. He's coming to pick up the sketches and make sure that I haven't totally maimed you."

"What business is it of his if you have?"

"Now, that's not in keeping with your philosophy. Isn't everyone supposed to be their brother's keeper?"

"In a perfect world. This world isn't perfect. Why is this Galen worried about me?"

"He recommended me to Logan."

"So it's pure self-interest."

"Not entirely. Galen is one of the good guys. He's generally a cynical bastard, but he's like you—he wants to go around righting wrongs. He even tried to right a wrong done to me." He smiled faintly. "Everyone makes mistakes."

"If he's your friend, I wouldn't call that a mistake."

"There are friends and then there are friends."

"What's that supposed to mean? No, don't tell me. You wouldn't get close enough to commit to a friend."

"Not willingly. But even I'm not perfect."

"What does this Galen do? Is he a criminal like you?"

"He's an information specialist. He has contacts all over the world. He arranges things and smooths paths that need smoothing."

"Legally?"

"Sometimes." He handed her the sketches. "Look at them. If there are any changes, let me know."

She glanced through the sketches. "They look good to me. I can't see anything I'd want to change. You're really very good. I don't know how you— Wait. This isn't right." She was staring at the sketch of the shooter. "You've given him a tiny scar on his left cheek."

"Didn't you tell me to put that in?"

She shook her head. "I'm sure I— Maybe I did. I was so tired."

"That's an understatement. You were exhausted."

"It's hard to remember. It looks right. . . ."

"I can take it out."

"No." She shook her head. "Let me think about it."

"Whatever you say." He took the sketches from her. "I'll set them up against the wall. I put your camera over on that chair. I'd like you to take some shots of the sketches before we turn them over to Galen."

She nodded. "Good idea." She moved across the room. "I still think we should give the sketches to Leopold. You may trust this Galen, but I don't."

Dead Aim

"Well, then you'll have the photographs, won't you? Galen has contacts in areas that Leopold doesn't know exist. Logan has had him working on gathering information since your friend Sarah's shooting."

"Then I assume he's a criminal too?"

"Not exactly." He finished setting up the sketches. "No Leopold. Lester's demise will make things very difficult for me with the authorities. It doesn't matter that he was a scumbag and a murderer. It wouldn't matter that he tried to kill you. I'm the one who'd land in jail for a year or two while I waited for the courts to get around to me. They don't understand vigilante justice."

"Neither do I." She focused on the first sketch. "You could have called the police instead of killing Lester."

"Too much red tape. People get killed wading through red tape."

She shook her head.

"Look at it this way. Suppose you could have run across an associate of one of those kamikaze pilots in the ruins of the World Trade Center. Would you have called the police and trusted that the courts would kill him for you?"

Smoke, tears, pain, and helpless rage.

She took the picture. "It's not the same thing."

"Anything that strikes at the heart is always the exception to the rules we make for ourselves. Remember how you felt in that moment?"

"Every day. Every minute." She took the final photograph and turned away. "I'm finished. You can package the sketches to give to your friend."

"Does that mean you're resigned to letting me help you get these assholes?"

"It appears you've already gotten one of them."

"That's an evasion."

She met his gaze. "I'm not resigned to anything. I don't trust you. You told me I'd find a use for you and I did. If you had let me go, Leopold could have arranged for me to have a session with a police artist. I don't owe you anything."

"I didn't say you did. I'm the one who has a debt to pay off." He shrugged. "And it makes me uncomfortable. The sooner I get rid of it, the better."

"Take me back to Denver and we'll call it even. I don't want your help and I certainly don't want your company."

"Do you suppose you can put up with it while I check that wound? You can't do it yourself yet."

She opened her mouth to tell him no and then closed it. She sat down in the chair and opened his shirt that she wore as a pajama top. "Why not? You're responsible for it."

"That's what I like, a heart full of forgiveness." He unwound the bandage and lifted the pad. "The doctor did a good job. Very neat stitches. Couldn't have done better myself."

"You're a doctor as well as an artist?" she asked mockingly. "Amazing."

"Don't be ugly. I'm a man of many talents. I wouldn't have liked the job of extracting the splinters and cleaning out this wound, but I've had enough battlefield experience to sew you up."

She wished she hadn't let him touch her. Her flesh was tingling beneath his fingers. Not as it had in the stairwell at the hotel. There was no comfort, no security this time. It was . . . sensual . . . disturbing.

He must have felt the tension, because his gaze shifted to her face. His hands became still for an instant before he put a clean pad on the wound. "Looks like it's healing pretty well now." He wrapped the bandage over her shoulder. "Be sure you keep taking those antibiotics and pain pills."

"Of course. I'm not a masochist." She buttoned up the shirt. "I'm going to get well as quickly as I can."

"So that you can avenge yourself on me as well as the bad guys?"

"It's hard to distinguish between you." She moved toward

the bedroom. "I'm going to take another nap. Wake me when Galen gets here."

"I will. I wouldn't cheat you of the opportunity to meet him. He's truly an original."

And so was Judd Morgan, she thought as she closed the door. Hard as a diamond and just as brilliant, every facet shimmering with power and deception.

Deception. Yes, that had been the one constant since she first saw Morgan in that stairwell. He was an enigma. She had no idea which move he'd make next.

Or why.

She walked across the room and crawled back into bed. She'd be glad when she regained more strength. She'd been on her feet for less than thirty minutes and she was disgustingly weak and shaky. Maybe it was the pills. . . .

The pills?

No, she didn't think Morgan was keeping her doped up for any reason other than pain. If he'd wanted to keep her sedated, he could have done it when he brought her here from the hotel. Not that she could be sure. Well, all she could do was be patient until she was better and meanwhile take whatever help he offered. Let him be as mysterious as the Sphinx for all she cared. It didn't matter how he tried to deceive her as long as she didn't trust him.

Deceive.

Suddenly her lids flicked open. "Oh, Jesus."

"What the hell is happening?" Galen asked harshly when Judd picked up the telephone. "My God, Logan has been on my ass since I landed. He said that if I don't go after you, he will. You were supposed to keep her safe."

"She is safe."

"The hell she is. Not bloody likely."

"What are you so upset about? I told you the wound wasn't serious."

"Wound?" Silence. "Do you have a television there in the lodge?"

"Yes."

"Then turn it on to CNN. I just picked up my rental car at Stapleton Airport. I'll call you again when I get on the road. I should be there within an hour." Galen hung up.

Not good. Galen didn't lose his cool without reason.

Judd moved across the room and clicked on the television set.

Morgan opened Alex's door. "I think you'd better come out here and see this."

She sat up in bed. "Is Galen here?"

"Not yet. He should be here any minute." He stepped aside. "But you'd better see this news report before he gets here."

"News report?" She swung her feet to the floor. "What's wrong?" Panic surged through her. "Has something happened to Sarah?"

"No. Something's happened to you. Come on."

She was already following him. "What news story? Have they found out that Logan paid you to snatch me?"

"I wish." He nodded at the TV. "Damn, another commercial."

"Screw the commercial. Tell me what's happening."

"It would be better if you saw it for yourself. You're not likely to believe me." He shrugged. "Okay, you're being hunted by the FBI for involvement in the possible sabotage of Arapahoe Dam."

She stared at him incredulously. "You've got to be kidding."

He shook his head. "Jurgens made an announcement this morning. There's an all-points bulletin out for you."

Her knees felt weak and she dropped down into a chair. "It

doesn't make sense. I'm the one who's been telling everyone that the dam break had to be investigated."

"According to Jurgens, Homeland Security was already suspicious that the break was no accident. They didn't want to make their findings public until they had more proof of how the sabotage was done. They're almost sure that the job was done by Matanza, and you were in Guatemala, their home base, two years ago. The CIA believes that's when you were recruited. The FBI was about to make an announcement when Ken Nader was killed. You were under suspicion from the moment you were found at the site."

She shook her head dazedly. "I could have died in that landslide."

"And who would suspect a supposed victim of being involved in Nader's murder?"

"And what about that man who ran us off the road and shot Sarah?"

"But never touched you. It was entirely possible your accomplices arranged the attack to take any suspicion off you in Nader's death."

"This is crazy."

"Actually, it's pretty clever."

"I don't understand this. Why would the FBI—" She drew a deep breath. "I have to get in touch with them and straighten this out."

He shook his head. "Bad move. I'd bet you'd be dead within twenty-four hours."

"Bullshit. We're talking about a law-enforcement agency. They might put me in jail until I could get this mess cleared up, but no one's going to shoot me."

"No, you'd probably conveniently find a way to commit suicide in your cell—if you made it that far. It's more likely that you'd be killed when you were apprehended. Presto. No witness."

"You're saying you think the FBI is in collusion with those

men at the dam." She lifted her shaking hand to her mouth. "And there was something about the CIA too. . . . I just don't believe it."

"It's not necessarily a conspiracy that goes deep to the bone of either organization. But I believe someone high up is pulling strings and furnishing scenarios to them that may fry your ass."

She shook her head. "I won't believe it. You're talking about Americans who work every day to protect our country."

"Ah, more heroes?"

"Yes," she said defiantly.

"Heroes can be manipulated. Evidence can be planted. I'd bet every news story for the next few days will show Alex Graham's guilt unfold with all the drama of a soap opera."

"My God, you're cynical."

"I've been there. I know how it works." He turned away. "I'll make coffee. You may need a jolt of caffeine after you finish watching CNN."

She needed more than caffeine at the end of those fifteen minutes. She felt ill. Christ, even the photos they'd turned over to the news agencies appeared incriminating. She recognized one taken at the airport in Guatemala City that looked like a mug shot.

"Not your most flattering photo." Morgan handed her a cup of coffee. "And it may be the one that's broadcast and re-broadcast."

"They still haven't come up with a reason why I'd do something like this."

"The Fox affiliate has a few theories. Bitterness over your father's death at WTC comes high on the list. Several people heard you say that the government should have paid attention to information they received before 9/11."

"Hell, yes."

"And friends and employers say you changed after your father's death."

"Didn't everyone change after 9/11?"

He nodded. "But we're talking about you."

"It's ridiculous." She moistened her lips. "And I'm a journalist. I know the people in my profession. They're not going to be duped. They're going to go after their own stories."

"But by that time you may be dead news. With the emphasis on *dead*. Will they work their asses off to discover how innocent you were then?"

"Maybe."

"And maybe not. Every day is a new story. You'd better concentrate on—" He was interrupted by a knock on the door. "It's about time." He moved to the door. "Galen?"

"You're damn right. Let me in."

Morgan unlocked the door and stepped aside. "It took you long enough."

"You're the one who decided to move up here to the back of beyond." His gaze went to Alex. "Hi, I'm Sean Galen."

Galen was a man in his late thirties with close-cut dark hair and dark eyes snapping with vitality. Even his movements were charged with electricity as he came into the room. "I hear this idiot managed to get you banged up. How are you?"

"I was better before I saw that I'm some sort of fugitive."

"Yeah, that came as a shock to us too." He took off his jacket and tossed it on a chair. "Logan is foaming at the mouth."

"Then let him direct some of that anger at Jurgens," Alex said. "If Logan has so much clout, tell him to get me out of this mess."

"Believe me, he's trying." He glanced at Alex's cup. "Tell me that's hot coffee?" He didn't wait for an answer but headed for the kitchenette. "Elena wasn't pleased that I had to take off. She said we both should be involved in having this baby. I'm not happy with you, Judd."

"Alex's wound is my fault; I plead innocent to everything

else. Besides, Elena doesn't need you. She can handle anything. The baby will be a piece of cake to her."

Elena? Alex had a vague memory of Morgan mentioning the name. The woman who wanted to cut his throat . . . Smart woman. "And what's Logan doing to straighten this out?"

"He's called Jurgens and is in contact with Homeland Security. So far they're not responding very positively."

"They've got to realize it's a mistake."

Galen glanced at Morgan. "Mistake?"

"Setup."

"That's what I think. So that means the dam break probably had some sort of government connection."

Morgan nodded.

They were both ignoring her. "Or that it's a mistake that I can straighten out if I can just get someone to listen. Maybe some hotshot in the Bureau developed this theory about me and they're running with it."

They both just looked at her.

Her hands clenched into fists. "Dammit, this doesn't have to be a conspiracy."

"No, but it makes more sense than a bureaucratic blunder," Morgan said. "Have they turned loose all their dogs, Galen?"

Galen nodded. "According to Logan it's going to be a witch hunt and no one's listening to him."

"CIA's involved. How high up?"

"Danley broke the news on the recent discovery of Alex's connection with Matanza. You can't get much higher than that. Do you know Danley?"

Morgan shook his head. "My contact in the CIA was Al Leary. But Leary was ambitious as hell and I'd bet he's in Danley's pocket." He thought about it. "Which may not be bad for us. He might know—" He shook his head. "Later. We don't have time for this. As I told you when you called me back on the phone, we have to get Alex out of here. That doctor I had up here to treat her isn't about to take this kind of heat. He'll be on the line to the police the minute he sees a photo and makes the connection. Have you found a place for her and arranged for a helicopter?"

Galen nodded. "I called from the car on the way here."

"Wait a minute." Alex stood up. "You're not listening to me. What part of what I said didn't you understand? I'm not running away and hiding."

Galen and Morgan exchanged glances.

Morgan shrugged. "I was expecting this. Unfortunately, she's an idealist. She wants to believe the good guys are always good."

"Nice." Galen smiled at Alex. "I'd like to believe that too. But it's always better to hedge your bet."

"And that means?"

"Let us get you to someplace safer and then start a dialogue with the FBI."

She hesitated.

"Why not?" Galen asked. "If we're wrong, then you'll be able to rub our noses in our dastardly suspicions. If we're right, then you'll be alive and kicking." His eyes twinkled. "Preferably not us."

This situation was so bizarre anything could happen. It wouldn't hurt to be cautious. "Okay." She turned toward her bedroom. "Let me throw some clothes on and we'll get out of here."

"Good. Galen, you call and tell the helicopter we're ready for pickup." Morgan moved toward the study. "I'll go down to the bottom of the road and keep watch."

"You talk as if we may be under siege," Alex said sarcastically. "As far as I'm concerned, this is merely a precaution. Nothing is going to—" Morgan had come out of the study carrying a rifle. "What are you doing? You look like you're going to war. I don't want anyone hurt, and I won't be party to any violence."

"You're not invited." Morgan headed for the front door.

"And if it makes you feel any better, I'll try not to damage anyone too badly. I won't be the one to start the war."

"Are you taking the Land Rover?" Galen asked.

Morgan shook his head. "I'll walk. We'll leave the lights on and the Land Rover in the driveway. I want the house to look occupied. I'll get back here as soon as I see the helicopter. Take care of her, Galen."

"It's my pleasure," Galen said to Alex as the door slammed behind Morgan. "Let me know if you need any help getting dressed."

"Thanks." She was probably crazy for going along with this, she thought as she went into her bedroom and started to dress. She didn't know Galen, she didn't trust Morgan, and she was only a pawn to Logan. She didn't believe anyone in the FBI was intentionally conspiring against her. So why the hell had she given in to their arguments?

Waco. Ruby Ridge. WTC.

Government agencies that made mistakes could cause tragedy and endless regret. It only made sense to avoid any confrontation until she was in a position to show everyone how ridiculous the suspicions were.

She slipped on her strollers, draped her plaid shirt over her shoulders, and grabbed her jacket. Galen would have to help her put on the rest of these clothes. This blasted shoulder was too sore to punish it anymore.

Galen was leafing through the sketches when she came out of the bedroom. "These are very detailed. You have a good memory."

"They aren't faces I'd forget. Morgan was determined I'd remember every single detail. He nagged me until I was ready to throw the pad at him." She added grudgingly, "But he did a brilliant job. He's exceptionally talented."

"Yes, he is. In any number of areas. A jack-of-all-trades—and master of all of them."

"Including assassin. He told me he killed George Lester."

Dead Aim

"Before George Lester could kill you."

She remembered the tingle of shock she had felt when she saw Morgan walk out of the study with that rifle. He looked totally at ease with the weapon, as if it were an extension of his body. "But I think it was too easy for him. Human life is precious. Destroying it should be difficult, if not impossible." She crossed the room to stand before Galen. "Can you help me get this shirt on?"

"Sure." He put down the sketches and helped her with the shirt and quickly buttoned it. "Sorry about this. I'm sure Judd didn't mean for you to be—"

"It doesn't matter what he meant. It happened. And it wouldn't have happened if he hadn't brought me here." She gave him a level stare. "And you're as much to blame, for arranging it."

He gave a mock shiver. "It's dropped a few degrees in here. Let me help you put on that coat."

"Son of a bitch."

Morgan cursed steadily beneath his breath as he trained his binoculars on the caravan of cars in the valley below. He could see two police cars trailing at least four unmarked vehicles.

He quickly dialed Galen. "Get the hell out of there. It's too late for the pickup. They're on their way. Six cars."

"I'll change the pickup to the valley. We're heading for the car now. We should reach your position in a few minutes."

"You'll run right into them if you keep on going down the mountain. There's a thick stand of trees about a mile down from the lodge. Hide in the shrubbery until they get past you."

"Where will you be?"

"Guarding your back." He hung up.

"Six cars?" Alex echoed as they pulled into the stand of trees. "To capture me?"

"Evidently you're a very dangerous person." Galen's tone was abstracted as he reached for his phone. "A change of plan, Dave," he said into the phone after dialing quickly. "Send the copter to the valley. Give us fifteen minutes." He hung up and said to Alex, "No problem."

She could see any number of potential problems. "Where's Morgan?"

He nodded at the pines surrounding them. "Somewhere out there. He has a fondness for climbing trees. Though pines aren't his favorite. Not enough cover."

"Isn't he coming with us?"

"Probably."

"What do you mean? Either he is or—"

"Here they come," Galen murmured, his gaze on the road. "I'd say they're moving with a definite sense of purpose, wouldn't you?"

There was no question of that, Alex thought in bewilderment. The caravan of cars was traveling swiftly up the road toward the lodge. The sheer number of cars was threatening. What the devil was happening here?

The cars approached and then passed the stand of trees where they were hiding.

"We'll give them a few minutes more." Galen started the car. "But they seem fairly focused on their mission."

Jesus, and she was that mission. It was too macabre.

"Okay, we're out of here." Galen put the car in gear and drove out of the trees. "If they're playing nice, we should be down the mountain before they get into the lodge."

"And what's playing nice?"

"Calling out for surrender, surrounding the place, tossing a few tear-gas grenades. Standard operations. That all takes time."

"Tear gas? For God's sake, that's ridiculous. There's no way that I'd be enough threat to warrant—"

Dead Aim

The vibration that shook the car came a second before the sound of an explosion.

Her gaze flew to the rearview mirror. The lodge at the top of the mountain was engulfed in flames.

Galen stepped on the accelerator. "Evidently they decided not to play nice."

She couldn't take her horrified gaze from the burning lodge. "If I were in there, there's no way I'd be able to get out to surrender."

"Does that tell you anything?"

She couldn't answer. All she could do was watch in helpless fascination as the devouring flames destroyed the lodge.

"My God, Jurgens, why didn't you wait?" Leopold stared in horror at the burning building. "You didn't give her a chance."

"You heard me call out and tell her to surrender," Jurgens said. "Didn't you see that rifle aimed at us from that window to the right of the door?"

"No."

"I did. From the doctor who called in the tip we confirmed that there's at least one other perpetrator. There's no telling who else is in there with her."

"So you lobbed in a rocket?"

"I had to make sure. We haven't got any cover here. We're sitting ducks. I had to do it."

"You should have given her a chance."

"Did she give those people at Arapahoe Junction a chance?"

"So you convicted her before she had her day in court."

"Well, if she's in there, we won't need to go to the expense of a trial." He frowned. "But it may be some time before we're able to go in and verify. We'd better search the area to make sure they didn't escape."

"So you can hunt her down and shoot her?"

"I only did my job." Jurgens smiled sardonically. "These

days this country is very aware of how vulnerable it is, and people don't like it. They want to strike back when they're hurt. What side do you think Joe Public will weigh in on when all the details concerning Graham's crime come to light?"

"How do you know they will?"

"It's a certainty. We have more evidence than we revealed to the media."

"Or to us?"

"We would have shared if Graham had surrendered peacefully." He turned to the agent next to him. "Take four men and search the road and brush. Don't take chances. These are criminals who— What the hell is that?"

The metallic throbbing of rotors was followed by the sight of a helicopter coming through the pass. The aircraft dipped and then started a descent into the valley below.

"I don't like this." Jurgens ran toward his car. "Leopold, have one of your cars stay here. You come along. We may need you. . . . The rest of you pile into those cars and get down there."

"Screw you," Leopold said. "I'm not taking orders from a gun-happy son of a bitch who—"

"Suit yourself." Jurgens jumped behind the wheel of the car, and the vehicle leaped forward as he jammed on the accelerator.

"They're coming like bats out of hell." Galen glanced over his shoulder at the four cars speeding down the mountain road. In a matter of seconds they'd reach the valley. "It's going to be close."

The helicopter was landing in a snow-covered field a half mile from them. Jesus, it seemed like a hundred to Alex. "Are we going to make it?"

"We'll make it, but with all their firepower the takeoff may be pretty chancy."

Dead Aim

Ken's helicopter. Exploding. Flaming. Splintering.

"Or maybe not . . ." Galen murmured, his gaze on the rearview mirror. "I believe Judd may be doing his thing."

"What?" She looked over her shoulder in time to see the lead car swerve violently and then crash into a tree.

The second car's front tire blew and the driver frantically tried to right the car, but it spun sideways and the third car piled into it.

"One more, Judd," Galen said as he parked the car beside the helicopter. "One more."

The fourth car's front tire blew, but the driver managed to stop before he piled into the other two cars.

"Bull's-eye." Galen jumped out of the car and ran toward the helicopter. "Let's get out of here."

She was right behind him. "What about Morgan? Are we just going to leave him?"

"He said he'd contact us later." He opened the door of the helicopter and lifted her inside. "I don't think we have to worry. He seems to have the situation in hand."

"He's on foot and he's just shot the tires out of four FBI cars. I don't call that having the situation in hand. They're going to go after him."

"He'll have a head start." He waved at the pilot to take off. "That's all he needs."

"He's on foot. They'll catch him."

"He was on foot in Afghanistan after he took out a warlord who was sheltering Al Qaeda terrorists. He had to travel seventy miles through unfriendly territory before he was able to arrange a pickup."

"He told you that?"

Galen shook his head. "Judd doesn't talk much. But he's something of a legend to the Rangers."

She gazed out the window at the wreckage on the hillside as the helicopter rose from the ground. A man had gotten out of the car that crashed into the tree and was striding toward the pileup. He was holding his arm and there was blood on his cheek. There was something familiar about him, but his head was down and she couldn't identify him. But she could identify the rage and tension that characterized the man's every movement.

And that anger would be directed at Judd Morgan, who had stayed behind so that they could escape.

"Call him," she told Galen. "Set up a meeting place near here. We're not leaving him."

"He said to get you to somewhere safe. They may have already radioed for helicopters and reinforcements. Besides, he's probably nowhere near that pileup. He took his shots and got out of there."

"Call him."

He smiled. "Whatever you say." He pulled out his phone and dialed. A moment later he shook his head. "He's got his phone turned off. Makes sense. He sure as hell wouldn't want it to go off at a sensitive moment. Now, may we get the hell out of here?"

"I guess we can't do anything else." She gazed down at the scene below. More agents were getting out of the cars. They were talking on phones, and the first man who'd gotten out of the car was standing and staring up at the helicopter.

"My God, it's Jurgens."

"Why are you surprised? He's the one who put that all-points bulletin out on you."

"I know . . . it's just . . . I guess what you told me about him never really hit home until I saw him down there." Her lips twisted sardonically. "And he told me he wanted to set me up in a safe house."

Galen's gaze shifted to the burning lodge. "Then I'd say you were smart to turn down his offer."

Her glance followed Galen's. No safety, only death there. No safety anywhere.

6

Morgan didn't call Galen until the helicopter had landed at a small airport north of Denver.

"I'm on my way. I picked up a rental car at Colorado Springs. Where am I going?"

"The airport at Fort Collins. I just let Dave out here and I'm flying the helicopter for the rest of the trip. We'll set down and pick you up."

"Not smart. Just tell me the final destination."

"I have a mutiny on my hands. Alex is feeling guilty about leaving you. I told her that the world would be better off without you, but she won't listen."

"Really? Amazing. Okay, I should be at Fort Collins in about two hours."

Galen turned to Alex as he hung up. "He's on his way."

Alex nodded. "You lied. I don't feel guilty. It's just that right is right."

"Refreshing."

"Where are we going after we pick him up?"

"A ranch near Sibley. It's a small town near Jackson Hole, Wyoming."

"Why are we going there?"

"It's the closest place I have contacts where you and Judd can go to ground. The heat's going to be very hot and heavy on you. We have to get you out of sight quick."

She shook her head dazedly. "I don't understand any of this. It's a nightmare."

"Yep. And the only way you can get away from a nightmare is to wake up." He met her gaze. "What happened at the lodge was ugly. Until then I thought there might be the smallest chance you were right about this all being a big mistake."

"Morgan didn't."

"Morgan isn't prone to think any government agency is clean since he's in hot water himself with them."

"And how could a so-called legend get himself in trouble?"

"Patriotism and trust. I believe at one time Judd must have been as idealistic as you are."

"No way."

"It's always the most devout who become the greatest cynics when they're disillusioned."

She shook her head.

"I can't say I blame you for not thinking well of him, considering he kidnapped you."

"How understanding," she said dryly. "You're not my man of the moment either. Nothing that's happened has changed that."

"Maybe we'll grow on you."

"I doubt it."

"It would be better for you if we did since we appear to be the only ones in your corner. Unless you count Sarah Logan, and I don't think you want to involve her in this mess."

"Certainly not. Though John Logan is another matter entirely."

"Sometimes things become clearer if you take them apart and put them back together. Think about it. Who knows? You may decide Judd is the best thing that's happened to you since Nader's death."

"Bull."

"Just a suggestion." He changed the subject. "How's your shoulder?"

"Okay."

"Which means it probably hurts. Why don't you try to nap until we get to Fort Collins?"

Nap? She knew damn well if she closed her eyes all she'd see would be that lodge in flames. She still felt her stomach clench whenever she remembered that first moment of shock. "That's a lousy idea."

Galen nodded as he studied her face. "Then try to relax. We moved fast enough so that we're probably ahead of the game." He smiled. "Though if you see any F-15s trailing us, forget everything I said."

"That's right, I'm a big-time threat, aren't I?" She shook her head and whispered, "Crazy. The entire thing's crazy."

Morgan was standing on the runway, waiting, as the helicopter set down.

He was looking up at them and was still carrying the rifle. Alex again had that odd feeling that the weapon was part of him. The cold wind from the rotors was tearing at his hair and pressing his jacket to his body.

Warrior. The word immediately jumped into her mind. Why not? Galen had just been talking about Morgan's experiences in the Rangers.

No, it was more than that. She could sense—

"Let's go." Morgan opened the door and jumped into the helicopter. "This is pretty dumb. You should have let me make my own way."

"Talk to Alex." Galen lifted off. "I couldn't convince her. She said right is right."

"And dead is dead," Morgan said. "You don't sacrifice a mission for one man."

"And you don't leave behind someone who's helped you," Alex said. "So shut up with all that military garbage."

He blinked, and then a slow smile lit his face. "Sorry. I didn't mean to bore you. I lived with that 'garbage' for a number of years. It's second nature to me."

"Galen told me." She looked away from him. "But this isn't Afghanistan. Did you have any trouble?"

"I did some dodging."

That was all he was going to say. Well, she didn't want to know anyway. "Bob Jurgens was in that first car you wrecked."

"You recognized him?"

"He was the FBI agent who interviewed me."

"He wanted to put her in a safe house," Galen added.

Morgan gave a low whistle. "Interesting."

"It's more than interesting to me," she said. "It's damn world-shaking. He seemed . . . I thought he was starting to believe me."

"I'm sure he did."

She shook her head. "I'm not sure of anything right now."

Except that she might have died today if Morgan hadn't been there. That fact was as bewildering as everything else that had happened to her.

"It's natural for you to be confused," Morgan said quietly. "It's against your instincts to doubt the authorities. You want to believe them."

"I'm not sure that I don't."

"Yes, you are," Morgan said. "Listen to your gut feelings."

She couldn't do that. Her gut feelings were telling her to run and hide, and that wasn't an option she could live with.

The ranch outside Sibley was located twenty miles from the town and set some three miles back from the road. From the air the house looked to be a nice, clean little wooden cottage with a wraparound porch.

Dead Aim

Galen set the helicopter down in a meadow to the south of the house. "You two get inside. I have to find a way of camouflaging this chopper. There should be a key underneath the phony rock beside the porch."

"Some security," Morgan said.

"It's that kind of town. Most people don't lock their doors here at night."

"I always wanted to live in a town like that," Alex said as she walked toward the house. "Fourth of July parades where everyone knows everybody. Picnics. Bands playing in a gazebo in the park."

"Sounds nice," Judd said. "But I notice you chose to spend your life globe-trotting instead."

"It just happened. At first, I was curious about everything and anything. After my father died . . . I needed to work. I went where I was sent. Where I was needed."

"But you still like the idea of your small town with unlocked doors."

"I guess I feel a little vulnerable. Going back to the way things were fifty years ago is like feather beds and mashed potatoes. Comfort."

"But we're not in a comfort zone right now." He moved ahead of her and retrieved the key from beneath the rock. "So stay outside until I check out the house."

"Galen said this place was safe."

"More soldiers are killed when they think they're safe than at any other time." He unlocked the door. "Oops, sorry. More military garbage." He disappeared inside the house but returned in a few minutes. "All clear."

"Galen would have been upset if it hadn't been," Alex said as she entered the house, whose furnishings reflected the same hominess as the exterior. It was all chintz slipcovers and pine cabinets. There was even a rocking chair in the corner. "He seems to take pride in his ability to move us around like chess pieces."

"He's proud that he's good at his job." Morgan was at the fireplace, kneeling to light the kindling. "But he has no desire to move the pawns around the board. Neither do I. Too many people in my life have pulled my strings. All I want is to be left alone."

"But evidently you made an executive decision when you snatched me."

He shrugged. "I'd committed myself to keeping you alive. I had no choice." He rose to his feet. "I'll go raid the kitchen and see if I can find coffee and some food. Those three doors leading off the living room are bedrooms. Why don't you choose one and wash up?"

"I will." As she moved toward the first door, she noticed a television set against the far wall. "And why don't you see if you can get some news on that television? I want to see if I'm wanted for the murder of any of those FBI men you shot as well as for blowing up the dam."

"I was as careful as I could be. I hit them when they were almost down to the valley and wouldn't go off the mountain. I targeted the tires. You said you didn't want anyone hurt."

"Jurgens was holding his arm. I think it might have been broken."

"So I'm not perfect. I try to make sure I don't have to calculate car speed on a target. It's very tricky. And no one has ever wanted me to take out cars instead of men." He opened a cabinet over the sink. "Ah, coffee. If you want to take a nap, I promise not to drink the entire pot."

"I'm not going to take a nap. Why do you keep trying to get me to go to sleep? We need to talk."

He glanced at her as he took down the coffee canister. "That sounds ominous."

"What happened last night was ominous. It scared me to death." She opened the door. "I don't like to be scared. I don't like to feel helpless. And I sure as hell don't like being made a target. I have to know what's happening." She didn't wait for him to reply but closed the door and leaned against it. Lord, she was exhausted. She needed sleep. Her shoulder throbbed and she felt as if she'd been through a war.

Morgan knew about wars. They were his stock-in-trade.

Well, they weren't her trade. She hated violence. Which made the fact that she had been forced into defending herself against this hideous charge all the more sickening.

Flames consuming the lodge, clawing at the sky.

No, she hadn't even been given the chance to defend herself.

So forget about rest. She had to figure out why this had happened and what she was going to do.

Morgan was still alone in the living room when Alex came out of the bedroom an hour later.

"Did you change your mind about that nap?" he asked. "I was just going to check and see if you were all right."

"No, I just wanted a little time to myself. Where's Galen?"

"We're low on groceries. He went to town to pick some up."

"How? I thought Sibley was twenty miles away."

"There was an old Ford pickup in the barn. Nothing fancy, but it works."

"Why did I even question? Galen seems to fill all needs."

"Thank God." He went to the cabinet. "I'll get you a cup of coffee. This is the second pot. Galen and I killed the first one."

"I could use the caffeine." She sat down on the couch in front of the television set. "Was there anything about the attack on the lodge?"

He nodded. "You and your accomplices resisted arrest and they had to fire. They haven't been able to go into the lodge yet to get DNA evidence, but they're almost sure you escaped. Particularly since the fine forces of law and order were ambushed while they were in pursuit of a suspicious vehicle."

"Resisted arrest? There was no one in that lodge."

He shrugged. "Poltergeists?" He handed her the cup. "And

they've identified me as one of your accomplices. I was wondering when they'd decide to put me in the hot seat too."

"You're probably used to it."

"Yes, and you'll be glad to know that the injuries I inflicted were minor. Jurgens has a broken arm, and one of his men has a minor concussion."

"I'm not sure I am glad."

He gazed at her with raised brows.

"Or maybe I am." She took a sip of coffee. "I just don't know. I still find it difficult to believe the FBI is out to get me."

"Then maybe you should consider that organizations like the FBI and CIA are so spread out and secretive that sometimes one department doesn't know what another is doing. Much less what each other is up to. That was one of the prime outcries after September eleventh." He poured himself a cup of coffee. "It's entirely possible that we have a bad apple in a fine, healthy bushel."

"Jurgens?"

He nodded. "But you've got to be aware that he might not be alone."

"So much for your theory."

"This attack on you has pretty wicked firepower. The media mentioned Homeland Security."

"Oh, for God's sake. Now you're saying they're involved? Why not the President?"

"Jesus, I hope not. I like Andreas. By the way, his trip to the dam has been postponed at the request of Homeland Security until the Secret Service can verify there's no threat from Matanza."

"Or me?"

"Or you. And all I'm saying is that Homeland Security must have been brought into the picture by either hard evidence supplied by the FBI and CIA or the influence of someone pretty high up."

Dead Aim

"There was no hard evidence against me. I didn't *do* anything."

"Except be in the wrong place at the wrong time." He smiled faintly. "And then refuse to go away and forget about it. You're a very obstinate woman."

"Obstinate? I was at Arapahoe Junction. I dug and dug, and all the time I knew. . . ." She had to steady her voice. "You're damn right I'm obstinate."

"I'm not complaining. I like it. Which is unusual considering what problems it's causing me."

"I don't care whether you complain or not. For the last few weeks my life has been a nightmare. I've been caught in a landslide, forced to jump into floodwaters, shot at, run off the road, and now this. For God's sake, it's like something from *The Perils of Pauline.*"

"You haven't been tied to the railway tracks yet."

"That's probably next. All I want is a way out of this mess." She stared him in the eye. "And you've got to help me."

"I told you that I'd find the men who tried to kill you."

"The circle seems to be growing by leaps and bounds. And it's going to keep growing until I find out what happened at Arapahoe Junction." She drew a deep breath. "So you're going to be with me all the way."

"Am I?"

"Yes."

"Why?"

"Because if you don't and they catch me, I'll tell them whatever I'm guilty of I did on your orders."

He stared at her for a moment and then threw back his head and laughed. "My God. You're wonderful. In a Lucrezia Borgia kind of way."

"I'm fighting for my life."

"And you're quite right not to trust me with it. You shouldn't trust anyone with anything that precious. It's too easy to take away." He dropped down into a chair. "So what exactly are you blackmailing me to do?"

"First, get Galen and Logan to find out what's going on with this witch hunt. I can't fight them if I don't know who is behind it. Second, I want to know what happened that night at the dam. There wasn't any explosion. I don't know what they did, but it was like . . ." She tried to remember. "A sort of . . . rumbling, shaking."

"Anything else?"

"Oh, yes." She paused. "I want you to tell me how and what you know about the last man we sketched yesterday."

"I beg your pardon?"

"The helicopter pilot. I didn't tell you he had a scar. I didn't even remember it until I saw the sketch. But you sketched it in. Later, I thought about it and realized that I wasn't that tired. I would have remembered telling you." She added, "My first thought was that you were in collusion with them. But then I remembered your reaction while you were drawing the sketch. You were shocked. You recovered quickly, but you didn't know that was the face you were going to draw."

"This is all supposition."

"Yes. Tell me one thing. Why did you think I'd be gullible enough to swallow that 'too exhausted to remember' excuse?"

"I didn't. I took a chance. It was the only out I had if I was going to send the sketch to Galen with every detail. I had to do that. I needed to know who that bastard was."

"And you don't?"

"I only saw him once, and the circumstances weren't conducive to exchanging either names or pleasantries."

"Why not?"

He didn't answer.

"Dammit, why won't you talk to me?"

"I've always subscribed to the policy of 'need to know.' " He held up his hand. "I know. More military garbage."

Dead Aim

"I need to know."

"Don't be greedy. I've caved in to your blackmail on the other things. I'm going to need some time to decide if I want to confide an episode that may have nothing to do with any of this. I'm a very cautious man."

She had a fleeting memory of Morgan, rifle in hand, standing on that tarmac as the helicopter descended. "I haven't noticed. And you said 'may have nothing to do with.' If you're not sure, then I should be told what—" He was shaking his head. "Dammit, you're not being fair. You're making me trust you in a situation where it could mean my neck."

"You do trust me. Not to any great depth, but you've worked your way through all the facts and our history to date and come out with the conclusion that I'm not on the bad guys' side."

"Right now."

"I stand corrected."

"And I'd be a lot more certain if you'd tell me where you saw that man in the sketch."

"Too bad. We all have to live with uncertainties."

He wasn't going to budge. She temporarily abandoned the battle and went back to fortifying the gains she'd made. "Have you really caved on those other issues?"

"Sure. I'm wallowing in the dirt and being pulled behind your chariot wheels."

"Bull. Stop it. Just give me your promise that you won't jump to the other side if the going gets rough."

His smile faded. "You must have been talking to Galen."

"I don't know what you mean."

He studied her expression. "Maybe you don't." He finished his coffee. "I don't like to make promises. It's too confining."

"That's why I want one from you."

"Would you trust me if I did give you my word?"

She thought about it. "I . . . think I would."

He chuckled. "What enthusiasm."

"I can't read you. Most of the time I don't know what you're thinking. I just have to rely on instinct."

"That can be scary. And a truckload of scary things have happened to you lately." He rose to his feet and took her cup. "If it makes you feel better, you have my promise I won't jump ship on you."

It did make her feel better. It was totally unreasonable that his words brought this sudden surge of warmth and reassurance.

The same warmth she had felt when he touched her wrist that day in the stairwell.

But that was different, that was deception and deliberate manipulation. And since she knew he was fully capable of both, why did she put stock in his word?

"You're fretting about why you're trusting me," he said over his shoulder as he headed for the kitchen. "It's pretty amazing to me too."

Evidently he had no trouble reading her, she thought in frustration. It wasn't fair.

"But it feels kind of good." He didn't look at her as he put the cups in the dishwasher. "Sort of like feather beds and mashed potatoes."

"Are you making fun of me?"

"I wouldn't think of it." He raised his gaze to meet hers. "Unless I thought I could get away with it."

"Well, you can't, and I wish—"

My God.

She quickly glanced away from him. Where had that come from? One minute she had been irritated and the next . . . *aware.* It was like that moment when he'd touched her when he changed her bandage. "How long do you think Logan will take to find out anything about this mess?"

He didn't answer for a second. "It depends. I'm sure he's on it now. Your friend Sarah must be very persuasive. Have you known each other long?"

"Yes." Sarah was a safe topic. Skid away from that weird, intimate moment. "Years. I ran into her during the first earthquake I covered near Istanbul. I was very green, and she saved me from being shot by one of the soldiers protecting the site. And then she saved me from breaking down any number of times when they started recovering the bodies." She shook her head. "It broke my heart. It still does."

"Then why do you go back?"

"Because I can help. It's not right to pass responsibility on to someone else because it hurts."

Confidences. Intimacy again. She had to break the spiral. She stood up and moved toward the bedroom. "Maybe I will rest for a while. Call me when Galen gets here."

Morgan nodded. "I'll be in to check your bandage in a little while."

"No, it's fine," she said quickly.

He met her gaze and then slowly nodded. "Whatever you say."

She moistened her lips. "Arapahoe Junction. That wasn't an explosion. I know it wasn't."

"I believe you." He turned away. "Rest well."

"She said it wasn't an explosion," Morgan told Galen as he watched him prepare supper. "She's positive."

"Then what brought the hill down? Earthquake?"

"That was one of the possible explanations brought up by the FBI." He shook his head. "But who the hell could trigger an earthquake? No, I'm not sure what it was."

Galen looked up from the chicken he was basting. "But you have an idea."

"I didn't say that."

"You don't say a tenth of what you're thinking, you secretive bastard." He picked up the pan and headed for the oven. "It's a wonder I don't give up on you."

Iris Johansen

"Yes, it is. You should. Why don't you?"

"I'm a masochist." He closed the oven door. "But not enough to stay away from Elena for much longer. Now that I've finished playing superhero, I'm going to cut you loose and go home." He grinned. "I'm enjoying the hell out of being a henpecked husband."

"Elena is no hen. Is there such a thing as tiger-pecked?"

"I'll find out, if she has to go through much more of this pregnancy without me. That's not going to happen. I'm not going to miss it." He went to the stovetop and started to stir the vegetables. "But you're going to miss me. Even though I bought plenty of frozen dinners for you."

"We'll survive. You're opting out entirely?"

"Anything I can do on the phone or through contacts, I'm your man. I'll start out by getting an ID on those two sketches. But the only thing that would get me to leave Elena again is if you or Alex were about to be drawn and quartered. And then only with Elena's permission."

Morgan made a face. "Not likely."

"I don't know. Maybe she's mellowing with pregnancy." He chuckled and shook his head. "Nah."

"I didn't think so."

"I'll get you transport. I'll get you experienced men for on-site help. I'll use my brilliant mind and persuasive talents to clear your path. As long as it doesn't take me more than thirty feet from Elena."

"Okay, okay. I hear you loud and clear. When do you leave?"

"Tomorrow morning. I'll probably be gone before you wake."

"No, you won't."

Galen smiled. "That's right. You'll be on guard duty, won't you?"

"I'm going to stay alive. And she's going to stay alive."

"Why did you let her think you'd given in to blackmail?

Dead Aim

You couldn't be in worse shape with the government than you are now."

"It didn't matter. It made her feel more in control. Those bastards have shredded her confidence in practically everything she believes in. She needed to feel she was doing something positive."

"And blackmail is positive? Never mind. It always depends on the situation." He glanced at the clock on the wall. "The chicken will be out in fifteen minutes. Do you want to wake her?"

"In a little while. Since you're between courses, why don't you get on the phone to Logan?"

"And what am I to tell him?"

"That you're opting out and I'm going to expect him to fill in the gap." He paused. "And if he doesn't, I'm going after his ass."

Galen gave a low whistle. "You don't talk to Logan that way."

"You can say it however you want to say it. Just make the point."

"No threats. He wants Alex kept alive. He'll cooperate."

"With you. He has to cooperate with me, and he's not sure which way I'll jump." He paused. "What about a bribe?"

"For God's sake, he's a billionaire."

"There are all kinds of bribes. Tell him I may be able to turn up something very beneficial to him."

"What? Okay, don't tell me. But I'm not going to offer Logan a bribe." He added, "Any more than I would you."

Morgan chuckled. "Galen, you offered me a bribe to draw me into this."

"Well, that was different."

"Yeah, you won't give up trying to save my ass."

"Someday I will." Galen pulled out his phone. "I'll handle Logan. Anything else you want me to tell him?"

"No. But I have something else I want you to do. Send a man down to Fairfax, Texas. It's a horse-and-buggy town near Brownsville. Make sure he's good and very careful."

"And?"

"There's a textile plant on the edge of town. Have him skirt around and see what he can come up with."

"What do you expect him to come up with?"

"I'm not sure. Maybe something . . . unusual."

"You've got it." He dialed Logan's number and when he picked up said, "We're safe, we've roosted, and I have a chicken in the oven." He flinched. "Hey, I wanted to see what kind of follow-up we need. Quiet down." He walked out onto the porch, talking fast.

Evidently Logan wasn't pleased at the way things were going. Well, neither were any of them, Morgan thought wearily. It was going to be a hell of a job just keeping them all alive.

He could walk away. He hadn't counted on the noose tightening around him like this.

Bull. He'd had a suspicion there might be a connection between Arapahoe Junction and Fairfax. It wasn't the carrot that Logan had held out to him that had brought him here. Nor was it Alex Graham's dossier and that fascinating face that had influenced him.

He had used Alex for an excuse to stop hiding and confront what had happened at Fairfax.

"No sign of her?" Betworth asked. "My God, she couldn't just disappear. She had half the law-enforcement officers in Colorado after her."

"We'll get her," Jurgens said. "We're processing the number on the helicopter now. The car they abandoned was rented at the airport by a Dave Simmons from Baltimore. Of course, we believe his ID was phony. But his description doesn't match the one the doctor gave us of the man who brought him to the lodge when Graham was injured. So it wasn't Morgan."

"What a surprise."

"I'm doing everything I can. Look, I put my ass on the line

when I blew that lodge. There were two local detectives there who were mad as hell."

"Then we'll take care of them."

"Powers?"

"No violence. I'll call Tim Rolfe in Homeland Security and ask him if he doesn't think a gag order regarding Graham would be wise."

"He'll go along?"

"He has so far. He's an ambitious man who knows who's going to hold the power. He wants to stay on my good side." Betworth paused. "As you do, Jurgens. You've done a good job, but I'm going to ask more of you. You have to move faster. We're getting too close to Z-3. I can't have any loose ends."

"Perhaps you could postpone it?"

"After four years of planning? No, Jurgens. I have to strike while the iron is hot. I may never get another opportunity. Which means you may not get another opportunity." Betworth added gently, "You're very clever and I know you'll do whatever is necessary. Just find them and remove them so that we can concentrate on what's important to us."

7

"I'm glad you enjoyed my chicken, Alex. Not that I expected anything else." Galen stood up and started to clear the table. "I thought you deserved a good meal, considering Morgan is entirely lacking in that skill."

"It was delicious." She stood up and started to stack the dishes. "I'll help you wash up."

"I usually leave that for Morgan. The drudgery factor is humbling, and God knows he needs it."

Morgan's gaze was narrowed on Alex's face. "I'll pass tonight." He stood up. "I be'ieve she wants to do something besides wash dishes. I'll go scout around the grounds."

He was too damn perceptive, she thought in frustration as she carried the plates into the kitchen.

Galen followed her and started putting dishes into the dishwasher. "Is he right?"

"Yes. Morgan says you're leaving in the morning."

"Yep, but I'm not totally deserting you."

"Morgan told me that too. But I'm going to have to rely principally on him. That makes me very uneasy."

"It shouldn't. In many ways he's savvier than I am.

Though I hate to admit it." He paused. "Nah, scratch that. It's just that we've had experiences in different areas."

She smiled reluctantly. It was difficult not to smile at Galen. Morgan was right, he was an original. "I don't care about his experiences. I care about his character. I can't read him."

"And you don't trust him."

"Dammit, he kills people."

"True."

"Isn't that enough to cause anyone to take a step back?"

"In your experience, has he killed anyone who didn't deserve killing?"

"That's not the point."

"If it makes you feel better, he's not in the business any longer. He's retired. He took this job as a favor to me."

"And what else could tempt him to return to the 'business'?"

"I don't know. He's a bit of a puzzle at times."

"My thought exactly. But I can't afford puzzles. I have to know—I have to trust him."

"Then you'll have to make up your own mind."

"But you trust him."

He nodded. "But it's always been instinct. I'd rather have him in my corner than anyone except my wife."

"And he said she wanted to cut his throat."

Galen nodded. "Elena doesn't forgive and forget."

"And she has something to forgive?"

"Oh, yes."

"But you don't agree with her?"

"Not entirely."

"You're not going to talk about it."

"It wouldn't inspire you with confidence." He started the dishwasher. "Suppose I fill you in on all I know about Judd's background instead?"

"I'll take whatever I can get."

He started to wipe off the countertops. "Well, I guess I should start with the North Korea debacle. . . ."

The kitchen was clean and the dishwasher was humming through its cycle when he finished speaking. He gave her a puckish grin. "And that's all you'll get out of me. You can beat me. You can tear out my fingernails, but I won't—"

"Shut up, Galen." She was trying to digest everything he'd told her. "I don't know much more than when I started about how he thinks, do I? You don't know anything else about him?"

"Let's see, he's mentioned he was an Air Force brat and grew up all over the world. He speaks six languages fluently. I guess going into the service was a logical step for him." He turned to face her. "You're right, all this isn't going to help you. You're probably going to have to rely on instinct, like me."

"That's scary."

"It depends on the instinct." He smiled. "I'm going to call Elena and then I'm going to bed. When Judd comes back, tell him I've spilled my guts to you. I wouldn't like him to think I'd go behind his back."

She watched him leave the kitchen and then moved toward the front door. A cold blast of air struck her as she went out on the porch.

"You should put on a coat if you're going to be out here very long." Morgan was moving down the walk toward her. "It's almost freezing."

"I thought you might be lurking on the porch."

"I don't lurk. I did what I told you I'd do. I needed to familiarize myself with the area." He climbed the steps and opened the front door. "You never know when it might come in handy. Get inside. You're having problems with maintaining body temperature anyway."

"Not anymore. I'm fine." But the warmth of the room felt

good as she went inside. "Galen told me to tell you that he spilled his guts to me."

"Not a pretty phrase." He took off his coat and hung it in the closet. "Not a great thing to do. But I expected you to squeeze it out of him." He turned to face her. "He probably knew it wouldn't make any difference in the long run."

"Is that why you left us alone?"

"Yes. Do you feel better now?"

"Why should I feel better? You're already in so much hot water that I have no hold on you."

"Sorry." He studied her for a moment. "What can I do to help?"

She stared at him and then laughed incredulously. "I believe you really mean that."

"I do. I want you comfortable with me."

"Then tell me about that man in the sketch. Tell me about the man who shot Ken down."

He didn't answer her for a moment. "I ran into him several months ago in Fairfax, Texas. I was sent there for a job and I saw him earlier that night."

"You're sure it was him?"

He nodded. "That night is pretty well engraved on my memory."

"Did you see any of the other men?"

"No. But that doesn't mean they weren't there. The place was a beehive of activity."

"What kind of beehive?"

"Labs. I thought it was a damn strange place for Morales to be."

"Morales?"

"The target. Juan Morales, big-time narcotics and arms dealer. At the time I speculated that maybe the Fairfax factory was purifying heroin or manufacturing crack or ecstasy."

"At the time? Not now?"

He shook his head. "You want some coffee?"

"Am I going to need it?"

He shook his head again. "Nothing very horrific happened that night. Well, I guess it might be to you. My orders were to take out Morales at the hotel in town and retrieve a briefcase he was carrying. It was supposed to be jammed full of money. I couldn't get a shot at the hotel, so I followed Morales to this little textile factory on the outskirts of town. He was met at the gate by your shooter in the sketch. There was lots of security, so I waited outside. When he came out, I followed him back to town, got an opportunity, and took my shot."

"You killed him?"

"I don't miss. Since I didn't get a chance to do the job before he went to the factory, I thought I'd better check the briefcase to make sure he didn't give the money to the man who met him at the gate."

"And?"

"No money. Just three sets of engineering plans with interesting notations. Strategic locations where to place explosives to bring down the structure. They even had suggestions as to what kind of explosives would work best."

"What structures?"

He shook his head. "I don't know. There were no names. The plans were labeled Z-1, Z-2, and Z-3."

"What did you do with them?"

"I did as I was ordered. I took the briefcase to Al Leary, my CIA contact, and told him the job was done but there was no money, only the plans. I could tell he wasn't pleased that I'd opened the briefcase, but he covered it almost immediately. Two days later I was sent to North Korea. The rest is history. I didn't even connect the two jobs until I saw the story about Arapahoe Dam on the news."

She stiffened. "What?"

"Two of the diagrams were of multistoried structures. But one of the plans was a dam: Z-1."

"Jesus."

"But the report on Arapahoe Dam was that no sabotage had been detected. Particularly no explosives. It could have been coincidental."

"And you did nothing?"

"I'm on the run. Was I supposed to go to Colorado and investigate a disaster that was probably natural?"

"You could have told someone, called—"

"Who? The CIA? If Arapahoe Dam was Z-1, then maybe the fact that I had had a look at those plans was the reason I was set up and sanctioned. FBI? Too chancy. They work pretty closely with the CIA these days." He met her gaze. "I decided to preserve my neck. I'm not one of your heroes. I'd spent years doing the dirtiest job on earth to form some sort of barrier between my country and the ugliness out there. All I got for it was a stab in the back. I opted out. If you don't like it, too bad."

"You can't opt out. That doesn't solve anything."

"It solved the question of whether I lived or died."

"Past tense. Does that mean you're not opting out any longer?"

"The question is moot. I've been sucked into this and I've got to act or be pulled under."

She made a rude noise.

"I beg your pardon?"

"Don't try to give me that guff. You've had choices all along and you know it. You took the job Logan offered because you wanted to find out if Z-1 and Arapahoe Dam were the same. You just don't want to admit it to me."

"Why?"

"I don't know. Perhaps you're afraid I'll think you're not as cynical as you claim you are. Don't worry. I'm not about to make that mistake. Everyone has a right to one lapse."

His lips twitched. "I'm glad I haven't ruined my reputation.

You'll tell me if you believe I'm pretending to be heroic like all those role models you grew up with?"

She found herself smiling back at him. "You can bet on it." He looked warm and approachable, and she suddenly wanted to reach out and touch him. She glanced away hurriedly. "How long do we have to stay here?"

"It probably won't be for more than a few days. Safe houses don't stay safe for long when there's a massive search. I'd like to stay here until we get a report from Galen on Fairfax. He's going to send a man down there to see what he can find out. When we move, I'd like to have someplace to go and a reason to go there."

"And you think that will take only a few days?"

"It better not take much longer. We're running out of time."

Panic rippled through her. She had never felt this hunted before. Even that time in Iran, when she had been on the run, there had never been this sense of overwhelming odds weighing in against her.

"It's going to be okay." Morgan's gaze was fixed on her face. "It's a big country. It's much easier to get lost in a country this size. And people aren't as suspicious. They're like you. They want to believe that everyone is good."

"And you think that's naive."

"Yes, but I also find it heartwarming." He smiled. "And we've already established how cold I am." His stare was suddenly intent. "I need all the warming I can get."

She couldn't look away. He wasn't cold. She could feel heat move through her as— She tore her gaze away. What had they been talking about? "It's not naive to want to see the best in people." She moistened her lips. "What are we going to do until Galen contacts us?" Shit, she wished she could take the question back. Stupid. Stupid.

But he didn't respond with a double entendre as she'd

thought he might. "Suppose you let me try to see the best in you."

"What?"

"I said I wouldn't draw you unless you gave me permission."

"You're not going to get it. I hate sitting still."

"Then don't. But you're still weak enough to let me have time to occasionally catch you at rest. You give me my time and I'll take you with me when I go scouting every day. That should allay the boredom for both of us."

"Aren't you afraid I won't keep up?"

"Maybe. But then I'll just have to slow down. Because I won't leave you here alone."

"Give me back my gun."

"It's in my duffel. Get it whenever you like. But what good would your gun have been against that rocket Jurgens lobbed into the lodge? Our best bet is guerrilla warfare if they find we're here."

"Not run and hide?"

"Run, stop, strike, run. Doesn't that suit you better?"

She was about to tell him no and then decided he was right. "If it's the only way to survive. I don't want to be caught like a rat in a trap. It's not fair."

"What is?"

"But this arrangement's a little lopsided. If you draw me, I want a favor from you."

He shook his head. "No photographs."

"I wouldn't even try. You're not that pretty."

"Jesus, I hope not."

But a face that held that many secrets would be fascinating to try to capture. "I'd probably end up with a photo that resembled a stone wall. No, you once told me that if I got away from you that you'd track me, that you were good at it. Well, I want you to teach me how to do that."

"Why?"

"I've been in a couple situations where it would have come in handy. I'm not a complete novice. My dad took me hunting from the time I was a little girl. I'm pretty woods savvy."

"But why tracking?"

"I remember a few years ago in Turkey there was a child who wandered away from the village when I was photographing her parents. It took us four days to find her. She was dead. She'd fallen down a slope into a river. If we'd been able to find her sooner, it might not have happened."

"I should have known. Another way to save the world."

"No, just a three-year-old little girl. Deal?"

"You can't grasp much in a few days. I had an Apache teacher who devoted months to teaching me, and it still took—"

"I'll learn what I can learn. It might help. Deal?"

He smiled. "Deal."

"Then I'm going to bed." She turned to leave. "I'll see you in the morning."

"Good idea. You've had a big day."

"A terrible day."

"I wish I could tell you that the worst is behind you. I won't do that."

No, he'd offered her comfort, but not at the expense of honesty. "I didn't ask you to. Good night."

She didn't turn on the light in the bedroom as she took off her pants. The shirt was too much trouble with her bad shoulder and she was too tired to bother. She just pulled the cover over her and plumped up the pillow.

It had been a terrible, frightening day, as she'd told Morgan. A day of terror and revelation and a wild mixture of emotion. A day that had drawn her closer to Morgan than she was comfortable with.

She shouldn't be that surprised. In life-threatening situations, sexuality often raised its head. She had experienced it once before with a young doctor on the flooded plains of Bangladesh. It had vanished as quickly as the danger.

But it hadn't been this strong.

It didn't matter. She could handle it. And Morgan was clearly not going to pursue that intimacy. Jesus, she was actually disappointed, she realized in disgust. All she needed was to jump into bed with a man like Morgan.

Except there was no other man like Morgan. She had never met anyone this complex, and the more she learned about him, the fewer weapons she had against him. His ways were not her ways, but it was difficult to condemn a man who—

Stop thinking about him. If she had to stay awake, think of something that would help her get out of this predicament.

Z-1. No, the picture was bigger now. Bigger and more bewildering. If Z-1 was Arapahoe Dam and that target had been destroyed . . .

Wouldn't Z-2 be next?

"What's the progress on Z-2?" Betworth asked. "You haven't got much time, Powers."

"No problem. We'll meet the deadline."

"But with what kind of success?"

"I think you should know that I'll follow through. The only reason there's been any delay is that you told me to go after Graham."

"But that's not an excuse now. I gave that assignment to Jurgens."

"And he hasn't been too successful, has he?"

"He'll get her. You concentrate on Z-2." He hung up and leaned back in his chair. Keep calm. Everything would go as planned. He was handling all the details with his usual skill. Jurgens would find Graham and Morgan and take them out. Everything would be—

His phone rang.

"I can't find him, Betworth."

Runne.

"For God's sake, why haven't you returned my calls?"

"I need to find him. I've run out of leads. You get me one."

He drew a deep breath. No excuses. The arrogant, fanatical bastard was giving him orders. "Perhaps if you'd returned my calls, I could have given you some assistance."

"Can you?"

He wanted to hang up on him. That would be a mistake. Runne was a wild card, but Betworth had plans for him. Besides, he might be the one who could bring in Morgan. "He was in Colorado a few days ago. He might still be there, but I doubt it. Wherever he is, he's with a woman, Alex Graham."

"You're sure?"

"Oh, yes."

"Can you send me a photo of her?"

"I don't have to. Pick up a newspaper. Don't you ever read a newspaper or watch television?"

"No."

"Well, she's very hot. So it won't do any good to give you addresses or phone numbers."

"Then what good is she to me?"

"It's pretty obvious Morgan isn't going to abandon her, so that makes her an albatross. She'll slow him down. He doesn't have to slow down much for you to catch him, does he?"

"No, but fax me the information anyway. I'll call you back and give you the fax number in the town I'm in. I might be able to go through her people to locate her."

"I told you, everyone's searching for her."

"That doesn't make any difference. They'll stop, they'll hesitate, they'll wonder if they'll get caught if they go too far. I have the advantage. I don't care." He hung up.

Dead Aim

"Okay." Judd gazed out over the mountains. "I'll give you fifteen minutes' head start. You take off and hide from me. Get going."

"You're tracking me?" Alex said. "How am I going to learn anything?"

"You make the trail and then we go back over it and see what you did wrong."

"What I did wrong?"

"Sorry, wrong phrase. I'm used to hunting prey who don't want to be found. But it's the only way I know how to teach you. Take it or leave it."

"I'll take it." She took off running down the slope.

"Found." Judd pulled Alex out of the brush. "You must be getting tired. You were really clumsy that time."

"Thanks." She grimaced. "That's the third time. I'm getting depressed. If it's that easy to track someone, why couldn't we find that little girl?"

"It's not easy. It takes practice. There are all kinds of things that obscure signs. She might have wandered in the shallow part of the river for a while. Rain could have washed the signs away. Children don't weigh much, and her feet probably made little impression in the grass. If she walked for a long time in the mud, she might have picked up enough of it on her shoes to form a pillow of mud. That makes it almost impossible to identify a human footstep except by the stride. A large animal might have walked over her prints and destroyed them. Or maybe you were at the wrong place at the wrong time."

"What does that mean?"

"The angle of light." He studied her face. "You're tired. We'll go over your mistakes and then go back to the house." He turned away and moved up the slope. "You dislodged rocks over there." He pointed. "You flattened ground cover when you first started down this hill, and the color is a little different." He pointed again. "You broke the stem of that plant when you went into the bushes." He knelt down. "And here's a clear footprint."

"It doesn't look clear to me."

"See the curve where your toe pushed into the ground?"

She nodded. "It's like learning a foreign language."

"Your eyes just have to train themselves to see the signs. There are four indicators to watch out for. Flattening, when dirt, rocks, or twigs are pressed into the ground by the weight of a foot. Regularity, which is an effect caused by straight lines or geometric shapes or anything not generally found in nature. Color change, which is a difference in color or texture from the area that surrounds it. Disturbance, which is a recent change or rearrangement." He moved ahead of her. "Come on, we'll go to the first place you hid and we'll go over the signs there."

She hurried to keep up with him. "I might as well have left a sign pointing to where I was."

"Well, yes. But I didn't have to look at the ground when I got near those shrubs."

"Why not?"

"I smelled you."

She missed a step. "What?"

"Deodorants, toothpastes, shampoos are the scents of civilization. But nature gives everyone their own individual scents."

"You're saying I stink?"

He looked at her. "No, you smell intensely female. It couldn't be more enticing."

She glanced quickly away from him. "Or identifiable, evidently."

"I'd know you in the dark."

She inhaled sharply and searched wildly for something to say. "And did your Apache friend educate your nose as well as your eyes?"

Dead Aim

"No, it's a talent. I just had to refine it."

"Sarah's dog, Monty, has a wonderful nose."

He started to laugh. "You're comparing me to a dog?"

The tension was gone, she realized with relief. "Well, he's an exceptional dog."

"Then I guess I'll have to accept that as a compliment." He knelt down and pointed to a spot some forty yards away. "Here's where I first picked up your trail. Do you see the shine?"

She squatted down beside him. "Yes, how did I do that?"

"Your footprints pressed into dirt particles, which formed a reflective surface. But you can only see them in an oblique light angle."

"As shine."

"But you might miss them if you were right on top. That's why distance is good."

"Well, you're definitely an expert on distance."

"I'm not bad on top either."

She didn't make the mistake of looking at him this time. She quickly rose to her feet. "Let's go. I can't wait to see what else I did wrong."

"You're pretty incredible out there." She stared into the fire as she slowly sipped her hot chocolate. "How did you meet this Indian who taught you to track?"

"The Army sent me to him. It was part of my training." His pencil moved swiftly over the sketch pad. "You never know when you're going to have to seek out and find. Actually, it took me longer than it should have to become proficient. At first, I didn't like hunting. I had to learn to block out the thought of the final kill and concentrate on the chase itself. You know, you look really good in the firelight. . . ."

"You'd better draw fast. This heat is making me sleepy."

"Just a little while longer. . . . You said you went hunting with your father. That surprises me. I can't see you with a rifle."

"We didn't take rifles. My father didn't like shooting animals. We took cameras."

"Now I understand. Much more in character."

"Do most people in your profession have problems learning to"—she searched for a word—"hunt?"

"Kill. Say it." His gaze remained on the sketch. "Some do, some don't. Occasionally, you find someone who loves it. Loves the hunt. Loves the kill."

"Not you?"

"No."

"But you've known someone who does?"

He nodded. "And for a short while he infected me with his enthusiasm."

"Was he as good as you?"

"No, but he came close." He put the sketch pad on the end table beside him. "Go on to bed. I've captured the essence. I'll fill in the rest tomorrow."

He didn't want to answer any more questions. Well, she probably shouldn't ask any more. She wasn't sure whether those moments in the cold mountains or these last hours beside the blazing fire were the most intimate.

She rose to her feet. "You may have the best part of our deal. I have a hunch I'm not going to be very good at this tracking business."

"You'll be good. You have good eyes. You're smart and you learn fast. Tomorrow you'll remember everything I've said and it will be harder for me to find you."

"Until you get close enough to smell me. I'm still not sure I like that idea."

He smiled. "The teacher has to have some perks. Then the day after tomorrow I'll let you take me back over your trail and tell me how I tracked you."

"That soon?"

"Like I said, you have good eyes."

So did he. Ice blue, and yet right now they didn't look cold at all. . . .

"Good night." She moved toward the bedroom. "I'll try to give you a little more of a challenge tomorrow."

"Don't try too hard. Believe me, you're a constant challenge, Alex."

Where was Morgan?

Alex stamped to keep the circulation going in her feet. It had turned colder in the last hour and she was ready to go back to the ranch. It had snowed during the night, and Morgan had called off her tracking lesson because the snow would hide the signs beneath its white blanket. She was surprised how disappointed she'd been when he handed her camera to her and then left her on the hillside. She felt . . . abandoned.

God, how pathetic. Forget the cold. Forget Morgan.

She lifted the camera and focused on the tops of the Tetons, now wreathed in a cloudy mist.

"Are you ready?"

She whirled to find Morgan behind her. She should have been able to hear him on the ice-crusted snow, but she hadn't. "Where were you?"

He gestured to the tree-dotted hill to the south. "I needed to stretch myself."

"And I was keeping you back."

"Yes." He went past her down the slope that led to the ranch. "But you've kept up damn well the last couple days, considering your injury. I ran you hard."

"Considering my injury? How patronizing." She smiled. "Even if it's true. Give me a couple weeks and I'll meet your pace."

"We don't have a couple weeks."

"I know that." She had spoken without thinking. The last few days had been amazingly tranquil. It was as if they were caught in a time warp. Maybe it was being surrounded by all this beauty and serenity. Or maybe it was that she wanted to run away from all the turmoil her life had become. "Galen's not coming through for us, is he?"

"It'll happen. I told you, he said Ralph Scott was on his way to Texas yesterday. He gave him copies of the sketches of the two men at the dam. Galen should hear something from him by tonight."

"Do you know anything about Scott?"

"Only that Galen chose him. That's enough for me." He glanced at her. "But I'm not going to sit on my ass and hope everything's going to break if we don't hear from him. We've been here too long already."

"I didn't think you would. You don't impress me as a patient man. I'm surprised you haven't been more restless."

"Oh, I've been restless." He looked away from her. "And very impatient."

Dammit. She felt a wave of heat move through her. It wasn't the first remark he'd made that she recognized as boldly sexual. The sexual tension had been there, ebbing and flowing, ignored but always present.

Morgan wasn't ignoring it now. He wanted her to know, to bring it out in the open.

"It's okay." Morgan's gaze was once more on her face. "Don't panic. I'm not going to jump you. It's just . . . I need it. And I think you do too."

"You don't always take what you need."

"I do. These days I live every day as if it were my last. You never can tell."

"No, I guess you can't." She moistened her lips. "But that isn't how I want to live my life. It's a gift and I intend to cherish it."

"Cherish it. I'm not into making memories. Just come to bed with me. You'll like it, I'll like it, and that will be the end of it. You won't find me hanging on when you walk away." He climbed the porch steps and unlocked the door. "That's all I wanted to say. What do you want for supper?"

"What?"

He smiled. "Food isn't nearly as satisfying as sex, but it is a necessity. What about an omelette? I'll cook it, but you have to chop up the onions. They make my eyes tear in a most unmanly fashion."

He was backing away as he always had during the last few days, but it was too late. The words were said, and she wouldn't be able to forget them. He probably didn't want her to forget them. He wanted her to think, to envision them in bed together.

And she would, blast him.

She drew a deep breath and went past him into the house. "You have to chop onions under cold tap water. I'll show you."

He followed her and hung up his coat in the closet. "Always glad to profit from someone with experience. Teach me."

"I don't think you need anyone to teach you anything."

"Then share the experience." He headed for the kitchen. "That's always more fun anyway."

Morgan's phone rang when he was breaking the eggs for the omelette.

"Scott just called," Galen said. "He struck pay dirt at the hotel in Fairfax. The desk clerk recognized both men in the sketches. The shooter is Thomas Powers and the other man is Calvin Decker."

"He's certain?"

"About eighteen months ago Powers and Decker were in and out of town almost every week for an extended period. They told everyone they were designers for the textile company. The townspeople doubted that was true, but the money was good so they turned a blind eye."

"They thought they were into drugs?"

"There were all kinds of stories about what was going on at the plant. Fairfax is very close to the border. Drug running is rampant in South Texas."

"Had the clerk seen Powers any time lately?"

"Negative," Galen said. "But the last two weeks of his stay, he paid for the room rent by credit card. Scott bribed the clerk to look up the records and give him the credit-card number. I'm checking it out now. Scott's going out to the plant tonight to look around."

"There's a hell of a lot of security there."

"Not anymore. The plant closed down six months ago. It's deserted except for a night watchman. Scott said he'd call me from the plant."

"Call me when you hear from him."

"I'll do that. How's Alex? Putting up with you?"

"Barely. I've got to hang up. I'm making an omelette."

"You?"

Morgan looked at Alex. "I'm discovering all manner of skills and qualities I never knew existed. Let me know as soon as you do." He hung up. "The shooter's name is Thomas Powers. The other man is Calvin Decker. Galen is checking out one of Powers's credit-card receipts right now."

Alex's expression lit with excitement. "Hot dog." Then she frowned. "It could be an alias. It probably is."

"Or it might not be. Anyway, it's a lead."

"Yes, it is. At last something's going our way. I was getting discouraged."

"I'm still discouraged."

She tensed. "Why?"

He smiled. "You haven't chopped those onions for me. I'm afraid you're going to make me do it."

"I'll make coffee, you turn on the television," Morgan said after supper. "We need to see what the opposition is up to."

"I can hardly wait." She went into the living room and flipped on the television set. "Just what I need for indigestion."

She glanced up when Morgan came into the room carrying a tray with coffee cups and a carafe. "They're still searching Colorado for us. They're having trouble identifying the helicopter because the numbers on the aircraft were phony."

He poured her coffee. "Imagine that. Anything else?"

"Not about us. There's been another embassy bombing. This time it was in Quito. Same MO as the last one in Mexico City. The Matanza terrorist group. Same threats to President Andreas." She shook her head wearily. "Won't it ever stop? I used to feel so safe, and now I'm looking over my shoulder all the time. Hell, I wonder how Andreas feels. His neck is on the line twenty-four/seven."

"He's got a tough job." Judd sat down opposite her. "But he can handle it. I'd bet he's got guts to spare."

"I remember you said you liked him."

"I think he's honest. That elevates any politician to automatic sainthood." He took a swallow of his coffee. "We may have to have Logan try to get to him. I don't know who else we can trust."

Her eyes widened. "The President?"

"Galen says Logan has some pull with him these days."

She shook her head. "Without evidence we wouldn't have a shot."

"You may be right." He took the remote from her and turned off the TV. "That's enough news. You're getting depressed. Lean back in the chair. I'll get my sketchbook."

"Lord, you must have dozens of sketches of me now."

"I like your face." He sat back down and started to sketch. "It's a very special face."

"You like wimps?"

"That's what you saw, not what I drew." He stopped sketching and looked at her. "Why are you so afraid that I see you as a weakling?"

Iris Johansen

"I'm not. You just drew me as—" She was silent a moment. "I suppose I'm afraid that deep down I'm like that. I try not to be. But what if—"

"Bull."

"A person never knows how they're going to react. I fell apart once. I could again."

"The World Trade Center?"

"I was helpless. There was nothing I could do. He wasn't *there*. He wasn't anywhere. I went to the hospitals. I posted his picture everywhere." She could feel the tears sting her eyes. "I couldn't find him. No one has ever found him. I wailed and sobbed like a madwoman." She swallowed. "Yes, I'm afraid of being that helpless again. I *won't* be that helpless."

"So you overcompensate."

"The hell I do." She cleared her throat. "And you'd better not have made me look like that woman I was all that time ago. You had some excuse after I was injured, but not now."

"Would you like to see this one?"

"You're damn right."

She watched him come toward her. She shouldn't have confided in Morgan. She didn't feel more vulnerable, but she felt closer to him. Heaven knew, she didn't need to feel closer to Morgan.

He knelt beside her and put the sketch on her lap. "Alex."

And Alex was the name scrawled at the top of the sketch. Strength. Alertness. Intelligence. Radiance.

She couldn't speak for a moment. "I'm . . . overwhelmed."

"Good."

"Is that how I look to you?"

He grinned. "Hell, no. It's just a ploy to get you into bed. I use it on all the babes." His smile faded. "You know me well enough to know that I'll be honest with you. Even if I weren't honest with you, I'd be honest with the work. The work always has to be honest and clean and true." His fingers lightly traced the line of her cheek. "It was no problem with you. I had it all right in front of me."

She couldn't breathe. His fingers were warm and whisper-light, but it was as if she felt that touch in every nerve of her body. His face . . . hard, totally focused, intent.

She slowly lifted her fingers and touched his lips.

He went still. Then he moved his head so that his lips were pressed to her palm.

She went rigid. Heat. Jesus, her whole body was ready.

She shuddered as his tongue touched her palm. Then it was gone. He was gone as he rose to his feet. "No."

She watched him in bewilderment as he backed away from her. What did he mean, no? She was so hot she was about to melt into a puddle.

"Not fair. You were breaking apart from talking about your father and then I threw the damn sketch at you." His lips twisted. "And I did it on purpose. I was hard and hurting. I wanted you and it was a way to get you."

"What?"

"Manipulation. Only I forgot I wasn't dealing in that particular commodity anymore." He moved toward his bedroom. "You want me, you come and get me."

She sat there, dazed, as the door slammed behind him. What the hell? She felt as if she'd fallen into the center of a volcano, only to have it turn to ice. No, not ice. She was shocked, but she was still as sexually aroused as the moment he'd first touched her.

It had been totally unprincipled of him to try to manipulate her. Just what she'd expect of a man of his background.

But that was a generalization, and you couldn't generalize with Morgan. He was a law unto himself. Who knew what he'd do next?

You want me, you come and get me.

Damn him.

She got to her feet, strode toward his bedroom, and threw open the door. He was standing in the middle of the room, unbuttoning his shirt.

"Am I supposed to appreciate having to make the moves? Well, I don't. It's damn difficult." She drew a deep breath. "I want you. I've come to get you. Now, dammit, it's in your court. I want a little seduction."

"You're sure?"

She crossed the space between them and laid her head against his chest. His skin was smooth, warm, except for a thatch of springy hair. She rubbed her cheek against him and felt the muscles of his stomach clench as a shudder went through his body. "I don't want to be saved from you. I can save myself."

"You're not doing a very good job."

"Didn't you say live every moment as though it was my last?"

"But you don't agree with that philosophy."

"Tonight I do." Her voice was uneven. "It will take forever to get my shirt off with this blasted shoulder. Will you stop standing there and help me, dammit?"

His hands slowly closed on her shoulders. "Oh, yes. I'll help you. Any way, every way. Just tell me. . . ."

"Did I hurt you?"

She chuckled. "Which time? Isn't it a little late to worry about damaging me?"

"No. Did I hurt you?"

She pretended to solemnly consider the question. "I think I felt a twinge in my shoulder the third time, but it went away quickly. Or maybe I was just distracted." Her teeth sank playfully into his shoulder. "Gee, did I hurt you?"

"No, you aroused me. Want to go again?"

"Soon." She nestled closer. "Lord, you have stamina. I need a little break."

Dead Aim

"Okay." He sat up in bed. "I'll go get my sketch pad."

"Don't you dare." She jerked him back down. "I'm not about to pose nude."

"Just your face," he whispered. He kissed her. "I want to remember your face like this. You . . . glow."

She swallowed to ease the sudden tightness of her throat. "Yeah, sure, and someday when I least expect it, I'll find myself in a gallery window."

"No. If I did a nude of you it would be just for me. I'm feeling very possessive." He kissed the hollow of her throat. "Just your face . . ."

"Maybe later." She pulled his head down to her breasts. "Suddenly, I'm not feeling tired anymore. . . ."

8

Fairfax, Texas

If he was supposed to look for something unusual at this factory, then the trip was a washout.

Scott moved quietly down the hall, pausing for a moment to glance into the labs as he passed. No chemicals. Lots of electronic gadgetry. Charts . . .

He went into one of the labs and checked a chart. Nothing definitive. No names or places, just numbers, graphs, and percentages. No wonder they had been left behind when the plant had been closed down. They told absolutely nothing. Galen was going to be disappointed.

He dialed Galen's number. "No luck. No chemicals. A lot of electronic gadgets, a few graphs that tell *nada*."

"Have you covered the entire factory?"

"First and second floors." He opened the door and started down the stairs. "I'm going down to the basement now."

"What about the night watchman?"

"No sign of him. I'm keeping a lookout, but so far I can't see why they'd need one." He reached the landing and started down the second flight. "Long flights of stairs. Deep basement . . ."

"Were there any notes or papers in the desks?"

"Clean as a whistle. The drawers looked like they'd been

cleaned by a Shop-Vac." He'd reached the door and tried it. "Hold on. The basement door's locked. I've got to open it."

He got out his skeleton keys and patiently tried a dozen before one opened the door. "Got it." He swung the door open. "Now, let's see—dammit." He jumped back into the stairwell. "I almost fell in."

"Fell in where?"

"I don't know. I just felt myself going." He shone the flashlight into the darkness of the basement. "Holy shit."

"Talk."

"It's weird. There's no floor. The basement is huge. It probably runs under the plant and the grounds around it. It's just dirt and holes, deep holes that seem to go clear to China." He shone the light around the walls. "That's all there is here. Just dirt and those holes. I'd say this qualifies as unusual. I'll take a couple pictures and you can see for your—"

Hot pain exploded inside him. "Christ!"

He should have watched his back. Only amateurs . . . He should have . . .

Alex rubbed her cheek back and forth in the hollow of his shoulder. "Who's Runne?"

Morgan went tense. "What?"

"He must be someone pretty important to you to make you talk in your sleep."

His muscles relaxed. "Is that where you heard the name?"

"Where else?"

"Runne sometimes seems to be omnipresent." He kissed the top of her head. "He's just someone I used to know."

"Which means you're not going to tell me."

"Maybe someday. It's an ugly story and I'm not about to spoil a good thing when I've got it." His hand covered her breast. "And it's a very good thing."

Yes, it was. She had never had it this strong or hot or

sweet. Full of stormy power and tension . . . and tenderness. She had never imagined Morgan as tender, but she had learned gossamer gentleness always followed the storm. "I . . . liked it."

He chuckled. "You loved it. You just want to keep me in my place."

"And what is your place? Every time I turn around you keep moving and expanding the territory."

"But it's such intriguing territory." He brushed his lips over her nipple. "And you certainly didn't object to my moving a little while—" His phone rang on the bedside table. "Shit. Galen better not just be telling us he has nothing to tell us." He flipped on the phone. "What is it, Galen?"

"I think Scott's dead."

He froze. "How do you know?"

"I don't know. I was talking to him on the phone. I heard a shot."

"Get rid of your phone. They may be able to trace you."

"I doubt it. But I ditched it anyway. I'm talking on another unit. Scott said there was all kinds of electronic gadgetry at the factory, but all the paperwork was cleaned out. The machines probably wouldn't tell us anything if they left them here. But he went down to the basement and found something interesting. The dirt basement wasn't only under the building but extended under the entire grounds. And it was full of big holes. Scott said it looked like they were digging to China."

"What else?"

"Nothing else. If he saw anything more, he didn't get a chance to tell me. Bastards."

"Sorry about Scott. Was he a friend?"

"No, but I sent him there. So he was one of mine. This is getting very personal."

"Holes . . ."

"Very deep. Any ideas?"

"Not about the basement. But we need to find someone who can talk to us. Any news on Powers's credit card?"

"No, I'll call you when I have something. I'm catching the next plane to Brownsville. I have to make sure I'm right about Scott." He hung up.

"What is it?" Alex asked.

"Scott's probably dead. Shot." He got out of bed. "I'm going to shower and make some coffee. I don't think either of us is going to sleep any more tonight."

"Talk to me. What did he find?"

"Holes. Deep, deep holes."

"It's crazy." Alex took a sip of her coffee. "What were they doing down there in the basement?"

"Some kind of experiment, judging by all the lab facilities." He leaned back in his chair. "One that required electricity, not chemicals."

"That's pretty scanty."

"It's going to take some research even into the possibilities. How good are you at digging and compiling?"

"Pretty good. I'm a journalist. What are you getting at?"

"Something brought down the dam and started the landslides. Not explosives. Unless the story they put out was a big lie. I don't think so. They had too many scientists out there looking for the cause."

"Then what am I searching for?"

"Something different in technology . . . maybe new . . . could be old but discounted. An acorn that might grow a tree. I don't know."

"Neither do I." Her lips tightened. "But if it's there, I'll find it."

"What do you need?"

"A computer with a password that will get me into Lexis-Nexis programs. Time and luck."

"The computer and programs are no problem. We'll have to make the time and luck ourselves."

"And what are you going to be doing?"

"As soon as I hear from Galen, I'm going after Powers. If we have Powers, we won't need anything else. He'll tell us everything we need to know."

"Maybe."

"No," he said quietly. "He'll tell us. I promise you."

Her cup stopped midway to her lips as a chill went through her. Forty minutes ago she had been in bed with Morgan, warm, aroused, content. Now it was a different, intimidating man who was sitting across the table.

"Do you want me to pretend to be something I'm not?" Morgan was searching her face. "Powers can open the doors. He *will* open them, Alex."

"Or?"

"I'll break him, slowly, and with a great deal of pain. I don't think he'll find it worthwhile to keep his mouth shut for more than an hour or so."

"My God."

"Should I be soft and let him and his buddies cause another Arapahoe Junction? Perhaps you'd like to climb among the rubble and dig bodies from beneath—"

"No!"

"I didn't think so." His lips twisted. "But you're having trouble with my image again. Funny. Some women find the smell of death an aphrodisiac."

"What?"

He held up his hand. "What do you see?"

"You know what I see."

"Do you see death? It's there, waiting. A finger on the trigger, a steady hand, a keen eye."

"Stop talking like this. You're making me—"

"Come too close? No one wants to come too close. If it's done for them, they accept it, even while they condemn it.

Why not? But no one wants to know what it's like. Turn a blind eye. Maybe it will go away."

But it never went away for Morgan, she realized as she studied him. His expression was hard, with a hint of recklessness, but beneath that facade was . . . what? She didn't know, and she was too uneasy right now to explore the intricacies of what made Morgan tick. They said no one knew a man as well as a woman who slept with him. She had slept with Morgan and found him passionate, gentle, and considerate. Undoubtedly the best lover she had ever had. Yet now he was revealing a side of his character that had nothing to do with the man who had made love to her.

"Jack the Ripper?" Morgan's tone was mocking as he watched her face. "Attila the Hun?"

"Don't be ridiculous."

"I'm relieved." He stood up and took his cup to the sink. "But you're still not eager to jump back in bed with me."

"What do you expect? You may not be Jack the Ripper, but you sure do a good imitation of Jekyll and Hyde." Her eyes narrowed. "Or was that intentional? It's a great way to distance me. Isn't that your modus operandi? Distance?" She stood up. "Well, you're going to get it. I can't deal with split personalities at the moment. Get me my computer and let me get to work."

"I'll call Galen and have him send it right away." He headed for the front door. "But it can't happen in the next few hours. He's on his way to Brownsville. Let's get out of here and take a walk. We both need to blow off steam."

"You go. I'll stay here."

"No way. Nothing has changed as far as security goes. We're joined at the hip."

That's not how they'd been joined last night. Dammit, why had the memory popped into her head when she was trying to maintain her cool? Because she was confused and hurt and her body was still aching and sexually attuned to Morgan.

Just shut it off as he had done. "You're right. Nothing has changed. I'll get my coat."

They had been outside for only a little over an hour when Morgan's phone rang. "I didn't expect to hear from you this— Shit." He listened for a moment. "Okay, I'm on it. No, don't send anyone else. I'm on it." He hung up. "Galen called from the Houston airport. He was between flights when he heard about the explosion."

"Explosion?"

"The Fairfax Textile factory. The fire department probably won't be able to tell what caused it for weeks. They can't get the fire out."   .

"A cover-up."

"And an excellent way to dispose of an awkward corpse."

Corpse. She had never met Scott, but it seemed callous to refer to him in that impersonal manner. "You think they left him to burn up in the fire."

"Probably. If they heard him on the phone with Galen, then they'd know it was too risky not to destroy the plant. Now there's no plant and no Scott." He turned and headed back toward the house. "And by the time that plant collapses, there won't be any basement sporting holes to China."

She hurried to keep up with him. "You told Galen you were on it. Are you going to Houston?"

"No, he found an address on one of Powers's credit-card receipts. I'm going to Indiana. First I'm taking you to your friend Sarah's house on the coast. Logan will be able to deal with the security, and the devil with keeping you away from her. None of us ever thought we'd be in this situation."

"You're not taking me anywhere I don't want to go. I'm not going to be dumped like so much garbage. And if you think I'm going to risk landing all this mess on Sarah's doorstep, you're nuts. Where in Indiana?"

"Terre Haute."

"Do you think there's any chance of the credit-card info being legitimate?"

"A small one. If it's not, I may be able to trace it. Or there's always the goat for the tiger."

"And that means?"

"If he finds someone is trying to trace it, he may come hunting."

"And that's why you're the one who has to go. Because you want to catch the hunter."

"Exactly."

"Has it occurred to you that he may not be the only one waiting at the trap?"

"In which case I get out and try again another day." His pace quickened as they neared the house. "But I'll have a bead on him. I'll be that much nearer."

"*We'll* be that much nearer."

He paused before climbing the steps. "I can't talk you out of going with me?"

"Don't try. Just tell me how the devil we're going to wander around Terre Haute without being recognized?"

"We can handle that problem." He paused. "Let me take you to Logan, Alex. Please."

She moved past him up the steps. "What about false ID, credit cards?"

He nodded his head resignedly. "Galen."

"Always Galen." She waited until he unlocked the door. "Then tell him I'll need him to supply me with a laptop and those programs by the time we get to Terre Haute."

"Fairfax is gone?" Powers repeated. "But you thought we might need it for more backup experiments after Arapahoe. I could have blown it for you. All you had to do was say the word."

"It was more risk than it was worth after Kimble found

Scott in the basement. He was on the phone, and there's no telling who else knows about Fairfax." Betworth paused. "And you. He was making inquiries at the hotel. I understand you used a credit card. I believe I told you to use cash."

"I only used my Visa twice. I ran out of cash and I needed—"

"I'm not asking for excuses," Betworth said quietly. "If everything had gone well, there would have been no problem with a minor slip like that. But now we have to make sure it doesn't hurt us."

"Have you checked on Scott's background?"

"Jurgens ran a check on him. We tried to find out who he was talking to on the phone but drew a blank. He's a hired investigator, freelance, very good, very discreet. No records in his office that indicate who he was working for." Betworth idly doodled a hangman's gallows on the pad in front of him. "I'd bet on Morgan. He was the only one who had inside information about Fairfax. What do you think?"

"It makes sense."

"Scott had a sketch of you. Alex Graham knew what you looked like. So Graham is probably still with Morgan." He drew in a stick figure to the gallows. "What address will that credit card lead Morgan to?"

"Terre Haute. But it won't do him any good. I haven't lived there for five years. I took the credit card out when I was still married to my ex-wife. I arranged with her not to cancel it and to forward the bills to a post-office box. It kept anyone from pinning down my current address." He added quickly, "But I can cover my tracks. I'll send Mae on a nice pricy vacation. She'll eat it up."

"Why do that? It offers us an opportunity. Why don't you go back to the dear old Hoosier state and snap the trap on Morgan? We might catch Graham at the same time."

"If that's what you want me to do."

"That's definitely what I want you to do. Call me when

Morgan surfaces. Naturally, I'll have Jurgens there on standby to come in if anything goes wrong."

"Nothing will go wrong."

"I have complete trust in you." He drew a noose around the stick figure's neck. "Keep me informed." He hung up.

He quickly dialed again. To his surprise the call was answered immediately. "Where are you, Runne?"

"Fort Collins. This is too slow. I need more information."

"That's why I called. I may be able to help you. I've just sent a gentleman named Thomas Powers to a city in the Midwest. Judd Morgan is going there to find Powers, and Powers thinks he's going there to catch Judd Morgan."

"No!"

"I thought that would be your reaction. Don't worry, I wouldn't think of cheating you. Powers has become a handicap to the operation, but he may be able to draw Morgan out into the open. But you have to do me two favors if I give you Powers's address."

"What?"

"I want your word that you'll do the work on Z-3."

He didn't answer.

"I've been very patient with you. Now you have to commit, Runne. You've told me you didn't care about anything but getting Morgan. Prove it."

"The job may get in the way."

"Commit. After all, it's a job your father would be proud to send you to do."

"Maybe."

"Then do enjoy Colorado."

Silence. "I'll do it."

"Your promise."

"I promise. Where's Morgan?"

"One more thing. I want Powers erased as well as Morgan."

"Done." There was no hesitation. "Tell me where he is."

"At 1372 Oak Place, Terre Haute, Indiana."

The disconnect buzz sounded in Betworth's ear.

For once Runne's rudeness didn't bother him. He was feeling too satisfied. It was pure joy to be able to pull the strings and watch the puppets jump.

Set the wolf to go after the tiger and then set loose the cobra to dispose of the wolf.

He smiled as he slashed two lines on the pad to indicate the opening trapdoor of the gallows.

"I can't talk, dammit," Alex said. "I feel like I've got a mouth full of cotton."

"Sorry. Plastic bags are the best I can do right now." Morgan quickly parted her hair in the middle and combed it straight. "I told Galen to have a kit waiting for us in a locker at the Greyhound bus station in Des Moines, but we don't want to attract attention while we're traveling."

"And how are we traveling?"

"The old pickup truck in the barn to Des Moines and then a puddle jumper to Terre Haute. Do you have any foundation makeup?"

She shook her head. "I usually wear only lipstick and powder. The rest is too much trouble."

He nodded. "With that skin you don't need it. But it's a little inconvenient at the moment." He went outside for a minute and then came back in to the fireplace and got a handful of ashes before returning to her. "But this should make you sallow enough. . . ." He rubbed the ashes into her skin and wiped the excess off. Then he combed the ashes through her hair and reached into his pocket and gave her a small pebble. "Now, take off your left shoe and put this stone in it."

"What?"

"Your walk is very distinctive. Very free and open. This will change your gait."

She made a face. "You mean it will bug me and make me limp."

"A little." He stepped back and critically tilted his head. "You'll probably be okay. Winter coats are bulky, and that's a plus. We won't stop for anything but gas between here and Des Moines."

She stood up and went to the mirror in the bathroom. Her face looked plump, colorless, and ten years older. The middle part and cheek pads had completely changed the contours of her face.

"Remember to keep the cheek pads even or you'll look deformed." Morgan was standing beside her with a contact case in his hand. His skin had the same ashy, sallow cast as her own. "It will be easier once we get the kit. Those cheek pads are used with professional theatricals and are much more comfortable."

"I can hardly wait," she said dryly. "What other little accessories do you have in store for me?"

"Nostril inserts to widen your nose. Tanning solution. A wig with a different hair color and style." He was inserting the brown contact in his left eye. "It's not smart to get too complicated. If you're too uncomfortable you look uncomfortable, and that attracts attention. Or sometimes you forget to put something on and that can be fatal."

"You know a lot about disguises."

"It can help on occasion."

"Where did you get the contacts?"

"I usually carry them with me. They're small and no trouble. These blue eyes are damn noticeable. They've gotten me into trouble more than once, and there's no telling when I might need a little camouflage."

"Not in your business."

He turned to look at her. "Right, not in my business." He stuffed the case in his pocket. "Let's hit the road."

The White House

Andreas was grandstanding as usual, Betworth thought with contempt as he watched the President and his beautiful First Lady move down the line of guests. His charm was at full wattage, and every man in the room would vaguely remember him as being as protective as their father, as companionable as their brother. Mix in a strong dash of sex appeal for the ladies and he was almost unbeatable.

But Betworth could have beaten him. He knew how to finesse and charm as well as Andreas. It was only that invisible aura of power that surrounded any president that made Andreas seem like Superman to the people around him.

However, Betworth had never been able to insinuate himself into the tight-knit group that surrounded Andreas. The bastard had always kept him at a distance, and it had become obvious to the power brokers on the Washington scene. Oh, well, he'd jumped over that hurdle.

"He's one gutsy guy, isn't he?"

He glanced over his shoulder to see Hank Ellswyth, the Senate Majority Leader, staring admiringly at Andreas.

"You'd think with all the threats swirling around him that he'd cancel this kind of soiree." Ellswyth lifted his cocktail in a half salute. "Better him than me."

"Not much danger here in the White House with all this security." Betworth smiled. "But maybe you're right. Discretion is the better part of valor."

"I didn't say he was making a mistake," Ellswyth said quickly. "We can't let those terrorists scare us."

"You'd never do that," Betworth said. "Everyone knows

what you stand for, Hank. We all rely on you. Andreas most of all."

Andreas was pausing beside a distinguished older man with a mane of white hair and aristocratic features. A moment later the two strolled out onto the terrace.

"I wonder what he's up to with Shepard," Ellswyth murmured. "They usually don't have much to say to each other."

"No telling." Betworth shrugged. "Maybe he's trying to show everybody he and the Vice President are a united front."

"Well, Shepard's been right in the forefront lately. That speech at Arapahoe Junction was awesome. I didn't know he had it in him. His approval rating shot sky-high."

"Well, we all have to answer the call in days like these."

"I'm wondering what call the President is asking him to answer now," Ellswyth murmured.

"Who knows? He can be a bit secretive. Not like you, Hank. We all appreciate your openness."

Ellswyth smiled. "I'm just a simple guy from Missouri trying to do my job."

Bullshit. There was nothing simple about Ellswyth. He was scheming and tap-dancing his heart out trying to position himself for the next presidential nomination. Betworth had no quarrel with that. Ambitious men were easier to manipulate than idealists. You promised them the world and they'd follow you anywhere.

"I think I'll go and pay my respects to the First Lady," Ellswyth said as he put his drink on the tray of a passing waiter. "I haven't had a chance to talk to her this evening."

And Chelsea Andreas was standing near the French doors through which Andreas and Shepard had vanished, Betworth thought with amusement. Ellswyth was practically salivating to know what was going on between them.

So was Betworth. But he'd never make the mistake of calling attention to that curiosity. He'd find out eventually. Patience. In all things, patience.

"I have a favor to ask, Shepard." Andreas gazed out over the garden. "One that means a lot to me."

"You know that I'll do whatever I can, Mr. President." Carl Shepard smiled. "I'm honored. It's the first time in all these years you've personally asked anything of me. I was beginning to think you regretted choosing me as your running mate."

He hadn't chosen him, Andreas thought ruefully. The party had given him a choice of two candidates who could carry California, and he was the less objectionable. Shepard was too much the elder statesman for his taste. The country was in a climate of change, and its leaders had to be ready to change with it. Yet he might have been too hard on the man. Shepard had been doing everything he could to meet the challenge—traveling, making speeches, visiting the bereaved families of those diplomats killed at the embassies. "We haven't been together in the White House for more than a few days every month. We've been forced to go our separate ways."

Shepard chuckled. "Some of the reporters who cover the White House have started to call me the mystery man." His smile faded. "I don't mind. If it helps the country to have me away from Washington, that's where I need to be. I realize politics or your personal preferences don't enter into it."

"No, they don't." He turned to face Shepard. "But it's a personal favor I'm asking you. I want you to help get my wife away from the White House."

Shepard's gaze flew to Chelsea, who was chatting with Ellswyth inside. "That's not going to be easy. We hardly know each other."

"Your wife is chairperson of the National Foundation for Abused Children. It's one of Chelsea's passions. She's been associated with the organization for years. Ask her to speak at a conference or visit the facilities around the country. I don't

Dead Aim

care what you do." His voice roughened with suppressed violence. "Just get her away from me."

Shepard was silent a moment. "It's the threats from the terrorists who are responsible for the embassy bombings?"

"What do you think? Three embassies gone and they haven't been able to find more than a few leads. It's not like the usual hits. They're smart and they must have a hell of a lot of money and contacts. I can't be sure they're not moving closer."

"Keller's been doing a great job keeping you safe."

"Yes, but a dose of cyanide still managed to get as far as my kitchen, and before that an explosive device was discovered on the grounds outside my quarters."

"*Discovered* is the key word. And that was some time ago. I'm sure Keller's plugged every hole."

"So am I. I didn't bring you out here to ask for reassurance." His lips tightened. "It's okay that every threat is directed at me. I never expected anything else. It's in the job description. It's not okay that Chelsea may be targeted because she's standing beside me." He paused, his gaze on Chelsea as he added softly, "And she's always beside me. In every way."

"I'll do my best. I'll talk to Nancy tonight. How soon?"

"Yesterday. Today. As quick as you can. I've sent the children away to their stepsister in San Diego. It's only Chelsea who won't leave me." He clapped Shepard on the shoulder. "I appreciate this. I owe you."

"It's my honor, Mr. President. We all have to pull together in times like this."

Yes, they did, Andreas thought wearily as he opened the French doors. United we stand. But Chelsea mustn't stand united with him now.

He paused in the doorway and glanced around the room. There was no way of slipping in or out of any function, but

Iris Johansen

everyone seemed to be pretending they hadn't noticed he'd been gone.

Except Betworth. He smiled and bowed slightly before going back to his conversation with the Secretary of Labor. Bold as brass and full of personal magnetism.

Andreas coolly nodded his head in acknowledgment at him as he slipped his arm around Chelsea's waist and brushed a kiss on her temple. "Everything okay?"

"Fine." She smiled brightly at Ellswyth. "The Senator was telling me about St. Louis. But I'm sure he's much more interested in what you and Vice President Shepard were discussing." She sipped her orange juice. "Aren't you, Senator?"

Ellswyth blinked. "Not at all. I had no—"

"No? Then I must have been mistaken." She slipped her arm through Andreas's. "I think it's time to circulate and then say our good night to the Prime Minister. You've got that visit to the school for the handicapped early tomorrow morning." She gave Ellswyth a smile that made him forget his momentary embarrassment. "You'll excuse us?" She didn't wait for an answer as she gently nudged Andreas forward. "What the hell are you up to?" she murmured. "You have everyone in the room wondering what you said to Shepard."

"Then they can keep on wondering."

"Not me. I'm on the home team."

"Maybe it's top secret."

She searched his expression and then shook her head. "I don't think so."

He should have expected both the curiosity and the perceptiveness. They knew each other so well. They had been friends and partners as well as lovers for many years. "No," he said softly. "Drop it, Chelsea."

She studied him and then shrugged. "I'll find out." She turned her brilliant smile on the Prime Minister. "So good of you to honor us with your presence tonight. . . ."

9

Terre Haute

Morgan and Alex checked into a Motel 6 shortly before seven in the evening. They stopped at the convenience store on the corner for take-out sandwiches and toiletries before they went to their rooms.

"The rooms are adjoining," Morgan said as he handed her the key. "Lock your front door and put a chair in front of it. We'll enter and exit through my room. I have to make a phone call. Take your shower and then come in and have something to eat."

She nodded wearily. "Don't hold your breath. I have to wash all this ash out of my hair."

"Need help?"

"I can do it. It will just take a while. Who are you calling?"

"I had Galen set up an operative here in Terre Haute to watch the motel. I have to tell him we're here."

"Why is he watching our motel?"

"Because I'm not leaving you alone here."

"You're damn right you're not." She didn't like the sound of what Morgan had said, but she couldn't deal with it right now. She went into her room, shut the door, and locked it. She didn't move for a minute. After that puddle jumper from Des Moines, she felt as drained and lackluster as her appearance.

Well, she'd feel better after a shower—though she'd probably risk drowning, moving in and out of the spray to keep this blasted bandage from getting wet. She was glad Morgan hadn't been insistent about helping her. She didn't need that tension along with the hassle of dealing with her bum shoulder.

It took over an hour for her to shower and wash her hair, and she was more exhausted than ever by the time she finished. She wrapped a towel around herself, sank down in the chair by the desk, and closed her eyes. She'd just take a little time to rest. Not long. Perhaps only—

"Are you all right?"

Her lids flew open and she saw Morgan standing in the doorway of the adjoining room. "I'm fine. A little tired." She tightened the towel around her body. "I'll get dressed and be with you in a minute. Will you set up my laptop?"

"No." He crossed the room, unzipped her duffel, and pulled out his gray T-shirt she'd taken to using as nightwear. "You'll eat. We'll talk a little, make plans, and then you'll go to bed. You can get up at the break of dawn and hit the computer. But you rest first or you'll be no use to yourself or me." He pulled her to her feet, stripped the towel off her, jerked the T-shirt over her head, and stretched it until he could manipulate both arms into the sleeves. "Hair." He took the towel and started to dry it.

She took the towel away from him. "I can handle it."

"I'm sure you can." He turned. "Call if you need me. I'll see you in ten minutes."

God, he was bossy. She was tempted to tell him to go to hell and dig out the computer herself and—

But he had known exactly what he was doing by striking just the right note of annoyance to send a corresponding surge of adrenaline through her. How long the energy would last she had no idea, but she'd better use it while she had it.

She quickly towel-dried her hair and strode into his room. "Okay, what next, Nero?"

He flinched. "I don't mind being compared to an emperor but not one who was off his noggin." He gestured to the table. "Sit down and have a sandwich. You haven't had anything to eat since that layover in St. Louis."

"I'm not hungry." She sat down and picked up the tuna sandwich. "Or maybe I am. It looks pretty good." She bit into it. "So talk. What do we do about Powers?"

He sat down opposite her. "Nothing, until I do a little surveillance of the house and surroundings. I want to make sure I'm not walking into a trap."

"You keep speaking in the singular. Stop it."

"No, that's the way it's going to be." His words were cool and precise. "You don't interfere with my business. You don't get in my way. I won't have you messing up my job."

"Your job? Don't you think I'm affected just a little by—" She stopped. Stop this defensive bullshit. He was a professional and she wasn't. Too many times she'd seen well-meaning amateurs cause irreparable harm on disaster sites. And God knows this entire scenario was a disaster site. "How can I help?"

"Stay here and do that research."

"Are you sure you didn't make that up to keep me out of sight?"

"It occurred to me. But I think it's a job that needs doing. What do you think?"

Damn him, he'd turned the tables by throwing out that question. She made a face. "If I didn't think there was merit, I wouldn't have consented to do it. I hate research. But I have other talents. I'm a damn fine photographer, and I have a lens that's good a block away and can see the stripes on the back of a bee buzzing around a sunflower. You wouldn't have to get too near the house, and I can have the film developed within thirty minutes of getting back here."

He was silent a moment. "A block can be pretty close."

"But I make sense." She stared him in the eye. "Don't I?"

"Yes, damn you." He finished his sandwich. "Okay, but I do the preliminary surveillance myself to find you a place to do your shoot."

Her heart skipped a beat at the thought. But she had won too much to argue with him. "When?"

"Tonight." He stood up. "As soon as I rummage through that kit Galen gave us and find a wig and a few accessories to disguise my unforgettable mug."

He was joking, but his face was unforgettable. If she never saw him again she would always remember it. Christ, the thought had come out of nowhere and scared her to death. Ignore it, and for heaven's sake don't let him know. She leaned back in her chair. "What kind of wig?"

"We'll see." He opened his duffel and pulled out a brownish-red wig with gray at the temples. "Not exactly fashionable, but it's nowhere close to my real hair. That's a plus." He pulled out a denim jacket and tennis shoes. "You can't say Galen's choices aren't eclectic." He threw the clothes on the bed. "I hope he does better by you."

"I think my wig is red too. Curly as Orphan Annie's. Maybe we're supposed to be brother and sister." She moistened her lips. "You do think this is a trap, don't you?"

He nodded. "They've got to know we'd access the credit card. It's only smart to follow up. It's what I'd do in the same circumstances."

"Then you be careful." She pushed back the chair and rose to her feet. "You'll knock on my door when you get back?"

"You'll probably be asleep."

"Don't be absurd. I won't be asleep. How the hell could I be asleep when you're—" She steadied her voice. "You knock on my door and tell me what happened, or I'll get my gun and shoot you."

He smiled. "In that case, you can bet I'll knock the damn door down if you don't answer. I'm always out to protect my neck."

"See that you do." She left the room and shut the door. Idiot. She'd known Morgan in only the most volatile circumstances and slept with him one night. He was possibly the most wary man she'd ever met and he had no desire for anything but a sexual encounter. It was the height of foolishness to let herself feel this way. For Christ's sake, get a grip.

But foolish or not, she knew she wouldn't sleep until he got back. She'd make a list of developing chemicals for Morgan to pick up tomorrow. Then she figured she might as well get out the computer and surf the Net.

It was after three A.M. when she heard Morgan's door close.

Her fingers froze on the keyboard and she closed her eyes. Thank God.

She was already opening the adjoining door when he knocked on it a moment later. "What happened?"

"Nothing. I scouted around and didn't see anything suspicious. A little brick house on a quiet street. Late-model car in the driveway. Not a rental car—Indiana license plates—and it doesn't look like it's been taken care of any too well. It could belong to Powers's ex-wife. That doesn't mean there isn't a very neat trap ready to be sprung." He gazed beyond her to the laptop on the table. "I see you've been working. Stumble on anything?"

"I'd have to stumble. I don't have any idea where I'm going. I started with explosives and now I'm doing a search on water pressure." She rubbed her eyes. "I'm almost blind. Did you find a house where I can shoot my photos?"

He nodded. "A house for sale on the next block. Two stories, unoccupied, with a clear view of Powers's house from the corner bedroom. There are shutters on the window, so the camera can't be seen from outside."

"How did you get in?" She gestured. "Never mind. What a stupid question. That's just another facet of your business, right?"

"Absolutely. I'll slip you into the house tomorrow night. May I suggest you stop work and get some sleep?"

She nodded. "I'll try again tomorrow." She started to close the door and then stopped. "You didn't see anything?"

He shook his head as he turned away. "I didn't see anything."

Morgan stripped off his clothes, lay down, and pulled the sheet over him.

He had told the truth. He had seen nothing.

But there had been someone there, waiting. His every instinct, every nerve had been vibrating with the knowledge. He had been in the game too long not to have developed antennae. It was the reason he had spent an hour and a half driving around before coming back to the motel.

Government?

Probably not. CIA agents on jobs like these usually traveled in twos or threes, and he'd only met a few he couldn't spot.

Powers?

More than likely.

Runne?

It was possible. Everything seemed to be overlapping, and Runne might be allowing himself to be used.

It would be helpful to know who the antagonist was so that he could adjust his actions to each player. But he'd probably have to go in blind and trust to instinct until he saw the field.

And hope he could get Alex in and out before all hell broke loose.

"How long will it take you to get the photos?" Morgan asked as he led Alex up the stairs to the second floor.

"It depends on angles and what there is to shoot," Alex said, moving carefully in the darkness. "Can't we have the flashlight on?"

"No, I'd be watching any vacant house in the area. Though this window isn't much of a threat. It's out of range. I'd probably concentrate on the house for sale across the street."

She felt a chill as she always did when she was reminded of Morgan's profession. "Let's hope it isn't out of range for me to shoot." She knelt by the window and opened her camera bag. "Which house?"

"The white brick, next to the house on the corner."

She started shooting. Every window. The porches. Upstairs. The garbage cans next to the backyard fence. Then she began to photograph every aspect of every house on each side of the street.

"Get the tree in the backyard."

"The tree?"

Morgan likes trees.

She remembered Galen saying that about Morgan. Evidently he thought someone else might have the same fondness.

She focused and shot several photos of the tree in the back and then the smaller one on the front lawn. "Satisfied?"

"Are you?"

She shook her head. "Give me another hour. We have to get lucky, and you cut down your chances the less time you spend."

"I want you out of here."

"Another hour." She changed the film in her camera.

He muttered a curse and then moved closer to the window, his gaze raking the street and houses.

"Now?" he asked exactly one hour later.

She nodded as she put the camera in her bag. "I've covered the area thoroughly. I can only hope I caught something on film."

"Well, if you didn't, you're not coming back." He picked up her camera and nudged her out of the bedroom and down the stairs. "This is it."

"Here they are." Alex called Morgan into the bathroom, where she'd set up a makeshift developing room. "They're not dry yet, but I thought you'd want to take a look."

He moved to stand beside her and stared down at the pans. "My God, you took enough. It will take an hour to go through all these photos."

"I already scanned most of them as I did them." She pointed to the photo of garbage cans by the tall fence in the backyard. "Something interesting here. They're not in the same position in the photo taken an hour later. I thought maybe a dog . . . but they're not turned over. It looks like they've been neatly moved."

He nodded absently, his gaze shifting quickly from photo to photo. "Anything else?"

She pointed to a window on the first floor. "A man and woman. You can barely see them in the shadows to the left of the window."

"It doesn't look like much to me. You're sure?"

"I'm used to looking at photographs. I'm sure." She tapped a photo of a garage on the opposite side of the street from the brick house. "There's a shadow here that could be some-one. . . ." She shrugged. "But I can't be certain. It could be a play of light."

"Show me the pictures of the oak tree. Never mind. I see them. Which one was taken first?"

She pointed to a photo. "And this one was an hour later." She pointed to the second photo.

He studied them. "There's a shadow in the first one that's not there in the second one."

"It's very marginal." She got her magnifying glass and examined the shadow. "It could be wind moving the branches. It changes the entire composition."

"Maybe." He stood looking down at the photos. "Maybe not." He turned on his heel. "I'm going back out there. Stay in the room and lock the door."

"What?"

"Double cross." He moved toward the door. "What do you do with a man who knows too much and has taken to making mistakes?" His voice sharpened with rage. "Dammit, I'm not going to let Powers be taken out. I *need* him."

She grabbed her camera bag and hurried out the door after him toward the car. "I'm going with you."

"The hell you—" He jerked open the driver's door. "I don't have time to argue with you. If you come, you do what I say. Got it?"

"Got it." She jumped into the passenger's seat.

He peeled out of the parking spot. "Yeah, sure."

"I don't like this." Mae Powers frowned. "I told you five years ago that I didn't want to have anything to do with you or your dirty business."

"But you haven't minded taking my money, have you?" Powers stood to the side of the window so he couldn't be seen from the street. "And there'll be a nice little bonus for you for going along this time. I'm even using a silencer so your neighbors won't know you're not as holier-than-thou as you pretend." He didn't see anything on the street in front of the house. He'd stationed Decker in the alley across the street, but he couldn't see him at the moment. Well, he'd only have to phone him and he'd be here in a flash. There was no need to be this nervous. All the windows and doors were locked. He was still uneasy. He'd heard a lot about Morgan. He was one tough bastard, and used to getting past locks.

Well, he was tougher than Morgan. He gazed down at his gun with the attached silencer. All he had to do was sit here and wait and blow the son of a bitch out of the water.

"What's that?" Mae jerked upright in her chair, her gaze flying toward the kitchen. "It was one of the pots hanging over the bar. I thought you locked the kitchen door. I told you I didn't want to—"

He was already on his feet, running down the hall, past the staircase, toward the kitchen, gun in hand.

He heard a squeak on the stairs and whirled.

He didn't hear Mae's scream as the hurled knife entered his chest.

Shit.

Pain. Darkness.

Someone coming down the stairs.

Kill him. Kill him.

He lifted his gun.

"Stay here." Morgan braked at the curb on the cross street from the brick house. "No arguments. I don't want you in my way."

"That's a sure way to get me to— I'll stay out of your way unless I see something I don't like."

He muttered a curse as he took off running toward the backyard of Powers's house. Too dangerous to go in through the front. Climb the oak tree and get in through the second floor.

Like the shadowy figure Alex had not been able to confirm.

Dead Aim

He shinnied up the tree and went hand over hand up the branches until he reached the window.

The glass had been cut neatly out of the pane.

He swung silently from the branch to the windowsill and into the bedroom.

The door was open. He drew his gun, moved to press against the wall beside the doorway, and waited.

No sound.

No, that wasn't true.

A groan?

He moved out into the hall.

No, more like a whimper.

He looked over the stair railing into the hall below.

He could dimly see a man lying on his back at the bottom of the stairs. Powers? A woman in a red blouse was crumpled at the end of the hall.

And maybe someone else waiting in the shadows for Morgan to come down and be slaughtered?

He hesitated. Only one way to find out. Throw some light on the subject.

He hit the light switch on the wall and at the same time dropped to the floor, his gun aimed at the hall below.

Nothing. No movement. No sound.

He cautiously rose to his knees, his gaze on the end of the hall. He was a target. Not a good one, but enough to draw fire.

Nothing.

Powers whimpered again.

Take a chance. He had to get to Powers before the bastard died on him.

He jumped over the rail into the hall below and hit the ground running.

No one in the kitchen. He turned and ran past the woman, toward the living room.

Empty.

He checked the woman as he passed her on the way back

to Powers. Dead. Her throat had been cut. Messy. It had been hacked as if in a blind frenzy.

He knelt beside Powers. There was a deep knife wound in his chest.

"Save . . . me." Blood was bubbling out of his mouth. "Don't let me die."

"Why should I?" Morgan asked. "What good are you to me?"

Powers looked up at him. "Morgan?"

He nodded. "Who did this to you?"

"Betworth . . . dirty fucking bastard. Sent Runne. Got him, though. Shot him in the head."

"If you got him, his body would be here."

"Shot him. I'm hurting. . . . Call a doctor."

"When you tell me what I need to know. Where's Z-2?"

"You son of a bitch, I'm dying."

"Then you'd better talk fast so that I can call 911. Where's Z-2?"

"Fuckin' bastard . . ."

"Where is it?"

"West . . . Virginia. Not important . . . Z-3. Z-3 . . ."

"And Z-3 is important? Not Z-2?"

"Z-2 . . . It's all bunk—" He arched upward as agony struck him. "Son of a bitch. Screw him." Powers's eyes were glazing. "Screw Z-3."

Powers was rambling. Morgan went in another direction. "What was happening in Fairfax?"

"Vents . . . Fucking waste of time. Couldn't get . . . it right after we lost Lontana. Get . . . me . . . an ambulance."

"Who's Lontana?"

"Brazilian . . . Betworth gave all that money. Couldn't get it right."

"Who's—" Powers was drifting off again. "What happened at Arapahoe Junction?"

"Wrong side. Couldn't get it right. Lost Lontana." His hand was clenching. "Please . . . I don't want to die."

"None of us does. Z-3. Listen to me. Tell me about Z-3 and I'll call an ambulance."

"They'll get him there. No choice. Z-3 . . ."

"What's happening?" Alex was standing at the front door, gun in hand. She moved into the room until she was beside Morgan.

"Powers . . ." she whispered.

Morgan ignored her, his gaze on Powers. "Where's Z-3?"

He didn't answer. He was almost gone, dammit.

Morgan's hand closed on his shirt. "Answer me. Where's Z-3?"

"Kettle . . ." Powers's body stiffened and then convulsed. His mouth opened wide in a silent scream. It stayed open as life fled.

"He's dead. . . ." Alex murmured. "Who—"

"Not me. Believe me, I'd have found out what I needed before I stuck a knife in him." He was going through Powers's pockets. "He was almost useless to me."

"I heard you tell him you'd call an ambulance if he told you about Z-3."

"I lied. He was a dead man the minute that knife entered his chest. But it gave me a hold to squeeze information out of him." He saw her expression and his lips twisted. "What else would you expect from me?"

"I don't know. He was . . . dying."

"Does that make him holy? He was bad news, and if he'd recovered he'd still be bad news. He deserved what Runne did to him. I was lucky Runne didn't do his usual excellent job and left me a little to work with."

"Runne. Is that who he said did this?"

He nodded as he jammed Powers's wallet in his jacket pocket and rose to his feet. "Let's get out of here. I don't think we have much time." He grabbed her arm and ran toward the kitchen door. "And why the hell are you here?"

"I told you I'd stay unless I saw something I didn't like. I saw someone run out the front door, blood all over his face. I didn't like that at all."

"I can see why you'd be disturbed. Where did he go?"

"He ran down the street and around the corner. Runne?"

"Almost certainly."

"Well, you'll be able to be very certain after I get my film developed."

"You took his photo?"

"Hell, yes. I've regretted every minute that I didn't take Powers's picture at the dam instead of screaming like an idiot. I guarantee I didn't scream this time." She raced beside him across the yard and out into the alley. "Why don't we have much time?"

"Because the setup is too neat not to have a backup." He jerked open the car door. "We'll go back to the motel and grab our stuff. I'll call Galen and tell him to get us out of here. I don't believe the highways are going to be safe for us anywhere near this town."

"And where do we go?"

He thought about it, quickly going over the few coherent bits Powers had given him. "West Virginia."

Christ.

Runne patted his bloody cheek with the T-shirt he'd taken off when he reached the car. He couldn't stop the blood. He could feel the hole. . . . He'd ducked back and turned his head, or Powers's bullet would have blown his head off. Instead, the bullet had gone through his cheek and taken out part of his lip.

Damn squeaky stair. He'd tossed a slipper he'd found in the upstairs bedroom into the kitchen to draw Powers. Everything would have been fine if that stair had been—

Excuses. He'd learned in training as a boy to never make excuses. The unexpected happened, and one had to make adjustments.

Dead Aim

He'd made adjustments. He'd kept his deal with Betworth. Powers couldn't have lived for more than a few minutes.

Morgan.

Anguish tore through him. He'd meant to remove Powers and his wife and be there in the house when Morgan found a way to get to Powers.

It might not be too late.

Find a doctor. Get the bleeding stopped. Then go back and wait until Morgan walked into the house.

Find a doctor. . . .

"Powers and his wife are dead. We found Decker's body in the alley across the street," Jurgens said when Betworth picked up the phone. "No Morgan. No Graham. Runne must have screwed up."

"Runne did it?"

"Probably. You said he liked to work with a knife at close quarters. Decker's throat was slit, Powers had a knife wound in his chest, and his wife was pretty much butchered."

"Then there must have been a good reason why Runne didn't stick around to get Morgan. Maybe he's gone after him. How long has Powers been dead?"

"Not long. We sent a car by when he didn't call for his two-hour check-in. What do you want us to do?"

"Clean up the crime scene and get rid of Decker, Powers, and his wife. Then have a team stake out the house in case Morgan shows up."

"And?"

"Do I have to tell you everything? Make sure every car that leaves Terre Haute is stopped by the police."

"What do I tell them?"

"Anything. Just make sure they're stopped."

10

On the way back to the motel, the adrenaline was draining out of Alex and she had to clasp her hands tightly in her lap to keep from shaking. She'd been bombarded by too many sensations tonight. She couldn't forget the vision of Powers with his chest torn by that hideous knife wound and Morgan kneeling above him, tense, relentless, completely without pity.

But why should anyone pity Powers? He'd not taken pity on Ken that night he'd brought down the helicopter. Still, Morgan's hardness had managed to shock her again.

Morgan glanced sideways at her as they neared the motel. "What are you thinking?"

"What do you think happened to Powers's wife? She looked . . ."

"Like an animal had torn her throat apart," he finished. "I've heard Runne is usually much cleaner. I'd say that something went wrong with his plan and Powers managed to hurt him. He ran out to lick his wounds and she was in his way. He was hurting too much to be neat. He just wanted to get rid of her."

"You seem to understand him."

"Oh, yes." He stopped the car in the parking space in front

of the motel and opened the door. "I'm leaving the car running. Don't be neat. Just bundle everything in your duffel. I'll give Galen a quick call, but I want to be out of this motel in five minutes and out of this town in twenty."

She nodded jerkily. "I won't be long." She left her camera in the car and moved toward the door. "What did Powers tell you?"

"I'll tell you when we get on the road." He had the door open and was grabbing his duffel and throwing everything into it. "Be sure to take the computer."

"Roadblock."

Morgan turned left at the first corner when he saw the string of cars stretching two blocks ahead. He parked the car in a Target parking lot. "Come on, get out. We're on foot until we're out of town. Grab your camera bag. I'll get your duffel."

"Right." She fell into step with him. "I suppose you know how we're going to get out of this town?"

"I called Galen when you were packing. He has a man with a moving truck coming from Fort Wayne. We'll meet him at the rest stop five miles out of town."

"A moving truck?"

"It will be easy to hide among the furniture if we're stopped. The driver will have documents that say his load is being delivered to Charleston, West Virginia, from a house in Fort Wayne. Most cops don't want to climb around in the back if the paperwork looks okay. It's too much work." He turned right, his pace quickening. "We should be out of the city in about five blocks, and then we cut into the woods."

"I can hardly wait."

"It will be safer."

"I'm not arguing. I'm only asking one thing."

"What's that?"

"If I'm going to be doing all this walking, can I take this damn pebble out of my shoe?"

The name of the driver of the moving van was Chuck Fondren, and he was distinctly nervous. "Get in." He jerked open the back of the truck. "I was stopped once already on the way here, but that doesn't mean I'm out of hot water. Climb over that mattress and hunker down behind that couch."

The door slammed behind them as soon as Morgan and Alex climbed into the van.

Darkness.

Morgan tossed the duffels across the van, behind the couch. "Come on. Let's 'hunker down.'" He climbed over the mattress to the couch and then reached out a hand to help her over the back of the couch. He followed and settled down beside her.

She felt the throbbing vibration as the truck pulled out of the rest stop, and she leaned back against the wall. She should have felt safer than she had when they were running through the woods, but she didn't. The darkness was claustrophobic and she felt . . . helpless.

"Like being sealed up in a metal box," Morgan said quietly. "But a box isn't a coffin. There's always something you can do."

She should have known he'd realize what she was feeling. He seemed to have the knack. "Like what?"

He chuckled. "Damn if I know. I just thought I'd make you feel better. I should have known you'd call me on it."

She smiled. She did feel better. His honesty made her feel a sense of companionship and she was no longer alone. "Are you saying you'd be stumped if we had to get out of here?"

"No. I'm saying I'd have to stretch my capabilities and borrow some of yours." He leaned back beside her. "So let's hope nothing happens and try to get our minds off it. Want to have sex?"

She went rigid.

"No, I didn't think so."

"And you thought it safe to offer since you knew this wasn't the time or place I'd take you up on it."

"Oh, I don't know. And neither do you." He reached over to her duffel, pulled out the laptop, and gave it to her. "I'm going to go over my conversation with Powers before he died. I've been trained to remember details, but I want them down in black and white." He flipped open the laptop, and a gray glow lit the darkness. "You type them as I give them to you, word for word. Here we go."

He closed his eyes and said, "The first thing he said to me was 'Save me. . . . Don't let me die.' "

For the next five minutes Alex typed quickly, occasionally asking a question, but Morgan's memory was amazing. He remembered everything, including pauses and breaks in the flow of conversation.

When he stopped, she looked up at him. "Is that all?"

He made a face. "Not much, is it?"

"More than we had." She saved the document. "So that's why we're going to West Virginia. You think something's going to happen there."

"I don't know. Powers seemed to think that whatever was going to happen wasn't nearly as important as Z-3. He said it was bunk. But Powers doesn't give a shit. Arapahoe Junction was only a mistake to him."

"So West Virginia could be another Arapahoe Junction."

"And if Arapahoe Junction was only a minor mistake, it makes you wonder what Z-3 is going to be. . . ." He closed his eyes. "It's a long way to West Virginia. Think about it. Vents. Lontana. Z-2 . . ."

There was no question she'd think about it. Her head was awhirl with information and the ugliness of Powers even at his death. She closed the computer, and the dim glow of the screen disappeared.

Suffocating darkness.

Morgan's arm suddenly went around her, and he pulled her close so that her head rested on his shoulder. "Shh, you're not alone. I'm here. I'm not going away."

Comforting words, but not true. It didn't matter. In the darkness she could pretend they were true. In the darkness she could take comfort and healing.

After all, in this day and age nothing was permanent. Fire came from the sky and quakes ripped the ground from beneath your feet.

And *always* was only a word.

"We've closed all the roads," Jurgens said. "And we've run fingerprints in the Powers house. Morgan was there and I'm betting so was Graham. We found a knife under Powers's wife's body. But it's not Morgan's prints that are on the knife."

"Runne."

"Yes. Morgan must have come before or after."

"If he'd come before, those would have been his prints on the knife: He wouldn't have let Powers live. The question is, how much later? Could Powers have been alive to talk?"

"It's doubtful. The wound was—"

"I need more than doubtful. I need to know."

"Then you'd better ask Runne, don't you think?"

Hell, yes, if he could get in touch with the bastard. As usual, Runne hadn't answered his phone. "As soon as I make contact with him."

There was a pause. "There was blood on the front porch. Neither Powers nor his wife could have been out there."

"You think Runne was wounded?"

"The police say a local intern, Richard Dawson, has been reported missing from a hospital a few miles from the Powers house. His car is in the parking lot, but he never showed up for his shift." Another pause. "So maybe Runne isn't as good as you thought he was."

"And maybe he is." Betworth wasn't going to admit his own doubts to Jurgens. "He didn't get Morgan, but he managed to rid us of Powers. And you haven't gotten Morgan yet either."

"If you'd let us spring the trap, there wouldn't have been this problem."

"I needed Runne to spring it. I needed him to owe me."

"You believed he'd keep his word?"

"The psychological profile I have on him indicates that he'd rather be burned alive than break his word. It's part of the brainwashing he underwent in the camps. And it's a job he's been trained to do every minute since he was fourteen."

"Even if he has the will, he may not have the skill. He screwed up this job."

"Drop it. I'll make that determination." He managed to keep the edge from his tone. "Or are you volunteering to take over Runne's job at Z-3?"

"No way," Jurgens said. "I'll let you know when we catch Morgan." He hung up.

No, Jurgens didn't want any part of it. Betworth didn't blame him. Only an obsessive son of a bitch like Runne would take on that job. Providing Betworth remained convinced he could do it. The Powers disposal had not been clean, and that's what he must have at Z-3.

Clean and deadly.

Clean. It had to be clean.

Runne rolled the young intern's corpse into the hole he'd dug and began to shovel in dirt. Christ, his face hurt. He'd take some of the painkillers the doctor had given him after he finished, but the pain reminded him of his failure. And he had to remember so that he wouldn't repeat the mistake. Mistakes weren't tolerated. Carelessness was a cardinal sin. The shame of not being able to claim a clean kill with Powers was almost unbearable. It must never happen again, and no one must know he'd failed.

This kill had been clean. No one had seen him take the young intern at the hospital. No one had seen the death. Now he must smooth the grave and cover it with leaves.

The damn doctor had been too slow. Runne had threatened him, but his hands had been too shaky to hurry. Now it was too late to go back to Powers's house and hope to catch Morgan. But if he could keep Betworth from knowing of his shame, then he would be given another chance.

Ignore the pain. He deserved it.

Bury him deep. Smooth the earth. Cover it with leaves. . . .

"Out," Chuck Fondren said as he opened the door of the truck. "I want to get away from here."

"Where are we?" Alex asked as Morgan helped her from the van.

"Prescott, West Virginia. It's forty miles from Huntington." The driver nodded at a rickety cedar house down the road. "That's your destination. This is where I was told to bring you." He threw the duffels to the ground. "Good luck. I'm out of here."

"Thank you," Alex said. She couldn't blame him for being glad to be rid of them. He'd risked a good deal driving them here. But when Galen called, his people seemed to jump to it. She gazed ruefully at the ramshackle farmhouse as the moving van roared off down the road. "Have you noticed our abodes have been going downhill lately? You must have a talk with Galen."

"It's hard to get good help these days." He started down

the road. "Personally, I'm just happy if there's no welcoming committee." He stiffened, grabbed her arm, and pulled her into the bushes. "I spoke too soon. Who the hell is—"

Her gaze followed his to the man who'd come out onto the porch. She sighed with relief. "It's Logan. Don't you recognize him?"

"I've talked to him on the phone, but I've never met him in person." His body language was still tense. "And I'm not sure I like him dropping in. He looks pretty grim." He moved out of the bushes. "But we may as well find out what he wants. I doubt if he's brought the gendarmes." His gaze held Logan's as he strode toward him. "This is a surprise, Logan," he called as he neared the house. "And I thought you'd abandoned us."

"I'd like nothing better." Logan's glance shifted to Alex. "Are you okay? Galen said you'd had an accident."

"It's getting better. How's Sarah?"

"Furious. Ready to do battle with the FBI and the media." He grimaced. "And me. Particularly me. After this idiocy came out about you belonging to a terrorist group, I had to confess and reassure her you were being cared for." He looked back at Morgan. "Though I wasn't sure it was true."

"I kept her alive. That's what you asked me to do." Morgan stopped in front of him. "Now, are you going to stand here sniping at me or are you going to help? Something very nasty is in the works."

"So I gathered from Galen. Why the hell do you think I'm here? We have to sort this out, and I couldn't do it long distance." He turned on his heel and headed for the screened front door. "You'll be sorry to know that the interior of this hog pen is worse than the outside. But come inside and we'll talk."

"Betworth?" Logan repeated slowly. "Powers mentioned Betworth?"

Iris Johansen

"You know him?" Alex asked.

"Charles Betworth. Congressman from Texas. He's been in Congress for the last fifteen years."

"Then he's not been very visible," Alex said. "I don't remember ever hearing about him."

"He prefers to work behind the scenes these days. He pushes nice noncontroversial bills on the environment and public health. He was the Democratic Party's great hope about thirteen years ago, but he got caught up in a campaign-finance scandal. It says a lot about his personal charisma that he was able to overcome the stigma and get reelected twice." Logan's lips twisted. "But there's no way the party would ever nominate him for President with that dirty laundry in his background. I'm sure it's a bitter pill for him to swallow."

"Bitter enough for him to engineer the incident at Arapahoe Junction?"

"Not unless it would give him something besides revenge. Betworth is consumed with ambition."

"Not money?"

Logan shook his head. "I think that campaign scandal was more about manipulation and power plays than cash. He comes from oil money. That's how he was able to gloss over the smears at the polls." He paused. "No, it has to be ambition."

"To what aim?"

"I've no idea. But I guess I'd better find out." He stood up. "I'll go to Washington and see what I can dig up. You're right, something nasty is going down." His lips tightened. "And it makes me mad as hell that the threat is coming from our own people. It's not enough we have to worry about the nutcases from outside our borders."

"You believe that Jurgens and some people in the CIA are involved?" Morgan asked. "I thought you'd balk at that. Alex did."

Dead Aim

"I believe anyone involved in a power play on this scale would have wooed law enforcement. I believe that it takes only a few key people to lead a battalion where they want them to go. It's getting the key people and controlling them. I'm very uneasy that Betworth's in the picture."

"You seem to know a lot about him."

"He interested me. I could tell there was a hell of a lot going on beneath that schmooze. I've seen him come into a room at a party and immediately start working at attracting everyone with whom he comes in contact. He almost hypnotizes them. It may be calculated, but it never appears that way. He's bigger than life." He moved toward the door. "But then, so was Stalin." He paused as he opened the door. "I brought a box of groceries and a couple blankets for you. They're over there by the window. Galen said you'd need them here."

"Probably not for long. Powers said Z-2 was already in place. I hope to hell we can find out where it is before—" Morgan shrugged. "We've got to find it. No option."

"I'll call when I find out something," Logan said. "Try to keep from getting killed, Alex. It would upset Sarah."

"God forbid we upset Sarah," Morgan murmured.

Logan nodded. "Exactly."

Alex followed him as he walked around the house to a beige Saturn parked in back.

"Logan."

He paused, looking at her.

"Tell Sarah that I'm well. Tell her everything's going to turn out fine."

"Everything's got to turn out fine. My ass is on the line." He searched her face. "And are you well? Morgan is more of a rough diamond than I bargained for. He's treated you decently?"

She nodded. "But that's a bad analogy. There's nothing rough about him. He's pure Toledo steel." She tried to smile. "But as long as he's in my camp I've no quarrel with that.

And, yes, he's treated me decently." She turned to go back inside. "Give my love to Sarah."

He hesitated before he said, "I had to do it, Alex. And I'm not sorry."

"I didn't think you would be. Just keep Sarah out of this mess."

"It's difficult. The only way I managed to leave her at home this time was because I told her I'd let her talk to you on the phone after security makes sure the line's safe."

"Don't have her phone me. I don't want to take the chance. Sarah mustn't be drawn into my troubles."

"I believe that's what I said. But it didn't do me any good." He smiled. "So I guess we'd better just get this over with in a hurry so Sarah doesn't come barging into the situation." He got into the driver's seat and waved as he drove past her toward the road.

She shivered as she watched his taillights disappear around the curve. Logan was no friend to her, but he'd been a comforting presence nevertheless. He exuded confidence and power, and in his presence for a brief moment she'd felt safe.

"I was hoping you'd go with him."

She turned to see Morgan standing in the doorway. She shook her head. "My place is here."

"The hell it is," he said roughly. "Your place is behind walls, with an army of security to take care of you."

"That's what you were hired to do." She smiled faintly. "Remember?"

"I remember everything." He looked away from her. "Enough to know you were lying through your teeth when you told Logan I'd treated you decently."

"You shouldn't eavesdrop."

"It's one of my minor sins. You're already familiar with the big ones."

"You did treat me decently . . . in perspective. Galen told me once to go over everything that had happened since

Arapahoe and I'd probably find that you weren't as bad as I thought you were."

"Yeah, let's go over it. I drugged you, kidnapped you, drove a stake into your shoulder, and then I fucked you."

Pain rippled through her. "Did you fuck me? That's an ugly word and I don't think it was ugly at all. Do you?"

"Everything I touch seems to turn ugly, except my work. I had no right to—" He saw her expression and took an impulsive step forward before he stopped. "No, it wasn't ugly. It was damn beautiful. You were—" He was silent an instant before smiling mockingly. "You're being a little too generous. I'm waiting for the knockout punch."

"You'll wait a long time. I'm tired of fighting." She shook her head wearily. "I had a long time to think while we were in that van. Too much has happened for me to worry about pride or ego. I think maybe you've got a lot of problems, but I can't take them on right now."

"I never asked you to take them on."

"But I'm not like you. I can't stay at a distance. I have to dive in and start swimming. I . . . liked what we did. You made me feel . . ."

"Cherished?"

"I was afraid to say it." She met his eyes. "And you can mock all you please. But, yes, cherished. And you couldn't have made me feel like that if you hadn't felt something. You're not the man I would have chosen to make me feel that special, but it happened. So I'm having to take a good long look at you."

"I wouldn't look too deep. I show well at long range, but close up I've been known to—"

"Oh, shut up. I'm not even sure you know what kind of man you are."

"I know exactly who and what I am." He smiled. "And it's not a hero. You're not going to find your father in me, Alex."

"God, no. But my father wasn't a hero all the time. He

couldn't keep his marriage together. He was more a kid than a grown-up. He even forgot my high-school graduation and went to a Mets game." She swallowed to ease the tightness of her throat. "But he was sweet and kind and that's all that mattered. I knew when it really counted he'd be there for me." She started past him. "And I'm not sure you're any of those things, but if you're even one of them, watch out. You caught me off guard when you pushed me away. I usually don't discourage easily."

"Alex . . . this isn't—"

"I'm not talking about it any longer. I just had to get it out in the open. I can't live with my whole life in turmoil, and this is the only thing I have any control over." She patted his arm as she passed him. "Don't worry, you're safe for a while. Where's my duffel? I have to set up my computer. I want to print out your last conversation with Powers and study it."

"It's about time you answered, Runne," Betworth said. "Where the hell have you been?"

"I had some things to do. I did what you told me. Powers is dead. I couldn't get Morgan. You'll have to help me find him again."

"Oh, will I?"

"You'll help me. You promised you'd help me."

"But that was before you made a mess of the Powers job."

"I killed him. That's what you wanted."

"I wanted a clean death with no loose ends. But I understand Morgan and Alex Graham were in the house that night. Could Powers have told him anything?"

Shame and guilt rushed over Runne in a hot tide. Betworth mustn't know he'd failed. He was within an inch of discarding him, and Runne couldn't find Morgan without the bastard. "I don't make mistakes. He didn't see him before I got there."

"And Powers was dead before you left."

"He was dead before I left."

"Excellent. Not perfect. But we're able to do damage control."

"Tell me where Morgan went."

"We haven't discovered that as yet. But there's a good chance that he'll be at Z-3. He's been busy putting pieces together. You may be running into him there."

"I want him now."

"But it's no longer about what you want, Runne," he said softly. "I gave you an opportunity to kill Morgan and you screwed up. Now you're working on my schedule."

Rage flowed through him. "I can find him on my own."

"You haven't found him yet. And I can't give you free rein any longer. He's become too dangerous. I'll have to turn Jurgens and his men loose."

"No! He'll get in my way. You promised me Morgan." He drew a deep breath. "Don't send Jurgens after him and I'll wait until after the Z-3 job."

"How patient of you. But you won't have that long to wait."

"How long?"

"Eight days. If all goes well." Betworth added, "But I can't tolerate this lack of communication, Runne. The time's getting too short. If you fail to answer my calls, I'll be forced to reconsider my decision." He hung up.

Bastard. He was robbing Runne of his independence, making him another one of his puppets.

He could stand it. It would only be for another eight days.

One more job and Betworth would give him Morgan.

And then he'd go after Betworth.

But he might not have to rely on Betworth to find Morgan. Betworth had said the woman was still with him, and she had to be easier prey than Morgan.

He pulled out Alex Graham's photo and the dossier Betworth had sent him. She was soft, weak, a bleeding heart who wanted to change the world. He would study her background more carefully and then he might be able to predict what her next moves might be.

Would Morgan step into the trap if Runne captured and tortured the woman? Runne would not make that mistake, but Morgan had grown up in a puny, sickly culture and might not be able to overcome his ingrained weakness.

Runne would have to see. First things first.

Find the woman.

"You look excited."

Alex looked up from the laptop to see Morgan in the doorway. "It's too early to be excited, but I think I may be on the right track."

"Z-2?"

She shook her head. "I have no idea where Z-2 could be." She rubbed the back of her neck. She'd been hunched over this computer for hours and every muscle was complaining. "Vents. I kept thinking of those deep holes in the basement at Fairfax. They have to have some connection with what Powers was muttering. So what kind of vents are there? Mechanical, metal, air-conditioning vents . . ." She looked back at the computer screen. "But there's another kind of vent. A thermal vent."

"What's that?"

"It's a fissure in the earth's crust that allows the heat and steam from the earth's core to surface. You find it most often in the ocean and volcanic regions. In the case of a volcano, it also releases melted rock that vents as lava. The core holds temperatures that near five thousand degrees centigrade."

Morgan gave a low whistle. "Hot stuff."

"Powerful stuff. But we've never been able to tap either the core or the pressure to any great extent. We've used natural geothermal energy in limited situations throughout history. The Romans, Icelanders, some North American tribes used them for baths, heat, or food preparations, but they were exploiting natural geothermal vents. Today we also have some plants that use the energy to generate steam that heats homes and turns turbines. The environmental groups are loving the possibilities of using geothermal power to heat and cool, because it's clean as well as cheap."

"So how does it connect with Arapahoe Junction?"

"I don't know. I'm still searching. Go away and let me work. I think I'm getting there."

"Anything I can do?"

"He kept saying Lontana, didn't he? They lost Lontana and everything went wrong."

Morgan nodded. "And he may have been referring to him as the Brazilian. I've already given the name to Galen to run a check on."

"I'm running my own check. If he was connected to Fairfax and Arapahoe Junction, then he should have something to do with vents. I'll cross-reference and see what I come up with. . . ." She frowned as the results came on the screen. "Nothing. I'll try a new search engine. . . ."

Morgan watched her for a few minutes longer, but he knew she'd forgotten he was in the room. He moved out onto the porch again and sat down, his gaze on the road. It was irritating that his part in this was a passive one. He wanted to do something.

But it would come. He could feel it coming.

And until then he'd watch and wait . . . and protect.

"Logan is in town," Betworth said as he walked with Ben Danley toward the Capitol building. "He's asking questions. Nothing aggressive, Danley. But naturally we have to keep our eye on him. What Logan does on the surface is usually only the tip of the iceberg."

"What kind of questions?"

Iris Johansen

"Don't get nervous. He's asking about the FBI investigation of Alex Graham. It's perfectly logical, since the woman and his wife are such good friends."

"He may know something."

Betworth shook his head. "He may suspect something. No one knows anything. And in seven days it won't matter anyway. So calm down and just go about your job. I only told you because I didn't want you hearing from someone else and panicking."

"I'm not panicking. I'm anxious. You always underestimate me. I'm the one who set up Matanza. I have a right to be anxious."

"Of course you do." Danley's sudden rebellion surprised Betworth. "Anxiety is fine. It keeps the edge. Overconfidence can be fatal. Who's assigned to go down and keep Matanza in line?"

"I thought I'd go myself."

"No, I'll need you at Z-3. Besides, you're too visible. Andreas might miss you and ask questions."

"Then I'll send Al Leary. He's competent, and he worked out the deal between Morales and Matanza at Fairfax."

"Since Morales was taken down, I wouldn't say that would inspire much faith in the group."

"They don't have to have faith. We're giving them what they want and they're giving us what we want. If you don't need me, I'll leave Wednesday for Z-3."

Betworth felt a surge of excitement. It was going to happen. For years he'd worked and planned and now it was almost here. "Go ahead. If there's any emergency, I'll be in touch."

"There had better not be an emergency."

It sounded almost like a threat. Well, he could handle that later. He had plenty of ammunition to keep Danley in line. Right now it was time to use honey. "Everything is going smoothly, thanks to you. It's amazing what one intelligent man can accomplish." He stopped at the Capitol steps. "Now, smile and wave good-bye. A very casual good-bye."

Danley's gaze went to the head of the steps, where Carl Shepard was standing surrounded by congressmen. "What's he doing here?"

"Trying to swing votes for Andreas on the environmental bill. He probably won't succeed. He's no Andreas."

"You can say that again. But I hear he's done well working to improve Homeland Security."

"That's a piece of cake. Security is on everyone's mind these days. Environment is much more difficult. I'm the only one who can swing those votes. But I'll shake Shepard's hand and look properly impressed and flattered at the attention of the honorable Vice President. Then I'll fade into the background with my fellow congressmen."

"Not much chance of that." Danley turned and moved toward the parking lot.

He was right, Betworth thought. His star was ascending, not setting, and there was no way he was going to let it fade away.

11

"I found it." Alex threw the papers down on the table in front of Morgan. "Maybe."

"Well, that's definite." Morgan picked up the sheets. "Lontana?"

"Philip Lontana. A Brazilian oceanographer. Very well respected in the profession. He's done it all—written reports on the deterioration of the barrier reefs, searched for lost cities, drawn charts of unexplored undersea territory. One of his pet projects was the study of oceanic thermal vents."

"And that leads us where?"

"Two years ago he wrote a paper that was published in *Nautilus*. It's a fairly obscure professional journal and that's the reason it took me so long to find it. It dealt with the possibility of tapping deep into the earth's core itself, of creating vents that could be controlled by sonic technology. It would take a complicated mathematical formula each time to make the necessary insertion, but he was sure he was on the right track. He was already working on the device." She shook her head. "He was all excited about the prospect of an unlimited power source that would change the way we live."

"Or the way we die. He didn't think of the possibility of using it as a weapon?"

"He mentioned it but then skimmed right over any disadvantages, stressing an energy source that could save the planet. Let the UN take care of the problems."

"Not the Brazilian government?"

"Evidently he wasn't fond of the Brazilian government. Early in his career he'd located a sunken Spanish galleon and he had to give half his finder's fee to the government. He rambles on quite a bit about salvage rights and the rights of the individual. He sounds like an eccentric."

"Or a nut cake?"

"Maybe a brilliant nut cake. But evidently the scientific community didn't take him seriously. There are several follow-up replies to his report from other oceanographers. They said what he was proposing was impossible, since the earth's core lies nearly six thousand kilometers below the surface."

"Anything else?"

She shook her head. "But if everyone in his little world pooh-poohed his work, isn't it logical he'd try to take it to someone else?"

"Like Betworth, who's known as one of the shining beacons in U.S. environmental issues? So he set Lontana to work in the labs at Fairfax. Evidently with some success."

She frowned. "But Powers said they lost him. Everything went wrong because they lost him."

"Then we've got to find him. If he's still alive." He dialed Galen's number. "I'll see if this new information helps."

"It's all guesswork."

"That fits together." He walked out on the porch as he gave Galen a rundown on the computer info. "Have you found out anything else about him yet?"

"We didn't run across that report in *Nautilus*. We do know he no longer lives in Rio. He works out of Nassau in the

Bahamas. We haven't been able to get in touch with him. I have a man on his way to Nassau now."

"He may not be alive. When Powers said they lost him, he might have meant they had to dispose of him."

"Stop being a pessimist. It doesn't sound like that to me."

"Well, then here's something else you can be optimistic about. I want you to trace Al Leary and see what he's up to."

"Leary . . . Oh, your old CIA contact. What do you want to know?"

"Everything. Including his cell-phone number."

"Why?"

"Powers wasn't as much help as I'd hoped."

"But Leary will talk?"

"Oh, yes. I'm a little irritated with him about setting me up after Fairfax. He'll talk."

"Considering he's fully aware of your capabilities, I'd bet on it. What should I know about him?"

"He's smart, well educated, and gay. He's still in the closet because he thinks it's more politically advantageous for an ambitious man with the CIA."

"Dangerous?"

"Definitely lethal if he's cornered."

"Then we'll leave it to you to corner him." Galen changed the subject. "How did it go with Logan?"

"As well as could be expected. At least he's moving and shaking. Have you heard from him?"

"The first night. He said people weren't talking. It could be because there's so much tension about the embassy attacks, but he said he was running up against a blank wall."

"Shit."

"There's that pessimism again. Logan doesn't like blank walls. He has a habit of blowing holes in them. He said he'd call you if he heard anything. Expect him to call." He paused. "Thermal vents. That could be bad stuff to monkey around with."

"Not half as bad as trying to access core power. Who the hell knows what that would do? All that magma ... How's Elena?"

Galen chuckled. "Melted rock makes you think of Elena?"

"There are some similarities. But I really wanted to know if you'll be available if I need you."

"Maybe. Why don't you come and ask her?"

"I'm serious. I may want to bring Alex to you. She won't go with Logan, but that's because she knows he'd put walls around her."

"I'm not endangering Elena, Morgan."

"Ask her. She knows what it's like to be on the run."

He was silent. "Alex would come?"

"Maybe not right away. But there's going to come a time that I'm more danger to her than Jurgens or Betworth. She can't stay with me."

"I'll ask her. I don't promise anything." He hung up.

No promises, but Galen would do it. Elena was another matter. She was tough, protective of Galen, and she hated Morgan's guts. He would have to wait and see.

"Lontana's home base is Nassau," he told Alex when he came back into the house. "Galen's sent a man down to locate him."

"That's good." She looked back at the computer. "I wonder if I should access another site and see if—"

"No." His tone was firm. "You've done enough. Why don't you rest?"

"I'm too wired."

"Then I may as well take advantage of you." He went to the corner and got her duffel bag. "If I set up your developing equipment, will you develop that picture you took of the man running from Powers's place?"

"But you already think you know who it is, don't you?"

"I want to be sure. Will you do it?"

She nodded. "Set it up."

"I don't know if you can tell who he is." Alex wiped her hands on her towel. "There's blood all over his face."

Morgan gazed down at the picture. "I know who he is." Her eyes narrowed on his face. "Runne."

He nodded. "But you're right. No one else could tell who he was. And you may need to know." He got his sketch pad and his pencil moved quickly over the paper. "This is Runne."

She looked down at the sketch of a handsome young man with intense dark eyes, sensitive lips, and an expression so tormented it almost jumped from the page. "You did this sketch incredibly fast."

"I could do it in my sleep. I'm used to drawing him. You might say he's been my favorite subject for a long time." He smiled. "Except for you."

"His eyes are slanted just a little. Is he Asian?"

"Half Korean. Half American."

"He . . . looks tortured."

"He is." He took the sketch back. "This isn't correct now. It looks as if he's been wounded in the cheek and lips. He'll probably have to have stitches." He altered the sketch to reflect the wound. "That's as close as I can come. If you see anyone who looks like this, run like hell."

"Is that what you're doing?"

He nodded.

"Because you're afraid?"

"Yes."

She studied his face. "I don't believe you."

"He's been hunting me for a long time. Why else would I be hiding from him?"

"You tell me." She smiled crookedly. "But you won't tell me, will you? That would mean you'd have to lessen the distance." She turned and went to the camp stove across the room. "I'm going to make myself some instant coffee. Do you want some?"

"I guess."

His gaze followed her as she moved around the kitchen. A few minutes passed before he said abruptly, "He's only twenty-two years old."

"I hear rattlesnakes have their venom from birth." She handed him the cup. "I saw what he did to Powers's wife. I can't believe you're feeling pity for him."

"I don't. I suppose it's empathy. I look at him and see myself. I know what he's going to do next, because it's what I'd do." He gazed unseeingly at the cup in his hand. "His name is Runne Shin. He's the bastard son of an American prostitute and Ki Ho Shin, a North Korean general."

She froze. "The North Korean general you were sent to kill."

"The general I did kill." He lifted the cup to his lips. "I had no problem with taking on the job. Shin was as anti-American as they come. Not only was he involved in several human-rights abuses, but he was the guiding hand behind a terrorist training camp near Pyongyang. Runne attended the camp from the time he was fourteen until he was almost nineteen. Before that he lived in Tokyo with his mother. She wasn't permitted to resume her profession, since she was the mother of Shin's son, but she didn't have much to do with him. Evidently Shin kept her docile and cooperative with drugs until she overdosed when Runne was fifteen. His father's visits were the highlights of Runne's life, and when he decided to take Runne back to North Korea for training he was more than eager to go." He smiled sardonically. "He became a star pupil, and a star pupil had to be used. When he was nineteen, his father thought he should go back to Tokyo to the American university there and soak up a little red, white, and blue ambience before they shipped him out to the States. He'd absorbed too much propaganda and political zeal in the camp and would stick out like a sore thumb."

"Political zeal. Terrorism?"

"Oh, yes. He'd developed into a great killing machine. He was excellent with explosives and magnificent with a rifle. He'd successfully taken down four targets by the time he was sixteen. But he preferred knife work for close quarters."

"How did you learn all this about him?"

"I couldn't get to his father. He was too well protected. So I had to find a way under his guard. I went to Tokyo to the university where Runne was studying and enrolled in the same art course he was taking."

"Art?"

He shrugged. "He had a passion for it. His father had one of the finest art collections in the East, and I suppose he wanted to imitate his father in all things. The kid was a lousy painter, but he thought he was wonderful. And that's what I told him. It's amazing how quickly a bond can form when it's based on ego."

"And he was impressed by your work too."

"I didn't say it was all his ego." He shrugged. "He was young and eager and he reminded me of myself when I first went into the service. Hell, I . . . liked him."

"But you used him."

He nodded. "I found out that Runne was going back to North Korea to visit his father. They were going hunting and Runne was very excited. His father sometimes arranged very special hunts at his place in the country."

"Special?"

"Political prisoners. No one important. No one who would be missed."

Alex felt sick. "Charming."

"I found out exactly where and when they'd meet. I was there before them and I took my shot. I never saw Runne again."

"My God."

"It was my job." His voice was harsh. "I had to find a way to get to the target."

"But you didn't kill Runne."

"He wasn't my job."

Alex shook her head. "I don't think that's the reason."

"You believe I felt guilty about betraying Runne?"

"Maybe on some level. What do you think?"

"I think it was much more selfish. Like I said, I saw myself in him. If I'd taken him out it would have seemed like suicide."

"You're nothing like him."

"How do you know? You say I won't let you near."

"I'm getting there. It's just tough going. Is Runne the man you said loved to kill?"

"Yes. I went hunting with him a couple times, but not for his preferred prey."

She sipped her coffee. "And how did Runne find out it was you who killed his father?"

"My guess is that Betworth had the CIA pick him up and tell him after I slipped out of the trap they were setting. Al Leary probably brought him here, furnished him with papers and a mission. He'd be the perfect tool. He had all the skills and a hatred and obsessive desire to kill the target."

"And now Betworth has him working for him."

"But Runne doesn't like to be under anyone's thumb. He's an arrogant bastard." He smiled. "He almost caught me a couple times. But I've developed an instinct where he's concerned. I can *feel* him."

She shivered. "That's not something to bank on."

"Sometimes it's the only thing to bank on." He tapped the sketch. "Remember him. He won't stop. He won't hesitate. He won't let anything stand in his way."

"Like you?"

"Like me," he said quietly. "Now you're getting the picture."

"Well, you're not. I don't know what twisted bond holds you two together, but I don't think it's anything you've told me. Maybe on some subliminal level you want to save the son of a bitch."

"I'm no missionary, Alex."

"And you're not Runne. You're not the kid you were when you joined the service to see the world. You're not the man who shot Ki Ho Shin. You've changed, evolved."

He smiled mockingly. "You seem damn sure."

"I'm sure." She walked to him and put her head on his chest. She whispered, "I have to be."

He went still. "Don't do this to me."

She rubbed against him. "You started it. Live every minute. . . ."

"I've changed my mind."

"Too late."

His hands closed on her shoulders. "Listen to me. I'm not up to this."

"I'm trying to remedy that."

"Dammit, Alex, I want you safe." His voice was harsh. "I'm not safe. I've never been safe. Not for myself, not for anyone."

"Everyone makes their own safety." She kissed his chin. "Screw safety. All I want from you is a little companionship and a damn good lay. I'll take care of the rest."

"That isn't all you want from me. You want something I'll never be. You want a hero. That's who you've been searching for since your father died. That's why I keep trying to— Oh, hell." His arms closed around her. "It's a mistake. I'll hurt you."

She drew his head down. "Not if you stay alive . . ."

"Why?" Morgan stared into the darkness. "It's a big mistake, Alex."

"You didn't think so when you first convinced me that going to bed with you was the most sensible thing I could do."

"For God's sake, I'm a guy. You shouldn't have listened to me."

Dead Aim

"I would have missed a heck of a lot of fun." She rubbed her cheek in the hollow of his shoulder. "And I wouldn't have listened to you if I hadn't been almost there anyway."

"It's not permanent. This is just—"

"Wonderful. And stop giving me warnings. I'll settle for temporary for the time being." She raised herself on one elbow to look down at him. "Hey, we're terrific together. Why don't you relax and enjoy?"

"Because you're not—you'll get hurt. I've taken care of you and seen how vulnerable you can be. I can't stand it if—"

"You're getting boring." She moved on top of him. "And I'm getting tired of being aggressive. It's not my nature."

For a moment he continued to frown up at her, and then a slow smile touched his lips. "The hell it's not." He rolled her over. "Boring? What a challenge. I'll show you boring. . . ."

Galen called the next morning. "Lontana is in the middle of the Atlantic Ocean somewhere."

"Dead?"

"No, on his big-ass schooner, *Last Home*. My guy, Coleman, says he came straight down to Nassau from Fairfax a few months ago and weighed anchor the same day. He was in a hell of a hurry and no one's seen him since."

"No radio?"

"Yes, but he's not using it. I'd say he's on the run. You can't blame him for taking off for the high seas."

"What about crew?"

"Usually has three men, but there's no word on them either. They've been with him for years, and it's not likely they'd rat on him."

"Doesn't he have any friends or associates? Isn't anyone talking?"

"We're not the first who have been down there beating the bushes trying to find him. But I guarantee we're the least abusive. A couple of Lontana's friends got roughed up, and they're not trusting anyone." He paused. "But Coleman has one lead. Lontana has a foster child, a daughter, Melis Nemid. They usually work together, but Coleman heard she'd returned to their island in the Lesser Antilles."

"Then Lontana might be with her?"

"Possible. Or she might know something."

"If she did, then Betworth would have killed her. Whatever Coleman found out, Betworth's men would have found out."

"It may not have been so easy. They live on a private island Lontana purchased with his prize money from salvaging that Spanish galleon. There are difficulties reaching there. It's surrounded by rocks except for one inlet, and that's barricaded by nets."

"What?"

"His daughter studies and trains dolphins. She needs the nets to keep predators out of the waters."

"Human as well as our fishy friends. Lontana shouldn't have gotten mixed up in dirty tricks if he didn't want to deal with predators." Morgan paused. "Does she have a telephone?"

"Yes, a satellite phone, but you'll get her voice mail."

"Give me the number." He jotted the number down on a pad. "I'll call and see if I can leave a message that will get her to call me back."

"Good luck. In the meantime, I'll tell Coleman to keep on it."

"Get who to call you back?" Alex asked as Morgan hung up.

"Lontana's foster daughter, Melis Nemid. She's on some island in the Antilles studying dolphins."

"And her father may be with her?"

He shrugged. "Who knows? If she saw him before he took off on his ship when he came back from Fairfax, he may be with her. Or she might know something we need to know."

"Let me call her."

"Why?"

"I'm less intimidating."

He smiled. "Only to people who don't know you."

"Let me try."

"Shucks, and I thought I was going to get something to do around here." He handed her the phone and the telephone number. "Be my guest. Galen said you're going to get her voice mail. What are you going to say?"

"The truth. What happened at Arapahoe Junction. What we're afraid is going to happen next. What else can I say? If she cares, she'll call back. If she doesn't, there isn't much we can do."

"Except storm the island and kidnap her dolphins."

"You seem to thrive on kidnapping." She dialed the number. "I think we'll skip that option."

Alex received a call back from Melis Nemid four hours later.

Morgan handed her the phone. "It seems she cares—I hope."

"Alex Graham," she said into the phone.

"Phil isn't to blame," Melis Nemid said. "He didn't know what they were going to do. He didn't know anything about it."

"Phil?"

"Philip Lontana. He didn't know. No one can blame him for— Of course they can blame him. No one is going to believe him. They're going to try to crucify him."

"Is he there with you?"

"Do you think I'd tell you if he was? How do I know you're not some con artist that Betworth hired?"

"If you've watched the news, then you must know that I'm on the run."

"I don't watch the news. And you could have made a deal."

"That's true. But I didn't, and if you don't help, then you'll be responsible for anything else that happens."

"Don't try to give me a guilt trip. All I want is to be left alone."

"So did all those people at Arapahoe Junction."

"It wasn't his fault."

Alex wasn't getting anywhere. Try to find a hole in the armor. "I can understand how you'd want to be left alone. You're a scientist, aren't you? You study dolphins?"

"Yes."

"I have a friend, Sarah, who has a search-and-rescue dog. Monty's wonderful. Sometimes I think I like him better than I do most people. Maybe you feel like that too."

"Is that supposed to soften me up?" She was silent a moment. "If you want to talk to me any more, it won't be on the telephone. Come to the island."

"It's difficult for us to travel, as you can imagine. It may be impossible."

"Then forget it. It's difficult for me too. I don't care about your problems. I care about Phil. And I need to see your face."

"How the heck do you expect us to get there? We can't move about freely."

"Come to the island." She hung up.

"She wants us to come to her," Alex told Morgan. "And I think it might be worth the trip. She wouldn't say whether Lontana was there, but she was very defensive. Can we manage to get to her without getting caught?"

"It's risky."

"I know it's risky. Do you think I'm an idiot? Can we do it?"

He thought about it. "With Galen and Logan pulling out all the stops, we have a good chance they can smuggle us down there. But we'd still be a hell of a lot safer right here."

"And we'll be safe right up to the time when they blow up another dam and kill more people. Get us there. If she knows anything at all that can help, then it's worth going." She moistened her lips. "Do you remember what you told me about having a feeling when Runne was near? Well, that's the way I feel about Z-2 or Z-3 or whatever: It's going to happen. And it's going to happen soon."

"You're preaching to the converted. I was just giving you the possible consequences." He added, "And wondering if maybe I shouldn't go down there alone. You could go to Galen and Elena and—"

"No."

He sighed. "That's what I thought. I'll call Galen."

The White House

"You're not eating." Andreas smiled at Chelsea across the candlelit table. "Fred's going to be upset and blame me. He always thinks it's my fault if you don't have an appetite."

"That doesn't surprise me. Why shouldn't that be your fault too?"

He slowly put down his fork and leaned back in the chair. "Would you like to explain that remark?"

"Not particularly." She took a sip of her wine. "I have to have my own secrets. Why should we share confidences? After all, we've only been married a decade or so."

She was glittering, barbed, and he'd better be very careful. "Would you like me to tell you exactly how long we've been married? I know it down to the minute." He stared her directly in the eye. "Because every minute has been a treasure."

She finally tore her gaze away. "Damn you. Why do you have to be so goddamn sincere? It's not fair."

"You're angry with me. May I ask why?"

"I didn't think it would be like this when you ran for the presidency. I knew it would be tough and I was willing to go for the long haul. But I didn't know everyone in the country would believe you were some kind of god." She waved a hand. "Andreas points his finger and lightning flashes. He touches a child and hunger vanishes."

"What are you saying?"

"What do you think?" Her eyes shone with unshed tears. "I'm scared to death. Since September eleventh you mean too much to too many people. That's why Matanza is so determined to kill you. They can strike a blow at the entire country by murdering you."

"Cordoba's only threatened, Chelsea. I've been threatened before."

"But he's getting closer. If he wasn't getting closer, then you wouldn't have sicced Nancy Shepard on me."

"I beg your pardon?"

"Don't you dare be evasive. You know very well that you told her to ask me to kick off the National Foundation for Abused Children's fund-raiser in Pittsburgh. Did you think I wouldn't guess?"

"No, but I hoped you'd pretend you didn't."

"Why?"

"Because it would have made it easier for both of us."

"I'm not going anywhere. I told her to get someone else."

He shook his head. "You're going to Pittsburgh."

"I'm not leaving you."

"You'll go." He smiled. "Because if you don't, I'll tell Nancy Shepard that I'll kick off the drive. I'll travel to every large city in the Northeast. I'll speak at convention centers and whistle stops. I'll shake hands and go to—"

"No!"

"Make your choice. You or me."

"You're safe here."

"Nowhere is perfectly safe, Chelsea."

"Okay, I know that. Why do you think I didn't argue when you sent the children away? But you're much safer here.

Dead Aim

Keller can control the security as long as you don't leave your ordinary stamping grounds."

"You or me."

"Damn you." She drew a long shaky breath. "Me."

"You'll do a wonderful job, my love."

"Yes, I will." Her voice was uneven. "And don't you dare let them kill you and make you a martyr while I'm gone. You know I look ghastly in black."

12

The huge net was stretched from shore to shore across the entire opening of the inlet and four feet above the surface of the water.

"So what do we do now?" Alex murmured. "Cut the net?"

Morgan shook his head. "We wait." He cut the motor of the speedboat. "You called and left a message we were coming. It's her move."

"We may be out here awhile." Her gaze fastened on the small stone-and-wood house hugging the shore. Christ, this was a beautiful place. Jewel-blue water, green mountains, and tropical breezes swaying the trees. It was like something from a travel brochure. "I don't see any sign of stirring. Maybe we should try shouting or making— There's someone."

A woman had appeared from around the back of the house and was heading for the pier. Or Alex guessed she was a woman. She wore khaki shorts and a T-shirt, and her feet were bare. She was small and delicately built, with the shining fair hair usually seen in small children. But there was nothing fragile or childlike about the way she jumped into the motorboat at the pier and took off. She breathed competence, forcefulness, and vitality as she gunned the boat toward them.

She stopped fifteen yards on the other side of the net and studied them.

She was stunning, Alex realized, and no child. She was probably in her mid-twenties. Huge dark eyes and features that combined delicacy and boldness to form an extraordinary face. The boldness was definitely on the ascent in the cool glance she was giving Alex. "Alex Graham?"

Alex nodded.

"You don't look like the picture they have of you on CNN."

"God, I hope not. You're Melis Nemid?"

The woman nodded.

"Then how do you know what I look like on CNN? I thought you told me you never watched the news."

"I don't. But I had to make sure you were who you said you were."

"Are you satisfied?"

"That you're Alex Graham and that you're up to your ass in trouble? Yes." Her gaze narrowed on Morgan. "But you may be in bad company."

Alex shook her head. "I'd be in a hell of a lot more trouble if he hadn't been around. You can trust him."

"Ah, trust at last," Morgan murmured.

"I don't trust either of you." Melis Nemid was silent a moment and then shrugged. "But I don't have much choice." She started the boat and came slowly toward the net, skimming beside it until she reached a spot a few yards from where Alex and Morgan waited. She bent over the side of the boat, and a moment later a ten-foot-wide section of wire net fell to the surface. "Start your motor and then cut it when you reach the net and coast over," she called.

Morgan obeyed, and the moment they were on the other side of the net Melis Nemid rehooked it and drew the rope that lifted it to its former height. Then she was turning the boat and speeding back toward the shore.

"I guess that means we follow?" Morgan started the motor. "Must be. What a warm welcome. You'd think we'd come without an invitation."

Melis Nemid had already tied up her boat and was striding toward the house when Alex and Morgan reached the pier. She glanced over her shoulder. "Come on. I can't be all day. I have things to do."

"Sorry." Morgan helped Alex out of the boat. "We won't be hurt if you start without us."

She stared coldly at them. "This isn't funny. None of it."

"We know that better than you." Alex stared her in the eye. "And we're not going to be put off or intimidated by rudeness or bad temper. We came for a reason, and you want to supply us with that information or you wouldn't have let us come. Now, can we get on with it, Ms. Nemid?"

She blinked, and then a slight smile touched her lips. "Maybe I do trust you . . . a little. At least you don't bullshit. Call me Melis." She turned and threw open the front door. "Come in and have an iced tea."

"We'd rather have conversation," Morgan said as they followed her into the house. "And Philip Lontana."

"Then you'll be disappointed. I never told you he was here." She went toward the kitchen and opened the refrigerator. "So take the iced tea. It's a long, hot trip back to Tobago."

"Thank you," Alex said. She wasn't about to turn down any peace offering, no matter how small. "If he's not here, where is he?"

"Somewhere in the Azores, I think." She poured the tea and set the glasses down on the bar in front of Morgan and Alex. "Or maybe the Canary Islands. At any rate, you can't get in touch with him. Forget it."

"We can't forget it," Morgan said. "He may know something we need to know."

Dead Aim

"You can't see him," she repeated. "You talk to me. I told him to get lost and stay lost. Phil doesn't usually pay a lot of attention to me, but he will this time. He got scared at Fairfax."

"Why?"

"Why do you think? He was in over his head. He thought he was going to save the world, and he found out that he'd been lied to. It's a wonder he got out alive. Phil's always been transparent as glass."

"He found out about Arapahoe Junction?"

"No." Her tone was sharp. "Neither of us knew that the thermal-sonic apparatus had even been used there. Not until you left the message on the phone. Phil only came to suspect his device might be developed for weaponry instead of geothermal energy."

"The scientists said there were seismograph readings that indicated an earthquake at Arapahoe Dam. Could those have been caused by Lontana's apparatus?"

She nodded. "Theoretically." She shook her head. "No, that's a word Phil uses when he doesn't want to face the truth. Hell, yes, it could have caused an earthquake. One that would be severe enough to impact the dam. I can't tell you how many times Phil told me how careful he had to be about developing probe techniques that would strike a balance."

"Evidently he wasn't that careful at Fairfax."

"For a long time he was so absorbed in the research that he didn't pay much attention to what was going on around him. After working there for a while, he gradually began to distrust Betworth and Powers and the other people who were in and out of the facility. So one night about three months ago he took his notes, destroyed the prototypes he'd developed at Fairfax, and took off."

"I'm surprised they let him."

"He was smarter than they thought. Phil's a little eccentric, and that fools a lot of people. They considered him the typical absentminded professor. Brilliant, but no common sense. In a way they were right. Phil's always lost in his own world."

"But I'd bet you aren't. Why didn't you stop him from going to Betworth?"

"It's his life. I don't interfere with—" She shrugged. "He didn't tell me. He knew I wouldn't approve, so he took off without saying anything. It wasn't that unusual. Phil was always going off on exploration trips without me. Then he'd show up excited or depressed and stay with me until the next time, the next adventure. I didn't even know where he was until he called me and told me he'd meet me in Nassau and to ready the *Last Home*."

"Then why are you here?"

"I didn't leave him in the lurch," she said defensively. "I'd never do that to Phil. I got him on the ship and out of port, but I had sickness here. I had to come home."

"We need to see him."

"No, he's out of it. I told him to stay away until I let him know it was safe. He can remain out to sea for years if he has to." Her lips tightened. "And he may have to do that. Thanks to those bastards. If they don't kill him, they'll frame him, won't they?"

"Probably," Morgan said. "But I'd bet on the former."

She shook her head. "I won't let that happen. Why do you think you're here? I can't trust the government. Betworth has too much influence. I can't really trust you either, but you're in hot water and you're going to be moving fast and trying your best to take Betworth down. Right?"

"Yes."

"I won't let you near Phil, but you can have me. I had Phil tell me everything that happened at Fairfax in case something happened to him. What do you need to know?"

"What are Z-2 and Z-3?"

She stared at him blankly.

Dead Aim

"Okay, let's try another tack. While the experiments were going on, did they concentrate on any particular vent areas?"

"The Rocky Mountains. The coal-mining country in West Virginia. The offshore hydro vents near Baltimore."

"Offshore?"

She nodded. "Those really interested Phil. He's always more intrigued by anything underwater."

"The Rocky Mountains," Alex repeated. "Arapahoe Junction . . ."

"He didn't know that," Melis said quickly. "I tell you, it was just scientific experimentation as far as he was concerned. He wouldn't hurt—"

"Okay. Okay." Morgan held up his hand to stop her. "Where are these coal mines in West Virginia?"

"He didn't know. Somewhere south, he thought. They were having him work very hard on the mathematical equations for that area." Her lips twisted. "Phil thought it was wonderful that they'd concentrated on such a poor region for geothermal benefits."

"Yeah, Betworth is all heart. What about the Baltimore hydro vents?"

Melis shook her head. "They abandoned them halfway through the initial survey."

"Why? Not practical?"

"Phil thought it the most promising of the three. But Betworth said that it wouldn't work. That it wouldn't bring the effect he wanted. He told Powers that they'd have to contact a man named Morales. They needed more bang for the buck."

"And that meant?"

"Phil had no idea. But by that time he was getting pretty pissed off at the entire operation. Not enough to abandon his work, but he just gave up arguing and concentrated on West Virginia."

"And they called in Morales?"

She nodded. "Phil saw him a couple times at the plant before he was introduced to him. He said he didn't look or talk much like a scientist, but it wasn't his business. He didn't have to work with him. Morales was glued to Powers and Betworth most of the time."

"Morales was there often?"

"Yes, but he came and went. He must have been sort of a visiting consultant."

"You might call him that," Morgan murmured.

"Anyway, he was evidently put in charge of the Baltimore operation. Phil didn't like it. It didn't make any sense to him. He didn't want anyone else to handle his apparatus, and Betworth seemed to be handing his pet project over to Morales."

"So he cut out?"

"Not then. He was still too intrigued, and evidently Betworth lost faith in Morales, because a few months later he stopped coming around the plant."

"And that made Lontana number one again."

"You've got to understand. It wasn't just professional jealousy. He was getting uneasy. There was more talk about volcano and earthquake effects than tapping reserves for thermal power. Phil has a big ego, but he felt deeply about this project. He didn't want it compromised." She looked down into her glass. "But it was compromised. Jesus, was it compromised."

"How did they manage to sabotage Arapahoe Junction without him?"

"I don't know. He said he took all but one prototype with him, and that one was in Washington with Betworth. But he didn't think it would be of any use without the mathematical calculations that he'd refused to turn over to the team."

"They evidently tried it on Arapahoe anyway," Morgan said. "Powers said it went wrong. That they'd lost Lontana and it had gone wrong."

"What went wrong?" Alex asked. "They destroyed the dam and Arapahoe Junction."

Melis shook her head. "How could you expect Phil to know that? He didn't have any knowledge of how those bastards were going to use the sonic apparatus."

"And he never heard of Z-2 or Z-3?"

"No."

"No references to places or dates?"

Melis frowned. "No places other than what I've already told you. But Phil said they kept pushing him to move faster. Betworth had a target date by which they had to have a successful launch to present to Congress."

"What date?"

"November twelfth."

And it was November 8 today, Alex realized. The knowledge sent a ripple of tension through her.

"D-Day?" Morgan asked speculatively.

"But they lost Lontana," Alex said. "That might have changed everything."

"Or it might not." He turned back to Melis. "I need to know more about why Morales was at Fairfax. Did Lontana say anything more about him?"

"Just that he didn't like him. But then, Phil's very competitive. He wouldn't have liked anyone who took over one of his projects." Her forehead creased in thought. "He said he overheard a lot of talk about a suitcase."

"Could it have been a briefcase?" Alex asked. "Morgan said Morales was carrying a briefcase the night he saw him."

Melis glanced at Morgan. "You saw Morales? You met him?"

"No, it was a very short encounter. But Alex is right, he was carrying a briefcase, not a suitcase."

"It could have been a briefcase, I suppose. Phil's not always precise, except in his work." Melis shrugged. "I'll ask him next time I talk to him." She checked her watch. "Is that all? It's time I gave Susie her medicine."

"Unless you can think of anything else."

She shook her head.

"Or will let us talk to Lontana."

"I told you, no one talks to Phil."

Alex smiled. "You're being very protective."

"Someone has to take care of him. He's a good man. It's not his fault he wants to believe everyone is as good as he is."

"That sounds familiar," Morgan said. "I believe I know someone else who's similarly inclined."

Melis looked at Alex. "You? Then I feel sorry for you. You get hurt a lot less if you don't let yourself trust people."

"I'm sure you don't suffer from that affliction to any great degree," Morgan said. "May we leave now? I watched you, and I think I can lower the net."

"If you don't hook it in the correct order, you'll get a hell of an electric shock. I'll come with you and let you out." She opened the refrigerator and took out a wrapped parcel. "As soon as I tend to Susie." She crossed the room, opened the sliding glass doors, and went out onto the lanai. "Five minutes."

"I believe we'll tag along," Morgan said. "Not that we don't trust you. I just believe your philosophy is absolutely sound."

"Come along. I don't care." She moved across the lanai and around the corner.

They followed, to find her sitting on the edge of the lanai, which was built out over the sea. Her bare feet were hanging in the water and she was unwrapping the parcel she'd taken out of the refrigerator. "Be quiet. She's not usually skittish, but she's been ill." She raised her voice. "Susie."

Nothing.

"Susie. Stop being a baby. It's wrapped in fish."

A high-pitched squeak and a gray head suddenly emerged five feet from where Melis sat.

"Not you, Pete. You chowhound. Go get Susie."

"Galen mentioned that you work with dolphins," Alex said.

"I don't work, I slave," Melis said. "And the ungrateful creatures won't even come when I call them. Susie!"

Two white snouts appeared not two feet from where she was sitting. "It's about time." She took one of the pieces of fish and threw it to the smaller dolphin. The mammal caught it and gulped it down. "That's a good girl." She tossed the other piece to the other dolphin. "Thanks, Pete."

The two dolphins swam closer, rubbing affectionately against her bare legs in the water, softly squeaking.

She stroked the female's head. "I love you too," she whispered. "But you've got to take the medicine, baby. No more hiding, okay?"

The dolphin squeaked, nodding, and then disappeared beneath the water.

Melis sighed. "Yeah, sure. Keep an eye on her, Pete."

The other dolphin glided away after the female.

Melis stared after them, her expression soft, almost radiant. Her demeanor was completely different from the guarded, tough exterior she'd shown Alex and Morgan.

"What's wrong with Susie?" Alex asked.

"A digestive-tract parasite. Nothing that can't be fixed." Melis stood up. "If I can get her to take her medicine. She doesn't like the taste. I've disguised it half a dozen ways, but half the time she won't come when I call her."

"Then what do you do?"

"Get on my scuba gear and go after her." She moved past them into the house. "As soon as I contact Phil, I'll call you and let you know if there's anything else he remembers." She glanced back over her shoulder and said fiercely, "I helped you. Now you go work your buns off and make sure he's safe."

"If you'd been concerned only for Lontana, you'd never have called me back," Alex said. "I believe you realize there are a few other people concerned in this. It's a big world, Melis."

"Not my world." She jumped into her motorboat. "My world is here." She started the engine. "I'll go ahead and lower the net."

"Are you totally alone on the island?" Morgan asked. "It's risky. I'm surprised Betworth hasn't sent someone here."

"He did. Two boatloads of assholes. I electrified the fence."

"Electrified?"

"I told you Phil was brilliant. The net gives off only a small charge to discourage sharks or other predators. But I can rev it up." She grinned. "I told them Phil wasn't here and they still tried to cut the nets and come and see for themselves. After a couple of them were literally blown out of the water, they decided I was telling the truth. For a few weeks I saw someone far out to sea keeping watch on the place with binoculars, but no one lately."

"They could come back."

"Let them. As you've noticed, this island is pretty inaccessible."

"By sea."

"The island is so lush with trees and vegetation that you can't even get a helicopter down. Besides, I'd know they were coming and I have weapons. I'd be ready for them." She peeled out over the water, toward the nets.

Alex glanced back at Melis as she skimmed toward her house on the island. Twilight burnished the waves and bathed the woman and her light-colored boat in a golden haze. "Beautiful . . ."

"Yes, she is."

"No, I mean . . . Of course she's beautiful. But the island and the sea and those dolphins. I wonder what it must be like to live on an island and be able to close everyone out as she does."

"She wasn't able to close us out. She had to let us in. She had to get medicine for her dolphin, so she had to use outside help for that."

"Because she chose to do it."

"But if Betworth's guys hadn't been told that Lontana shipped out in the *Last Home,* she'd probably have had a much more determined crew to deal with. In that case, the choice wouldn't have been hers either. The island concept is nice, but it seldom works. Civilization always interferes, emotion interferes."

"I'd like to try it sometime."

He shook his head. "You couldn't stand it. You're too involved with life. Give it a month and you'd be risking your neck on the Gaza Strip or digging through some ruin with Sarah Logan and her dog."

"But you could. You could stand on the outside and watch the world go by."

"Sure I could." He glanced at her and his lips tightened. "We're different, Alex. That's what I've been telling you."

She quickly looked back at the island to mask the pain that went through her. "It must be a really strange relationship between Melis and Lontana. She seems more the protective parent than he does. He evidently leaves her out here in the middle of nowhere for months on end."

"I wouldn't worry about her. She's definitely no victim."

"I didn't say I was worried. I just don't like the idea of anyone being that isolated." She grimaced. "We didn't find out much, did we? Except about the coal mine. How many coal mines are there in West Virginia?"

"I don't know, but we'd better find out soon," he said grimly.

She felt the same sense of urgency. They seemed to be taking only the tiniest steps forward, and again she had the panicky feeling that time was running out. "It's like trying to work a picture puzzle with half the pieces missing."

"But we're gradually finding those pieces. We know Betworth originally hired Lontana because they thought they had a foolproof way of accomplishing their ends without being found out. But evidently there was some reason why they thought the sonic apparatus wouldn't give them the effect they wanted on the last project in Baltimore. So they brought in Morales to handle it and evidently also to give them backup plans in case Lontana's technology didn't work."

"And after they got what they needed, they called you to get rid of him so he couldn't talk," Alex said. "And when Lontana took off for the high seas and ruined their nice little scenario, they had to backtrack and rely on Morales's original plans."

"See, we're making progress."

"Yeah, some progress. We don't know why, when, or where. As a journalist I was taught those questions were the essentials for any story."

"Well, we know who. Betworth. The rest will fall into place."

She hoped it would fall into place in time. "Do you think Lontana is as innocent as she claimed?"

"Maybe. He bailed out before Arapahoe. Did he suspect? It's possible. But Betworth evidently didn't think he'd picked up enough information to be dangerous or he'd never have gotten out of Fairfax alive." He frowned. "What I'm wondering about is Morales's involvement in this Baltimore project. It's logical that it would be Z-3. But the diagram in Morales's briefcase looked more like a skyscraper than anything to do with a seaport. And Morales dealt in drugs and arms. Betworth wouldn't have trusted him to have anything to do with this thermal-sonic apparatus. He had to have some other job to do in Baltimore."

"What?"

He shook his head. "I don't know and he can't tell us. But

maybe someone else can. Most arms dealers don't work alone. The transactions are too involved and complicated. They have partners or at least contacts."

"Did Morales?"

"I didn't do an in-depth investigation of him before the hit. It was going to be a simple job. No problems." He reached for his phone. "I told Galen to run a check on him, but it's time to let him know we might need something in a hurry." When Galen picked up, Morgan went through everything they'd learned from Melis Nemid. "Finding that coal mine should take top priority. But I don't like that info on Morales. I didn't realize he was that much involved in the project. It could be those diagrams are just the tip of the iceberg."

"Then I'll see if I can find the rest of the berg." Galen paused. "We have your transport set out of Tobago, but you don't have to come back here. You could stay out of the country. It would be safer. Or you could leave Alex down there."

"No way. Alex and I have just been discussing islands and the fact that Alex couldn't live on one and certainly couldn't be one. So I guess I'll go along for the ride." He hung up and said to Alex, "Though he's right, it would be safer to stay down here in paradise. And much pleasanter than that shack in West Virginia."

"That wouldn't take much."

"But the answer's no?"

She looked back at the island, which was almost out of sight in the distance. She was so tired of fighting, and it would be heaven to find a place like that to rest and heal. The idea was beautiful and tempting . . . and completely out of the question. "The answer's no."

Galen called Morgan back when they were driving down a dirt road to a private airport on the island of Tobago. "I've found Al Leary."

"Where is he?"

"Guatemala City."

"What?"

"He left Washington two days ago and we followed him to Guatemala City. Actually, he's in a small town south of the city. He's staying at the Rio Hotel, a Matanza hangout. One of Juan Cordoba's whores lives there, and he uses her place for his more sensitive meetings."

Morgan could feel Alex's gaze on him and carefully kept his face expressionless. "You're sure?"

"No doubt about it. And I don't think Leary's down there trying to catch the bad guys. If he were, he'd be dead by now. It looks dirty to me. You're going after him?"

"Yes."

"You need transport?"

"Of course."

"You don't want to talk right now, do you?" Galen said. "Call me back as soon as you can. I'll have Marco Salazar pick you up at the airport in Guatemala City. He'll try to help you, but it's really going to be your show. Matanza practically owns the town." He paused. "And Leary's being pretty brassy. He wasn't as hard to find as he should have been. Be careful."

"You know it." He hung up.

"What's happened?" Alex asked.

"Logan is still in Washington, but hasn't found out anything. No other news." He put his phone away. "There's the airport. I hope this wind dies down. That prop plane doesn't look like it could stand much buffeting around."

Don Garver, the same pilot who'd flown them from Miami, gave them a sunny smile as he threw open the door for them to board. "Have a good trip? This one may not be so hot. It's going to be a little rough today."

Dead Aim

"Should we be flying?" Alex asked.

"Sure. I wouldn't risk that pretty neck." He went back to the cockpit. "But I don't promise not to cause your stomach to do a few flip-flops."

"We'll survive." Morgan helped Alex into the plane and settled her in her seat. "That's what seat belts are for."

"Speak for yourself," Alex said. "I don't travel well in bumpy weather."

"I promise that you won't even feel it this time." Morgan smiled down at her. "Trust me."

"That's a first." She smiled back at him. "Lately you've been trying to convince me you can't be trusted."

He put his hand caressingly on the side of her neck. "No one ever said I was consistent."

"Good, because I do trust—" Her eyes widened. "What are—" She slumped down in the seat.

"You won't trust me when you wake up. Sleep well." He brushed a kiss on her forehead and turned to Garver, who was staring wide-eyed at him. "Take her to Miami and don't let her leave the plane until Galen gets there."

"What did you do to her? Hit her?"

"Sort of. And she's going to be mad as hell when she wakes up. If I were you, I'd want to be out of this turbulence before I had to deal with her." He turned and headed for the door. "Tell her it was necessary. I had no choice. Galen will explain it to her."

The White House

"I have to talk to you, Mr. President," Keller said.

"Not now. I'm late." Andreas moved quickly down the hall. "I was supposed to be at the dedication of that statue at the Pentagon ten min—" He stopped when he saw Keller's face. "My God, what's wrong?"

"Plummock Falls. We believe it's . . . gone."

Andreas halted in his tracks. "You told me it couldn't happen again. You told me it was safe."

"That's what I was assured by both the FBI and the CIA."

"Assurances. God, I'm tired of assurances. Was anyone hurt?"

"You'll be glad to know that, thanks to your orders, our people were not—"

"Was anyone hurt?"

"Unfortunately, the explosion undermined the integrity of the surrounding acreage. Thirty-four miners are buried. We don't know if there are any fatalities yet."

"Thirty-four—" He felt sick, and he knew that horror must be reflected on his face. He had to get to somewhere less public. He was the President. He mustn't show fear or disgust and most of all he mustn't show despair. He was the icon, the symbol. God, he was tired of that too.

Well, too bad. It went with the territory. He drew Keller out of the corridor into the green room. "Now, tell me what the hell happened."

Miami, Florida

"What happened?" Alex glared at Galen as he helped her from the plane. "And where's Morgan? I'm going to kill him."

"I can't say I blame you." Galen took her duffel and led her toward a car parked beside a hangar at the private airport. "But I'm innocent. He didn't say anything to me about ditching you until it was a done deed. He called me after your plane had taken off."

"But you suspected, didn't you? What did you tell him when you called while we were on the way to the plane?"

"That Al Leary was hobnobbing in Guatemala City with Cordoba, the head man of Matanza."

"Leary . . ." She had to think for a minute before she made the connection. "He's the CIA agent who sent Morgan to North Korea."

"And set up the Morales hit. Morgan asked me to locate Leary."

And he hadn't mentioned anything about it to her. She felt a burst of anger and frustration—and sheer terror. "He's gone after Leary, hasn't he?"

"More than likely."

"You know damn well that's where he is." Her voice was shaking. "He wants answers and he thinks Leary will give them to him. It doesn't matter that he's down there with all those crazy butchers and killers and—" She had to stop to regain her composure. "And he didn't want me with him. He thought I'd get in the way. I'm not that dense. I would never have—" She drew a deep breath. "He said he'd call me, but he's more likely to phone you. You're not going to give him a guilt trip. So you have to let me know when he contacts you. No more secrets."

"Okay. I'd never think of disputing a lady as angry as you are." He opened the passenger door for her. "In the meantime, I promised Morgan I'd take you home with me until he could—"

"No way. Your wife's pregnant. I'm not going to put any more pressure on her than she has already. You can stash me back in that shack in Prescott and I'll wait until I hear—" She broke off as Galen's phone rang.

Morgan?

Galen shook his head to her unspoken question as he spoke into the phone.

The disappointment was so intense she had to turn away from Galen for a moment. What had she expected? Morgan might not even have reached Guatemala City yet.

Galen was cursing softly and her gaze flew back to his face. Grim. Very grim.

"What is it?" she asked as he hung up. "Your wife?"

He nodded. "But she's fine. She just wondered if I'd heard about Plummock Falls."

"What?"

"It's a coal mine south of Huntington, West Virginia. There's been a gas explosion and thirty-four miners are buried."

Horror surged through her. "No," she whispered.

"That's what I said."

"Z-2?"

"It could be a coincidence."

"I don't think so." Thirty-four miners caught in that smothering darkness beneath the earth. "What are the chances of getting them out?"

"It depends how unstable the mine's become and how much air is left down there."

"We should have been quicker. We should have been able to figure out where it was going to happen."

"How? You just found out about the possibility of coal mines being in the equation. Do you think you're some kind of fortune-teller?"

"I guess not." She felt numb. All she could think about were those men buried in that mine. "Why? Why would anyone do that?"

Galen shook his head.

"I have to know, Galen. You weren't at Arapahoe Junction. All those people, all those deaths. It can't keep happening. . . ." She tightened her lips to keep them from trembling. "I won't let it go on. It has to stop."

Galen touched her shoulder comfortingly. "Come home with me. I talked to Elena. She's good with it."

Alex shook her head. "I'm going to Plummock Falls."

"It's not a good idea. If it's sabotage, there will be all kinds of law enforcement there. And we've already established that some of those cops aren't as pure as they should be. They'll probably be expecting you."

"I don't care," she said fiercely. "I'm going. Even if you have to arrange plastic surgery to keep me from being recognized. I have to be there."

He studied her for a moment and then nodded. "Okay. You do what I tell you and we'll find a way for you to go. I'll call Logan and tell him I may have to ask for some help on this one." He smiled. "And we'll try to do without the plastic surgery. You can use the same disguise elements you did before. It would be a shame to take a knife to that face."

13

Plummock Falls . . .

Runne stared thoughtfully at the CNN shot of the mine. Betworth had done well. He hadn't heard one murmur of suspicion on any of the news channels. They appeared convinced it was caused by a buildup of gas in the mine. There was a bit of ranting and raving by environmental groups and union representatives, but they clearly didn't have a clue. All they could determine was that—

The dogs!

He sat up straight with excitement as the television camera caught a shot of the rescue workers and canine teams on the edge of the mine. That's what he'd been waiting for. Throughout most of her adult life, Graham had worked side by side with search-and-rescue workers. Even if she only suspected that Plummock Falls was Z-2, he doubted she could resist coming to help.

Besides, he'd made sure there was an added lure that would bring Alex Graham to the disaster site.

———

Dead Aim

"What do you mean you're at Plummock Falls?" Logan said. "For God's sake, Sarah, you're in no shape to work. Why the hell didn't you call me before you took off?"

"I'm calling you now," Sarah said. "And you have no room to complain about lack of communication. You still haven't told me where Alex is."

"She's safe."

"The devil she is. Look, I didn't call to argue with you. I have a job to do and it looks nasty. They won't let us near the mine shaft yet. There's too much debris and too many walls to be shored up."

"Then you shouldn't be near it. Your team shouldn't have asked you to come."

"Hey, I'm not the star here. The local Emergency Rescue Unit made a special request to headquarters to have Monty brought here."

"What?"

"You know Monty's nose gets more press than any dog's in the search-and-rescue field."

"Yes." But he didn't like any special requests being made. Not right now. "Look, Sarah, stay at the site. Don't be alone. Even for a minute."

There was a silence. "What are you saying?"

"I'm saying I don't like either you or Monty being singled out." He paused. "And if you get a call from Alex, don't go to meet her. She's already told me she won't be contacting you."

"And what if she changes her mind?"

"Don't go to meet her."

"What's happening, John?"

"I wish you'd just go home, dammit." But she wouldn't leave and she had to be warned. "We're not sure that Plummock Falls was an accident."

He heard the sharp intake of her breath. "Another Arapahoe Junction?"

"Possibly. At any rate we have to be very cautious."

"Those bastards."
"Yes. Will you go home?"
"No."
"Then will you be careful?"
"As careful as Monty will let me. We have to get those miners out." She didn't speak for a moment. "Why? This has to end, John."
"I'm working on it. And so is your friend Alex. You just concentrate on your job. I'll call you tomorrow. I love you."
"I love you too." She hung up.

Logan sat staring into space after he hung up the phone. Christ, it was too damn convenient that someone had called and made a special request for Monty. Where Monty went, there went Sarah. If it was a trap, then it had been baited by one clever son of a bitch.

He reached for the phone again to dial Alex Graham at the mobile home that Galen had found for her near Huntington.

"Sarah and Monty are at the site," Alex told Galen after she'd hung up the phone with Logan. "Logan's calling the local Emergency Rescue Unit to see if anyone there actually requested them to come here. He thinks they may have been brought here to be staked out."

"Could be. Betworth and his men can't be sure how much you know, but they're aware Morgan saw Morales's plans. This disaster is in the same category as Arapahoe Junction." He paused. "Are you sure you don't want to come home with me? What can you do here? You can't go digging like you did at the dam."

"I don't know. But I'm here, where the action is. I wouldn't be able to accomplish anything sitting and holding your wife's hand."

Galen chuckled. "You don't know how funny that is." He stood up. "But I have orders from Elena to stay near if you refused to come home. And I never disobey the lady. Anything I can do for you?"

She shook her head. "Tonight I'm going to hit the computer."

"And do what? Research?"

"No, I'm going to go over Powers's last words. God knows, I'm tired of looking at them. But there might be something I'm missing." Her lips tightened. "I'm going to try to see if I can figure out why, when, or where."

The computer screen was becoming a gray blur.

Alex rubbed her eyes and tried to focus. She should probably stop and try to get a little sleep. She sure as hell wasn't accomplishing anything in this shape. She'd been working all night, taking Powers's sentences apart and putting them back together. She'd come up with half a dozen possible explanations for every word he'd spoken. None of them made sense.

Or maybe they did and she was too tired to see it. She hoped Morgan was having better luck getting answers.

She instinctively shied away from that thought. She'd been trying not to think about Morgan or the fact that he hadn't called either her or Galen.

Maybe he was too busy. Maybe he was caught in a situation where it would be dangerous for him to—

Dammit, the bastard should have phoned. Didn't the cold son of a bitch know what he was doing to her? When he came back, she was going to make him—

If he came back.

He would come back. He had to come back.

Stop thinking about him. Focus on this damn computer screen.

Morgan's hand closed on his shirt. "Answer me. Where's Z-3?"

"*Kettle . . .*" Powers's body stiffened and then convulsed. His mouth opened wide in a silent scream. It stayed open as life fled.

"Kettle?" Alex repeated. "What the hell is that supposed to mean?" It might mean nothing. It could have been the confused meanderings of a dying man.

But he'd said Z-2 was in West Virginia, and he hadn't lied about that. He hadn't lied about Lontana.

He'd said Z-2 wasn't important. If it wasn't important, why had they buried those miners?

"*West . . . Virginia. Not important . . . Z-3. Z-3 . . .*"

"*And Z-3 is important? Not Z-2?*"

"*Z-2 . . . It's all bunk—*" He arched upward as agony struck him. "*Son of a bitch. Screw him.*" Powers's eyes were glazing. "*Screw Z-3.*"

Her phone rang.

Morgan?

She jumped for it. "Hello."

"Any luck?" Galen asked.

Disappointment tore through her. She tried to keep the emotion from her tone. "Not yet. Have you heard from Morgan?"

"No, but I heard from Salazar. He said that Morgan had all his plans in place and was going to contact Leary tomorrow night."

"Contact?"

"Well, that wasn't exactly the word he used. He said that Morgan was one tough bastard and he wouldn't be in Leary's shoes if they gave him a winning ticket to the lottery."

At least Morgan was still alive. She supposed she should be grateful for small favors. "I don't think that's why you called me in the middle of the night."

"No, I wanted to warn you. Logan checked on the request to bring Sarah and Monty to the disaster site. It was bogus."

It didn't surprise her. "Just so he's warned Sarah. And I don't think there's a chance in the world that he wasn't on the phone to her the minute he got word." She rubbed the back of her neck. "Now, if you don't mind, I'll try to figure out why Z-2 wasn't important. Why it was—" She jerked upright in her chair. "My God."

"Alex?"

"Hang up, Galen. I've got to call Logan."

"What?"

"I'll call you back." She hung up on him and dialed Logan's number. Her hand was icy cold as it clutched the phone. She listened to it ring.

Please pick up. Logan, for God's sake, *answer*.

Morgan called her at six the next morning. "It occurred to me that you might do something reckless just because you're angry with me. So I thought I'd let you get it out of your system."

Sweet Jesus, he was alive. She was almost limp with relief. "You persist in thinking I'm going to react like an idiot," she said unevenly. "When have I ever done that?"

"Touché."

"But that doesn't mean I'm not going to tear the hide off you when I see you. You bastard, how dare you lie to me?"

"I couldn't take you with me."

"So you played Spock and gave me the Vulcan knockout punch?"

"Actually, it was a Tibetan blow I learned from a monk who—"

"I don't care. It was wrong and you're going to pay for it." She drew a deep breath. "When I have time to spare from trying to figure out where this damn kettle is located."

"Kettle?"

"Remember Powers said that at the end? It has to be a topographical formation of some sort. I asked Logan to try to talk to the President. He'd know. But Logan can't get through to him. And who else is he going to trust when the FBI and CIA seem to be breeding grounds for—"

"Easy. Why would the President know about this kettle?"

"Bunkers. He'd have to know about the bunkers."

"Bunkers?"

"Remember when Powers said 'It's all bunk—' we thought he meant it wasn't important, that it was all bullshit. But he broke off because of the pain. He was trying to say they were all *bunkers*. Arapahoe Junction, Plummock Falls, and this kettle place." She moistened her lips. "Right after September eleventh it came out that bunkers had been established to make sure the U.S. government could still function if Washington came under direct attack. They were principally concerned with nuclear threats, so underground facilities were chosen."

"I recall hearing something about a facility at the Greenbrier. But that was abandoned years ago."

"But the bunker concept wasn't abandoned. When the press secretary was questioned at a news conference, she reluctantly admitted there was more than one bunker. No officials would say anything more, because it was a sensitive security issue. Later, a magazine article came out with an interview with an anonymous lower-echelon government official who described how personnel rotated into the bunkers every month and weren't permitted to tell even their families where they were going. They could only be contacted at an 800 number. Most of the time there were at least fifty personnel keeping the bunkers going, but very few high-profile members were called to serve at the bunkers. It was purely volunteer as far as they were concerned. Except for one cabinet member who was supposed to serve at all times."

"Why three bunkers?"

"There may be even more. But I don't think so. They'd need one near the West Coast in case the President was in that part of the country at the time of an attack. One in West

Dead Aim

Virginia, which is close to Washington, but not too close. The other one . . . I don't know. Baltimore? Those hydro vents Melis mentioned were near Baltimore."

"And Baltimore is practically next door to Washington. The sonic manipulation of a hydro vent offshore could directly affect Washington."

"Jesus."

"But Betworth wanted more bang for his buck, so he contacted Morales." Morgan was silent for a moment. "And what could Morales give him for more bang for his buck?"

She was afraid to guess. "I hope to hell you find out. You meet with Leary tonight?"

"If I'm lucky. I have a good many more questions to ask him now about those bunkers." He paused. "Sharp, very sharp, Alex."

"Then maybe you should have called me before."

"I had to brace myself to be flayed. I'll phone you after I finish with Leary."

She slowly hung up the phone. She didn't want to let him go. Maybe she shouldn't have jumped on him. What if she never saw—

Of course she should have done it. He was wrong. He was honest enough to realize that and expect her to—

Dear God, she wanted him here.

Forget it. Think about this blasted kettle. Think about those bunkers and why they were destroyed.

More bang for the buck.

Christ.

"I've verified your bunkers, Alex," Logan said. "No one in Congress wanted to talk, but I tapped one confidential source. Once he realized I already knew about it and only needed to be filled in, he opened up. The bunker wasn't in Arapahoe

Junction, it was on the other side of the dam, where you were taking your pictures."

"Powers said there was a screwup. They didn't have the technology right." Her lips twisted bitterly. "They blew the dam and buried the town of Arapahoe Junction. I'd say that was a big-time screwup. All those people . . ."

"My contact didn't know anything about any of the other bunkers. Since they're all underground, he said he'd bet that the installation at Plummock Falls is practically right beside the mine. The location picks were supposed to be in fairly populated areas so that the Congressmen's comings and goings wouldn't stick out like a sore thumb."

"And Plummock Falls is a bustling mining town."

"So they blow the bunker and take some of the coal mine with it."

"No information about Z-3?"

"Evidently everyone knows about their particular bunker and no other. It makes good security sense. Sorry, I'll keep trying."

"You found out quite a bit. At least one thing is going right."

"More than one. Sarah called me and told me they'd located the miners."

"Alive?"

"At least some of them. There was tapping."

"Thank God." She paused. "Have you gotten through to Andreas?"

"Not yet. There's a steel wall of security around him these days. I'll keep trying. Has Morgan phoned you?"

"Not since this morning. He said he'd call me when he could."

"Let me know when he does."

"I'll do that." If she heard from him. She was beginning to wonder if he— Stop wondering. Stop thinking. She had to believe he'd contact her when he could. He had his job to do and she had hers.

Dead Aim

She stared down at the open atlas on the coffee table in front of her.

The kettle . . .

Guatemala City

Jesus.

Morgan took a long drink of his bourbon as he stared at the television set over the bar.

Plummock Falls.

The cameras were panning the faces of the crowds gathered outside the fence that encircled the opening of the mine. Pain. Disbelief. Fear. Hope.

"It's terrible." The bartender shook his head. "But it's good that maybe some of them will be saved. To be buried alive would be anyone's nightmare."

"Yes." He tore his eyes from the television set. This wasn't the time to be distracted. He was only grateful Alex was so absorbed in trying to figure out the location of Z-3 that she wasn't one of those people behind the fence. He turned to Marco Salazar. "You're sure Leary will be alone?"

"Well, he won't be with anyone from the Matanza group." Salazar shrugged. "Cordoba doesn't approve of gays. This bar is *the* hangout for homosexuals in Guatemala City. Leary was here last night and went home with someone he met. He'll probably be back. He didn't impress me as the faithful type."

"He's not. I remember when we were in San Francisco for a couple weeks, he hit practically every bathhouse in town." He got off the stool. "Time to make myself a little less conspicuous. I'll be back in that booth in the corner. When he comes in, let me know."

Salazar nodded absently, his gaze focused on the TV set and the miners being carried out of the shaft.

Ten minutes later Al Leary walked into the bar.

Morgan didn't have to see Salazar's signal to know Leary was in the room. He blew in with his customary swagger and immediately began to talk to the bartender.

He was on the hunt, Morgan thought. He had seen Leary operate in dozens of cities around the world and it was always the same. Make contact with the bartender and let him know he was available, then get a line on the most attractive men who frequented the place.

He was turning toward Salazar, Morgan realized. He'd thought that would be his response to Salazar's dark good looks. Leary was all flashing white teeth and aggressive charm as he sat down on the stool next to Salazar.

Fifteen minutes later Morgan got up from his booth and moved toward the bathroom in the rear of the bar. It was empty, but no telling how long it would stay that way. He cracked open the door so that he could see the bar.

Come on, Salazar. Get the show moving.

As if he'd heard Morgan, Salazar got off the bar stool and touched Leary's arm and said something to him. Leary and Salazar left the bar and strolled toward the bathroom.

"It's good stuff," Salazar was saying as he pushed open the door. "Enough to give you a high but not interfere with—"

Morgan's arm encircled Leary's neck and jerked him backward.

Leary gasped, gurgling helplessly as he tried to breathe.

"We're leaving," Morgan said in his ear. "We're going to go out the back way and then get in the car in the alley. When we leave this bathroom, my arm's going to be around your shoulders and my hand is going to be affectionately on your neck. If you're not equally quiet and affectionate as we go through that crowd, I'm going to stop being affectionate and give you a shuto blow to the back of the neck and kill you. It will be over almost before you know it. You've seen me do it before."

Leary's eyes were wide with terror as he tried to speak.

Dead Aim

"Go and start the car, Salazar." Morgan loosened his arm around Leary's neck. "We'll be along in a minute."

"Morgan." Leary's voice was hoarse. "Don't kill me. It wasn't my—"

"Easy does it. This isn't the time." His arm slipped around Leary's shoulders. "Now, let's go. Salazar's arranged a place for us to have a little talk."

14

November 10
8:45 P.M.

"Danley tells me you're in position, Runne," Betworth said.

"Of course. We made a deal."

"You checked in at Z-3 last night. But no one's seen you since then."

"If they'd seen me, I wouldn't be doing my job, would I?"

"I want you to report to Danley again tomorrow. I have to know that you're ready. Not that I don't trust you."

"Just have that helicopter ready to get me out of there. I'll handle the rest."

"Report to Danley tomorrow or there won't be a helicopter."

"Don't bluff me. You want me out of there as much as I want to get out. When do I get Morgan?"

"He's still on the loose. Who knows? You may run into him at the Kettle." Betworth hung up.

And he might not, Runne thought. The surer bet was still the woman. He had been disappointed that she hadn't shown up at the mine. Time was running out. He'd been running back and forth between the mine and Z-3 for the last few days to placate Betworth and Danley, but now there were only two days left.

Dead Aim

If he was going to have the opportunity to get Morgan, it might be necessary to escalate matters.

He reached for his phone.

9:05 P.M.

Kettle.

Dammit, Alex had stared at the atlas of the northeastern United States until she was almost blind. No mention of topographical features anywhere in this area that might fit. No lakes or rocks that could be—

Screw it.

Her phone rang.

"Alex. This is Sarah." Her words came bullet-fast. "I'm only going to talk for a minute because I don't know if he's found a way he can trace the call. Hell, I don't know how he got my number. He must have finessed someone at rescue headquarters."

"He?"

"Someone called Runne Shin. He said you'd probably know who he was."

Alex stiffened. "Oh, yes."

"Look, I didn't even want to call you. But I decided I didn't have the right. I wouldn't want to be kept in the dark if it were me."

"In the dark about what?"

"He said that there was going to be another disaster worse than Plummock Falls if you didn't stop it. He said to tell you he didn't care about Betworth's plans. He only wants Morgan."

Shock rippled through her. "And how am I supposed to stop this so-called disaster?"

"He said to call him. He gave me the number." She rattled off the phone number and then paused. "And now that I've given you that bastard's message, I'm giving you one of my own. Don't be crazy. You can't be held responsible for the actions of this asshole. Stay away from him."

He only wants Morgan.

"That may be difficult to do."

"I'm hanging up now. I don't want to take any chances. But I'm calling John and telling him about this Runne Shin."

"He already knows about him."

"He doesn't know that he's setting you up," Sarah said grimly before she hung up.

Sarah was right. Alex would be stupid not to realize that Runne would do anything he had to do to her to draw Morgan.

Yet if she didn't call Runne, she was neglecting an opportunity to stop another tragedy and perhaps find a solution to this insane puzzle. She stared down at the phone number she'd jotted in the margin of a page of the atlas.

He only wants Morgan.

Well, he couldn't have him. She wasn't giving him up.

But Runne didn't have to know that. She quickly dialed the number Sarah had given her.

"What kind of disaster?" she demanded when the phone was answered.

"Alex Graham? I've been very eager to meet you since I've heard you're very close to our mutual friend. I trust Morgan has told you about me."

"Yes."

"I thought he would. You must be on intimate terms."

"That's none of your business."

"I know Morgan wouldn't have stayed with you for any length of time if he hadn't formed an attachment. I'm a little disappointed in him. After he killed my father, I studied his files and grew to admire his cool objectivity. I was going to model my lifestyle on him after I cut his throat, but I'm not sure now. You may have tainted his image."

Dead Aim

"Too bad. Where's the Kettle?"

He chuckled. "You know that much? I'm impressed."

"It's Z-3, isn't it? What's going to happen there?"

"What do you think?"

"Another Arapahoe Junction?"

"Nothing so cataclysmic. Morgan and I don't indulge in mass murder. We save ourselves for the special tasks. But I believe you'd consider this particular job a true disaster."

"But you're not going to tell me what it is."

"I'll tell you where it is. Well, not exactly tell. I'll take you there tonight."

"I saw what you did to Powers's wife. Do you think I'd trust you?"

"Of course not. But you're a woman who can't resist running to comfort the suffering. You'll find a way to get around your doubts so that you can do that."

"And you'll use me to get Morgan."

"If possible. I'll give him a better chance than he gave my father. There are two hundred acres of woods and mountains near the Kettle. I'll give him a head start and then track him. It will bring back the memory of old times and be much more satisfying than a quick kill. I've been waiting too long to have it over in a hurry." He chuckled. "And I'm sure you'll use me to try to save him and the target I'm going to take out the day after tomorrow."

"Where are you?"

"Very close to Plummock Falls, but I leave here in two hours. Let me know." He hung up.

Jesus.

She couldn't do it. There was no way she could be the bait in the trap that would snap on Morgan.

I believe you'd consider this particular job a true disaster.

We save ourselves for the special tasks.

She was starting to shake.

Iris Johansen

True disaster . . .
Dear God in heaven.

Guatemala City

"Let's get this very clear, Leary. I need answers," Morgan said. "Why, when, and where."

"I don't know what you're talking about." Leary moistened his lips. "I was just sent down here undercover. Matanza is causing all kinds of flak at the White House, and Danley thought if I came down and pretended to be a turncoat that—" Leary arched in pain as Morgan pressed on the nerve at the base of his neck. "I tell you, I don't know any—"

"You know." Morgan's tone was without expression. "And you'll tell me. It's only a question of whether it's before or after. Do you remember that Al Qaeda bastard we were assigned to find in India? He was very talented. No one is better at torture than a fanatic. Do you recall what the Marine he was holding as hostage looked like when he got through with him?"

"Yes."

"And do you remember what I did after I tracked that son of a bitch down and caught him?"

Leary swallowed. "Yes."

"I was very angry then, but that's not a patch on what I'm feeling toward you right now. Do you understand?"

"You can't get away with this. Cordoba will have all the Matanza searching for me. I'm valuable to them."

"Not when Salazar arranges to have them find out that you went off with your latest conquest for a weekend in the country."

"He'll contact Danley. Danley will send—" He screamed as Morgan applied pressure. "Damn you. I told them you should have been killed right after Fairfax. But that prick Danley

– 246 –

didn't want to risk any suspicion within the Company." He shrieked in agony. "Screw you. I'm not talking."

"You will," Morgan said softly. "Believe me, you will, Leary."

10:15 P.M.

Alex drove thirty miles south of Huntington before she phoned Runne. "I thought it over, and I've decided I'll let you lead me to Z-3."

"I said I'd take you, not lead you."

"But that would put me entirely in your power. I'd be foolish to even think about doing that. Will I be able to identify this place as the Kettle when I see it?"

"Definitely."

"Then when we reach there, I'll take off and you can try to catch me. If you do, then you'll have your bait for Morgan. I know it's him you want to hunt, but I may not be as easy prey as you think. I'm at the gas station at the intersection of Highways 5 and 22. What kind of car are you driving?"

"A tan Toyota 4Runner."

"Then when I see you, I'll leave the station and follow you. I'm sure you'll reconnoiter to make sure no one but me is around to trail you. But I have a gun, and if you try to lead me down a wrong road, either literally or figuratively, I won't hesitate to shoot you."

"Then the odds seem to be in your favor. Why should I go along with it?"

"Because I'm not a professional. I don't know how to hunt down and kill anyone. Morgan told me that you were an expert. Once we reach the Kettle, don't you believe that you can turn the tables on an amateur like me?"

"Oh, yes. With great certainty."

She felt a chill at the absolute confidence in his tone. "And after you catch me, do you think you'll be able to force me to call Morgan and beg him to come?"

"It will take no time at all."

"Then come and get me."

"There's a problem. I only have one day to track Morgan before I have to commit to my other duty. This small charade with you is going to eat into my time."

"But you're so sure that you'll get me in a heartbeat, and you said Morgan was the only thing that was important to you."

There was a silence. "And what do you hope to accomplish by this?"

"I hope to kill you."

He chuckled. "The hunted turned hunter?"

"Or I hope to remain free long enough to give Morgan a chance to kill you."

"A slightly greater chance."

"I'll call Morgan when we reach the Kettle and tell him where I am. He won't tell anyone else, because he'll be afraid that you'll kill me." She paused. "And he'll come after me. Isn't that what you want?"

"It's very tempting." He thought about it. "On one condition. Give me Morgan's phone number so that I can communicate with him. I'll be the one to call him from the Kettle and tell him where to come. You call Morgan right now and tell him what a tender sacrifice you're making for his sake. Don't think I'm fool enough to trust that you haven't had your car bugged so that you can be traced. There's a very simple device that will detect the signal and I'll use it."

"I've hardly had time to arrange anything that elaborate."

"And then I want to see you throw your phone and that gun you mentioned out the window of your car as you drive out of the gas station. I won't risk you calling someone else and giving them your location once you reach Z-3.   'l circle around and see if there's a gun with the phone. If there's no gun, I'll disappear and you can find Z-3 by yourself."

No phone. No gun. If she did that, she would be totally alone and isolated, with no way to call for help.

What was she quibbling about? It was only one more hazard in an almost suicidal situation.

"I'll call Morgan now." She hung up and drew a deep breath before she dialed Morgan.

No answer.

Then she got his voice mail.

No!

She hung up and leaned her head on the steering wheel in despair.

Okay, keep cool. He was meeting with Leary tonight. Naturally he wouldn't want his phone going off. He'd access his voice mail eventually.

When it might be too late.

She tried one more time.

Voice mail.

"Morgan, this is Alex." She steadied her voice. "I need you to listen carefully. I don't have much time. . . ."

11:05 P.M.

Morgan accessed his voice mail when he was on his way to the airport.

"Morgan, this is Alex. I need you to listen carefully. I don't have much time."

He tensed. His hands tightened on the steering wheel with white-knuckle force as he listened to the first few minutes of the message.

"I doubt if I can kill him. I won't have a gun. If he's as good as you say he is, I probably won't be able to do it. Hell, if he weren't good at all, I'd still have problems. So I figure my job is to keep on the move and out of his way until you can get here. It's not going to be easy. He's got to be so much more skilled than I am. But I can do that and I *will*. And if you don't get here in time, then I'll find a way to cope." She paused. "And don't start cursing me for getting us into this mess. I had to do it. I told you what he said about the kinds of jobs you both specialize in. Well, it finally hit me. God, if I hadn't been so focused on finding Z-3 and preventing another disaster, I'd have concentrated on why those bunkers were being destroyed. He's going to assassinate Andreas. He's the target. They brought Runne here to do the job in exchange for help in finding you. These days Andreas is surrounded by impregnable security, so how do you get to him? You cause an incident that would drive him out of his safe White House to a bunker. But you have to make sure he'll be taken to the right one so that you can set up the ambush. So you destroy the other bunkers. They tried to make it look like an earthquake at Arapahoe, but they had to go public when I stumbled on their attempt at cleanup. They had a good scapegoat in Matanza. And Logan said that he thought it likely the people who manned the bunkers knew only about their own. No one would make the connection except the people who had the overall view." She drew a deep, shaky breath. "But we can blow the bastards out of the water. They can't assassinate Andreas if we stop Runne. We have one day, Morgan." Another silence. "I have to throw away my phone, so this is the last time I'll be able to contact you. But I'm a survivor. I'm not going to let Runne kill me or use me. Get that thought out of your head. And I'm not going to say anything soppy like I love you." Her voice was uneven. "But I have to tell you that I've thought about it and decided that you have the makings of a genuine, grade-A hero, and I may not be able to let you go."

Morgan closed his eyes as the message came to an end. Jesus, he was scared.

And so was Alex. Yet it hadn't stopped the damn woman from rushing in and trying to save the world. He wanted to shake her. She didn't know what she was biting off when she'd pitted herself against Runne.

Yes, she knew. That was why she was frightened. And the thought of her scared and alone was making him sick.

Get a grip. He was at least four hours away from the action, and he had to start thinking and moving instead of sitting here frozen like a kid at his first funeral.

He called Galen. "I'm on my way. Salazar arranged for transport. Where the hell is Logan? I tried to call him as soon as I left Leary."

"He's been busy. There have been a few problems here."

"That's nothing compared to what's coming," Morgan said. "I need Logan to jump on the bandwagon and start cutting red tape. I'm not sure how many hours we have left."

"Left for what? You got Leary to talk?"

"He talked. He only had part of the picture. That seems to be Betworth's modus operandi, but it's a pretty nasty part. It took me longer than I thought to convince him the cavalry wasn't going to ride in and rescue him. Betworth had him convinced that he was going to be a big man in the new regime when he took power."

"You haven't asked me what kind of problems we had here." Galen paused. "Or do you know?"

"I know. Alex called me."

"She's safe?"

"For now." God, he hoped he was telling the truth.

"Logan called Alex thirty minutes after Sarah gave Alex the message. She didn't answer. The operative I had watching her called me twenty minutes later and told me she'd jumped in the car and taken off. He lost her. She didn't want to be followed. We've been searching for her ever since."

"I'm not blaming either of you. You couldn't have stopped her. I don't think I could have stopped her."

"What's happening, Judd?"

"Nothing you can help with now. Maybe later. There's enough for you to do in Washington. Call Logan and tell him Keller is okay, that Leary said he's sure he's not part of Betworth's group. Tell him to grab Keller and tell him that all hell's going to break loose there the day after tomorrow."

"Andreas and Keller are at Camp David. Andreas is working on the Mideast Pact and he's not receiving anyone."

"Shit." One more thing gone wrong. It was almost too coincidental that the President was incommunicado. Manipulation behind the scenes by Betworth?

"What's happening the day after tomorrow?"

"Morales sold Betworth a suitcase bomb as part of the package. Dirty. Radioactive."

"Christ."

"It's going to go off somewhere in the White House. Leary wasn't sure when or where. He said Danley would know. Pick up the bastard and grill him."

"If we can find him. He's disappeared from the radar scope for the last few days." He paused. "How dirty?"

"Small, but with enough radioactivity to cause a hell of a lot of contamination."

"How the hell could they get it into the White House?" He paused. "Alex found out where Z-3 is, didn't she? Do you know?"

"No."

"But you're going to find out. Call me, dammit. We have to know. It's not just your game this time, Judd."

"Then find a way to get in touch with Keller, but tell him to stay the hell away from Z-3 until I get back to you. It's the quickest way to get Alex killed. He has a little time. More than twenty-four hours. Nothing's supposed to happen until November twelfth." But they wouldn't care about Alex. To the Secret Service, everyone was expendable if it meant saving the President.

Well, Alex wasn't expendable. Let Logan and Galen race

around and save Andreas and the whole damn country. He'd given them their chance.

He was going after Alex.

Another hill . . .

Alex stumbled up it.

She could see her breath pluming in the cold night air as she struggled for air.

She glanced over her shoulder. Strong moonlight. She might be cursing it before the night was over.

No Runne yet. It had been ten minutes since she'd jumped out of her car and fled into the woods. Why wasn't he right behind her?

Or maybe he was ahead of her.

Don't think about it.

Keep on running.

He might be good, but no one was perfect.

She had a chance.

Keep on running. . . .

November 11
12:40 A.M.

Morgan's phone rang just before he was boarding his flight.

"Hello, Morgan," Runne said. "Have you been waiting for my call? I've been waiting for a long time too. But it's almost over now."

"I'm glad. I'm tired of leading you a chase. There was no challenge. Though why you think you can best me is pretty laughable. I was tracking and targeting hits when you were still a snotty-nosed kid."

"You're not going to make me angry. If there's one thing I've learned from you, it's to keep my emotions in check."

"It didn't look like it at the Powers place. That job could have been done by a teen slasher."

"I was hurt. I couldn't—" He stopped. "I'm not making excuses to you. I'm in control now."

"You're not in control until you have Alex Graham. You don't, do you?"

"Not yet. I'm giving her an hour's head start. Isn't that generous of me? After escaping me for so long, she'll be filled with hope. We both know how depriving prey of hope can crush them. I figure I should have her within twenty minutes or so after I start tracking. Shall I tell you what I'm going to do with her?"

"Don't play that charade with me. You'll have to catch her first. Are you going to tell me where you are or just keep on snarling like some third-grade hoodlum?"

There was silence. "Of course I am. That's what this is all about. And she'll pay for that ugly remark, Morgan. I want you to remember that. Take the Beltway out of D.C. to 270 north. Go forty miles to Frederick, Maryland, then take Highway 15 north. Turn left on Matthew Parkway and then right at the first intersection. Z-3 is two miles down the road. On your right you'll see a sign advertising the Copper Kettle Restaurant in Baltimore. Six miles from the sign you'll see a bluff. Beyond that bluff is a valley of two hundred acres of unoccupied Corps of Engineers woods and hills. When will you be here?"

"It may take me a few hours to get there. But I'll show up when you least expect me."

"Don't be too long. I might grow impatient and cut her throat."

"But then I wouldn't have any reason to continue with the hunt. What good is a dead woman to me?"

"Revenge?"

"Revenge is for fanatics like you. I'm sure you've found I don't let emotion enter into the mix."

"I learned it when you used me to kill my father. Do you

know, I'd never had a friend, but I thought I had one in you. I . . . thought you felt that way too."

"No, you were just a means to an end."

"You son of a bitch." Runne's voice was hoarse with pain. "And that's what the woman is to me. A means to an end. Your end, Morgan. Come and find us." He hung up.

When will you be here?

The question had filled him with frustration and terror. There was no way he could be at Z-3 in less than another five hours. How the hell was Alex going to survive on the run from that bastard for that long? She wouldn't surrender easily, and that meant Runne would use force—and force could be deadly.

He had to keep calm and cool as he'd learned through years of playing this ugly game.

But this time it wasn't a game. It was Alex.

"Runne called me ten minutes ago to report in," Danley said to Betworth when he answered the phone. "The bastard was almost cheerful. It makes me wonder."

"He should be cheerful. He's doing what he likes best," Betworth said. "But you know where he's going to take his shot?"

"From the top of the bluff."

"And you'll be there to take him out immediately? I don't want any mistakes."

"I'm doing it myself. He'll be dead ten seconds after he makes his shot. Is everything going well there?"

"As well as can be expected. I think Logan may be getting uncomfortably close, but once we go into high gear we can roll right over him." He paused; time to spread some honey. "By the way, the tech van you stationed near Camp David is functioning well. Good job."

"Thanks." Danley hesitated. "I haven't heard from Leary today."

"Is that a concern?"

"Not yet. Cordoba said he'd been bar-hopping every night since he arrived. I just want him in place to make sure Matanza doesn't go overboard."

"You said Leary was reliable. Besides, Cordoba has everything to gain. I wouldn't worry that he'll cooperate." Betworth glanced at the clock. "It's two-thirty in the morning, Danley. Just this one more day to get through and then we'll be going full steam ahead. I can't tell you how relieved I am to have a man of your ability in charge there. I'm coming down myself, but not until tomorrow. I won't be able to take off from here until right before I set everything in motion. Call me if you have any problems." He hung up and leaned back in his chair. He could feel the excitement flowing through him like fine wine. It was exhilarating to feel this all-powerful. Other men would probably have felt nervous and frightened along with this high.

But, then, other men wouldn't have been able to pull off a coup like this.

5:05 A.M.

"Danley's nowhere to be found," Logan said. "And, dammit, I can't get through to Camp David. I've been trying for hours. I keep getting told neither Keller nor the President will accept calls."

"Have you tried to get through to Chelsea Andreas?"

"I've got a call in to Pittsburgh, but Andreas has made sure her security is as tight as his own. Not much hope there."

"Weird," Galen said. "I can see Andreas refusing calls, but not Keller. If he refused a call, it would mean ignoring information. The Secret Service checks out every piece of info that comes their way. After Kennedy's assassination they even beefed up their policy."

Logan rubbed his temple. "I don't know. Maybe I'll have better luck later. It's only five in the morning."

"The time wouldn't make any difference to Keller." Galen moved toward the door. "I think I'll take a few men and go up there and see what I can find out."

"Be careful. They shoot first and ask questions later these days."

"Don't worry, I wouldn't dare not be careful. Elena would kill me." He paused. "How long are you going to wait before you call the cops or the media?"

"Do you know what kind of panic that would start? People get hurt when they're stampeding. It'll be a last resort if we can't get through to Andreas. Morgan said nothing was going to happen before tomorrow. We may have time." He grimaced. "If you can get me through to Andreas."

"I think I may have a handle on it. I'll call and let you know."

Cover your tracks.

Use everything she'd learned from Morgan.

She took the branch and carefully erased her tracks in the dirt before heading for the creek. If she waded in the creek for the next mile or so, she might be able to lose him for a while.

The icy water flooded her tennis shoes as she stepped into the stream.

She had been hot and panting only moments ago, but now the ice seemed to be trickling through every vein in her body.

Ignore it.

Keep going.

No Runne yet.

She had thought she heard a crashing behind her ten minutes ago near the bluff, but she must have been mistaken.

Unless he was toying with her.

That was defeatist mentality. She wouldn't give in to it.

She glanced at her watch. It was still too dark to see here beneath these overhanging branches. The last time she'd checked she'd been on the run for over four hours. She felt every minute of it in the aching muscles of her calves and thighs.

But he hadn't caught her.

How long before Morgan could get here?

Too long.

No, it wasn't too long. She'd make it.

Keep going.

The tech van was parked in the woods at least seven miles from Camp David.

Galen glanced down at his meter.

Pretty powerful to give off this strong a signal at that distance.

"Found it?" Kelly asked.

Galen nodded. "Go back to the car and get the guys." He started moving toward the woods. "I'll see if we have any sentries to worry about."

5:40 A.M.

The sky was beginning to turn the first pearl gray of dawn behind the bluff. Daylight that could be deadly for Alex, Morgan thought.

If she was still alive.

He jumped out of the car, grabbed his rifle and shells, and zigzagged into the brush. He was four miles south of the location Runne had given him, but that didn't mean he couldn't be waiting in ambush.

No shot.

He paused. Listening. Nothing unusual. He breathed deep. No smell of soap or sweat.

He started up the hill.

"Go ahead," Galen said when Logan answered. "I think you'll get through now. It was a tech van that was filtering and monitoring the calls."

"Was?"

Galen glanced at the charred and burning vehicle. "I had to make sure they didn't have time to alert anyone. That wouldn't have been smart. Try to make the call again."

"Stop arguing, Keller. I have to see Andreas," Logan said. "Now."

"And I'm expected to believe you?" Keller asked. "I'm aware of who you are and your contributions to the President's election campaign, but that doesn't mean anything now. Your wife has direct ties to Alex Graham, who's wanted by the FBI for connections to Matanza. I'd be insane to trust you."

"You don't have to trust me. Just do what you do best and protect Andreas—and send search parties to locate that suitcase bomb."

"Which may not exist."

"If it doesn't, you can tell everyone that you were conducting a test run." Logan paused. "Or would you rather wait until it blows and then make excuses?"

"I'm not afraid of being a scapegoat, Logan."

No, Logan had a hunch Keller was an honorable man trying to do his job. Which might make him more difficult to handle. "Look, I know we have more questions than answers right now. But we've got to find those answers fast." He wasn't getting through to the stubborn bastard. He tried a new direction. "I was having trouble reaching you because a tech van was stationed seven miles from there, intercepting and filtering your calls. Why would that happen?"

"It couldn't happen. We'd know about it."

"Not if it was done by someone who knew how to bypass your safeguards. Like Ben Danley. If you don't believe the van existed, send your men to see the remains. We thought it best to destroy it."

"A very violent move for a peaceful businessman."

"Will you let me see Andreas or not?"

There was a silence. "I'll talk to him. When can you get here?"

"I'm on my way. Galen and I should be arriving at your first checkpoint in fifteen minutes."

15

It was the third time Runne had lost the track.

It had taken him twenty minutes to discover that she'd coated her shoes with mud so that they formed pillows of dirt and blurred the imprint.

Fury tore through him as he scanned the ground for new signs. She was good, and her stamina was amazing. He thought he'd have caught her by now and be waiting for Morgan to show with the trap baited. Instead, he'd spent hours chasing the bitch.

He drew a deep breath. It couldn't last much longer. The last footprints he'd found had been almost dragging. She was tiring, and exhausted prey always made mistakes.

But now he was being forced to look over his own shoulder. Surely that bastard Morgan should be here by now.

If he was coming. Maybe he'd decided the woman wasn't worth the risk. It was the decision Runne would have made. But in their short time together he'd noticed that Morgan didn't hold the same contempt for women that he did. It was that weakness he was relying on.

Footprint!

She'd tried to erase it, but she was getting careless now.

He moved forward quickly, excitement driving, surging
through him.
Find the woman.
Bait the trap.
Kill Morgan.

Camp David
6:35 A.M.

Andreas didn't speak after Logan had finished.

"It's a wild story, sir," Keller said. "The idea that Matanza
has been set up as a paper dragon to front an assassination
attempt is bizarre. Danley would have had to be in the plot
up to his neck to pull that off."

"And Danley has been with me for years." Andreas stared
into the flames of the fireplace. "I trusted him."

"Past tense?" Logan asked.

"Maybe." He rubbed the back of his neck. "It's hard to
trust anyone these days and harder to give up that trust once
it's given. I want to hold on tight. Yet I can see Betworth cor-
rupting everyone around him. He's like the serpent in the
Garden of Eden. Only the fruit of temptation isn't knowledge,
it's ambition. My main problem is that I can't see why
Betworth would find it worthwhile to have me dead. I haven't
gotten in his way on any of the major bills. There's no way
he'd be able to climb over my corpse to get the next nomination. It doesn't make sense, Logan."

"No, it doesn't," Logan agreed. "And I wish I didn't have to
admit it. All I can tell you is what I know, and what I know
scares me."

And Andreas admired a man who could admit to fear. He'd
always liked what he'd known of Logan. He hesitated.
"Keller, do you have a list of our honorable colleagues who
were designated to serve at Z-3?"

Dead Aim

"In my briefcase, sir." Keller crossed to the desk. "I thought you'd want to see it."

"Why did you keep Plummock Falls as a bunker after what happened at Arapahoe?" Galen asked.

"I pulled our people out of the Arapahoe bunker as a precaution after the dam broke, and I stopped the rotation of personnel into the Plummock bunker. I hoped that what I'd been told was true," Andreas said, "that there couldn't be another security breach, it couldn't happen again. We handled all the bunkers completely separately. It seemed incredible that Matanza could buy that amount of sensitive information." His lips tightened. "I wish to hell we didn't even have to have those bunkers. But we do. Because the government *has* to be preserved and without them we could fall into anarchy. I won't let those bastards win that victory."

"Maybe you should have closed down Z-3 too."

"We discussed it," Keller said. "But there has to be at least one safe haven in case of nuclear attack. It was decided that the alternative vulnerability wasn't acceptable. We sent security teams to Z-3 to check for any possibility of sabotage, and it came up clean as a whistle." He opened his briefcase and drew out two documents. "Here's the bunker itself." He spread out the first diagram on the desk. He pointed to a solid rock wall. "It's built into the side of a mountain. Five-foot-thick steel doors and an elevator that goes down seven stories. It was the last bunker built, and we learned a lot from Arapahoe and Plummock Falls. Not that the other two bunkers weren't perfectly safe. It's just that the new technology we installed at Z-3 made it absolutely impregnable. The clearing where the helicopter lands is about two-thirds of a mile away. The helicopter has to go through this pass to land. The aircraft has to fly low and would be almost on the ground before anyone could get off a shot." He handed Andreas the second sheet of paper. "And this is the personnel list, sir. The list of volunteers is at the top."

Andreas smiled crookedly as he scanned the names. "Betworth. No surprise there." His smile faded. "Life in those bunkers isn't exactly luxurious. It was my understanding it was hard to get volunteers from the higher echelon. But here's Ellswyth, Johnson, Cornwall, Waterson. It reads like a fraternity of Betworth's cohorts. He stacked the deck with a powerhouse of his own players. Nolan, Thorpall . . ." He glanced up. "Shepard? I thought he was going to go to Plummock Falls in case of any problems. He was changed after the mine explosion?"

"No, after Arapahoe Dam. Z-3 was the stronger facility and more secure than Plummock Falls." Keller paused. "But Danley agreed it would be safer for the Vice President."

"Interesting."

"And Shepard did come to me and suggest that he'd feel better about a change to our strongest facility." He paused again. "Which might mean nothing, sir."

"And it could mean a hell of a lot," Logan said. "Where's Shepard now?"

"I'll find out." Keller pulled out his phone.

"It would fill in the missing blank," Logan said. "The reason why Betworth would instigate a chancy conspiracy like this."

"Don't push, Logan. I have to think about it." Andreas moved across the room to the window. It had been a bitter cold night and the glass was frosted. He felt cold and hollow himself. It wasn't every day a man found out he was scheduled to die in a little more than twenty-four hours. "You say this man, Morgan, is at Z-3?"

"So I understand from Galen."

"And is he good at what he does?"

"Yes, the best," Logan said. "No one can say he's a team player, but Galen trusts him."

"Mr. President."

Dead Aim

Andreas turned to see that Keller was off the phone. "Well?"

"Vice President Shepard is presently at Z-3. It's his scheduled time to spend a few days at the bunker."

"How convenient. Safe and sound and away from nasty suspicions."

"You believe Shepard is involved in the conspiracy?"

"If there *is* a conspiracy."

"What can I do to convince you?" Logan asked. "There's not much time. Any number of things could set Betworth off. Hell, if they discover we knocked out that tech van, that may escalate—"

"I told you not to push," Andreas said. "Okay, Shepard is a possibility. He's been grabbing the limelight frequently, taking my place at functions and acting more aggressively than I've ever seen him. That doesn't necessarily link him to—"

"The Homeland Infrastructure bill," Keller said suddenly.

"What's that?" Logan said.

"It's a bill Shepard's been pushing for the last year," Andreas said. "It's aimed at improving and shoring up vulnerable areas and infrastructure that might be targeted for sabotage or in danger from natural disasters. It's a general bill, nothing to send up any red flags, but the Arapahoe Dam disaster made Shepard look very smart."

"And presidential?" Galen asked. "You're probably the most popular President we've ever had. Shepard had some work to do to make himself over into your image. Betworth not only stocked Z-3 with his own crew and planned to destroy the rest of the bunkers, but he used their destruction to set up Shepard."

"You say the bomb was supposed to have been smuggled into the White House, Logan." Andreas shook his head. "That's almost unbelievable. Everyone who enters is searched thoroughly."

"Except you, Mr. President." Logan turned to Keller. "And you wouldn't insult the Vice President either, would you?"

"It's possible he could do it," Keller said cautiously.

"And if he brought it in piece by piece and Betworth sent a man in to assemble it later . . ."

"It's also possible he could have been instrumental in the other two attempts on my life," Andreas murmured. "Talk about an inside man. But you were too good, Keller. You made sure that every aspect of my life was impossible to penetrate without detection. They must have gotten nervous about getting caught and decided to go a different route."

"You believe us?" Logan asked.

"Shepard would take over the presidency if I was killed," Andreas said. "The presidency is the ultimate power, and Betworth has wanted it for years. And I'd judge Shepard a man who can be controlled by someone as clever as Betworth. Shepard takes over the presidency, has Matanza to blame for the assassination, and initiates a crusade against terrorism that immediately sends his approval rate soaring. In the meantime, Betworth is behind him pulling all the strings, with a nice little pocket of puppets in the FBI and CIA already in place. Matanza gets the glory, Shepard gets the presidency, Betworth gets the power." He grimaced. "And I get dead. I can't say I regard that as an acceptable scenario."

"It's supposition, sir," Keller said.

"Then I suggest you get on the phone and call your Secret Service people in charge of protecting Shepard and see if there's been any increase in contact between Betworth and Shepard in the last six months. I want a tap on Betworth's and Shepard's phones immediately. And get a tech van out to Betworth's place on the double to monitor and record any calls."

"The bomb first," Logan said, and then added politely, "sir."

Arrogant bastard. He *did* like him. "Start a search, Keller. But discreetly. Very discreetly. We don't want the son of a bitch to get suspicious and set it off ahead of schedule." He turned to Logan. "Satisfactory?"

"Splendid. Caution is good."

"I'm glad you approve. But it's what I'd have done anyway. What you've told me may be bull, and I'm certainly not disturbing the people of the United States with as little proof as you've given me. They've gone through too much already during these last years." He shook his head wearily. "And if we have to arrest Betworth and Shepard for this crime, it will be one more horror for them. They don't need their trust in their own government shaken."

"They don't need a bomb going off in the White House either," Logan said dryly.

"Anything else, sir?" Keller asked.

"Hell, yes, make sure you tell your men in the field to get my wife and children to a secure place." He headed for the door. "Now."

She could hear him behind her.

Alex shinnied up the tree and crawled to a nook cloaked in pine branches. It was daylight now, and she needed all the cover she could get.

Pray that no bird or animal would fly out of the tree and give her position away.

Don't make a sound.

Don't even breathe.

He was right below her.

No, he had moved on down the hill.

She was afraid to let out a sigh of relief. Stay here for a little while until she was sure she'd lost him.

Fifteen minutes passed.

Twenty minutes.

Twenty-five.

She climbed down from the tree.

Runne smiled.

The woman had turned and was circling back toward the bluff.

Perhaps she was in a panic and trying to reach the road.

Or perhaps she was trying to meet with Morgan.

Where the hell was he?

The anger and frustration had been growing in him for the last hour. He didn't know if he could wait for Morgan to show after he caught the woman. She'd hurt his pride, and that couldn't be tolerated. She needed a lesson, and he would give it to her.

He would slit her from belly to throat.

She couldn't hear him, but she knew he was close.

Her heart was beating hard, painfully, as she ran.

No use trying to be quiet now.

Run.

Too tired . . .

Keep running.

Her hand tightened on the branch she'd picked up after she climbed down from that last tree. It wasn't much of a weapon, but she was getting too exhausted. Soon she'd have no choice but to face him.

Not yet. The path that led up the bluff was just ahead. Morgan might be—

Her legs went out from under her.

Tackled!

He was on top of her, his hands on her throat, her mouth. "Shh."

She bit his hand and tried to swing the branch.

"Alex, dammit," he whispered.

Morgan.

She went limp.

Dead Aim

"Are you okay?"

"No." The tears were streaming down her cheeks. "I'm tired and cold and scared and that son of a bitch wouldn't give up. You took your time getting here."

He touched her cheek gently. "No supersonic jets from Guatemala City. I'm sorry."

"You should be." She tried to sit up. "Get off me. We have to hide. I don't know how far he is behind me."

"I do. We have a little time." He got off her but stayed on his knees beside her, his hands running over her body. "Christ, you're wet."

"I went through a couple streams. I thought it would kill my scent. It worked. Or maybe he can't smell as well as you can." He was drawing her into his arms. "Don't do that. I must feel like an icicle. I'll get you wet. I'm okay."

"You're more than okay," he said unevenly. "And this is for me, not you."

She didn't move. He was warm and strong and she wanted to stay there forever. Her arms tightened around him for a moment before she pushed him away. "No, after what I've gone through tonight I'm not taking any chances. We're going to stay alive." She got unsteadily to her feet. "Let's get out of here."

"You're about to collapse. You go to the side trail and hide there. I'll lead Runne up the bluff trail."

"Why?"

"I need him there."

"Need?" Her gaze searched his face. "Why not here?"

"Not now. Go and hide in the shrubbery."

"The hell I will. I don't know why the hell you want him up there, but I'm the one who'll get him there. He wants to catch me so bad by now he's probably salivating." She took the branch and erased their signs on the ground. "You wait in the shrubbery and then follow him." She dropped the branch and moved up the trail. "But don't take as long this time. Okay?"

"Alex, dammit."

She didn't listen. It was too difficult just putting one foot in front of the other. Get to the top of the bluff. She could make it.

It took her another five minutes to reach the top of the bluff, and by that time she was numb-weary. She moved toward a huge jagged rock and leaned against it.

Come on, Runne.

Come and get me. Bait for the trap.

He was coming.

She felt every muscle in her body freeze when she saw him appear at the top of the trail.

He was smiling with fierce satisfaction. "You've led me on a chase, you bitch."

"Because you're not as good as Morgan. He would have caught me in the first fifteen minutes."

His smile disappeared. "Look at you." He walked toward her. "How pitiful you are. Like my whore of a mother. Just a weak woman after all."

"Screw you."

"Bold words. Do you think Morgan is coming to rescue you?" He shook his head. "You're all alone. I killed him."

She froze. "You're lying."

He shook his head. "I killed him." He was only six yards away, and suddenly there was a knife in his hand. "So there's no reason to keep you alive. I can't tell you how much I'm going to enjoy killing you."

9:45 A.M.

"For God's sake, everything's going to hell, Betworth." Shepard's voice was panic-stricken. "I just got a call from Andreas at Camp David telling me to stay where I am. There's been an anthrax packet found in the Rose Garden.

Dead Aim

They've called in the CDC to make a search of the White House. They'll find it, dammit."

"Keep calm." He wasn't calm. His mind was flying in a hundred different directions. A search for anthrax? It was too damn convenient. "Was there any note claiming responsibility?"

"Hamas."

"Hang up. I'm calling to check."

"You don't have to check. It's all over CNN. I'm watching it right now. Set off the damn bomb before they find it."

"Listen, keep cool. We can handle this."

"This is your fault. I knew it would get out of control."

"All you knew was that you were scared to death to take care of Andreas up close and personal. Well, I fixed it for you. I made you a big man and now you've got to hang tough. Let me talk to Danley." When Danley was put on the phone, Betworth asked, "What do you know about this?"

"I called Jurgens as soon as I heard about it. He says it seems to be a legitimate anthrax scare. The CDC preliminary report confirms anthrax."

"It's too pat."

"Then why would Andreas call Shepard? Oh, who the hell knows? Maybe—shit!"

"What's wrong?"

"CNN . . . There was a big-ass explosion. Shepard's office, I think. Fire. Smoke."

Betworth switched on the TV set. He could barely see the White House for the haze of smoke. "I'll be damned." He suddenly started to chuckle. "Stupid blunderers. They set it off themselves." EMTs and firemen in bulky protective suits were running toward the White House. "Danley, in a few minutes they'll confirm the bomb was radioactive. Call Camp David and make sure Keller's following procedure and sending Andreas to Z-3."

"It's still a go?"

"I'm not stopping now. We've got a chance to win the whol

pot, and only cowards hesitate. Once Shepard's in power we'll be able to control any investigations. If there was a tip about the bomb, then they've cut their own throats by setting it off and destroying any evidence. If the anthrax was genuine, then Hamas and Matanza can fight over credit for killing Andreas. The confusion will only help us." He headed for the door. "I'm leaving now. If you can confirm that Andreas is boarding his helicopter and heading for Z-3, we'll proceed as planned. Notify Runne."

"The situation has escalated," Danley said on the phone. "Get in position, Runne."

"I'm in position. How long?"

"The President left Camp David five minutes ago. Fifteen minutes tops."

"I'll be ready."

Betworth's helicopter arrived five minutes later. Danley met him at the landing site and waved the helicopter off and away.

"He's on his way." Danley gestured to the bluff. "Runne's up there behind that rock. Here's the scenario. You and Shepard go forward to meet the President when the helicopter arrives. When Andreas goes down, you both hit the dirt. You wait for another shot—that will be mine taking out Runne. You get up and run to Andreas. Big grief scene for the benefit of the pilot and Keller."

"Fine. Except for one point. I want you to shoot me."

"What?"

"I'm going to crawl toward Andreas in a desperate attempt to save him. You shoot me. Everyone will assume it's Runne. A shoulder or arm wound. Nothing serious. Just enough to get me sympathy and a little glory. I may need it when I'm continually at Shepard's side after he takes office."

Dead Aim

"Whatever you say."

"And you'd better aim straight, Danley." He moved toward the bunker entrance. "Now, I'll get Shepard out of that hole and see if I can put a little iron in him. You start climbing that bluff."

"Here he comes," Betworth murmured as he watched the helicopter fly through the pass. "Keller's flying the chopper. Don't smile, Shepard. Look concerned. We have a national emergency here."

"I am concerned," Shepard said between his teeth. "I don't like things not to go as they're supposed to."

"Want to bail out?" Betworth asked. "This is the time. Say the word. Who wants to be the most powerful man in the world? You can go back and hide in your cave for the rest of your term and then retire quietly to the country."

"I didn't say I wanted to bail out. I just want him dead and all the unpleasant details—" He stopped as the door of the helicopter opened and Andreas appeared in the doorway. "Come on. Let's get it over with." He strode toward the helicopter. "This way, Mr. President. We have to get you inside and safe."

Andreas stepped to the ground. "You shouldn't have come out, Shepard. There's no telling what—"

A shot.

But Andreas was still standing, Betworth realized.

Dammit, Runne had missed.

Another shot.

Andreas was falling to the ground.

Finally.

"Hit the dirt," he shouted to Shepard. "The President's down." He dove for the ground. "Keller, for God's sake, do something. The President is—"

Keller wasn't moving to help Andreas.

And Shepard wasn't moving either. The Vice President

– 273 –

was crumpled on the ground a few feet from him. There was a small round hole in his temple.

Rage tore through him. Runne, that asshole. What fucking good did it do Betworth to kill the President if he killed Shepard too? All his plans blown by—

"Kill that son of a bitch, Danley!" he screamed. "Kill him now!"

Another shot.

Pain tore through his back.

Jesus. He'd told Danley not to hurt him. A shoulder wound . . .

Just enough to make him a hero . . .

He felt cold. He could taste the blood in his mouth.

He was dying, he realized incredulously.

"No!"

Logan, Galen, and Keller left the helicopter at a run, but Keller was the first to reach Andreas. "Are you okay, sir? I told you this was crazy. Why didn't you let me do my job?"

"Because I'm tired of sitting in that ivory tower and relying on everyone else." Andreas got to his feet and dusted off his pants. "If I'd had more hands-on interaction before this, maybe Betworth wouldn't have been able to take out those bunkers." He looked down at Betworth and Shepard. "Dead?"

Galen was kneeling beside Betworth and checking his pulse. "As a doornail." He glanced up at the bluff. "It's a really bad angle. He made a great shot."

"I never said I wanted them dead." Andreas's lips tightened. "Get Morgan down here."

Galen stood up and flipped open his phone. "Come on down, Judd. As usual, you've taken too much on yourself." He hung up and turned to Andreas. "I can't be sure he's going to obey your orders. He may take off. He's been a scapegoat before."

"So you've told me," Andreas said. "But that doesn't mean he has the right to arbitrarily kill the Vice President of the United States." He glanced down at Shepard. "And he took him out first. If there was to be an assassination, I'd have thought Betworth would have been the primary target."

"I'm sure Morgan had a reason," Logan said. "He's not a—"

"I'm here." Morgan was coming down the trail. "Stop making excuses for me, Logan. I can talk for myself."

"Be quiet, Morgan." Alex was trailing behind him. "Let him make excuses. You can use all the help you can get."

Morgan turned to Logan. "I know she shouldn't be here. She wouldn't stay on the bluff." He stopped in front of Andreas. "Any deal we make has to include a free pass for her."

"Deal? I don't make deals, Morgan."

"The hell you don't. As President you're the consummate deal-maker."

"I ordered Galen to tell you to eliminate a possible assassin on that bluff."

"And that's exactly what Galen told me."

"You weren't told to kill Betworth and Shepard. Keller could have arrested them and brought them to trial. That's the way we do things in this country."

"But that's not what you wanted. You didn't want the American people disillusioned with their government. They've gone through enough heartache lately. It might have taken years in court to convict them, and that would have been constant salt in the wounds."

"Is that what you told him?" Andreas asked Galen.

"I might have mentioned that you were a bit unhappy with the situation."

"No, he didn't," Morgan said. "It was pure intuition on my part. Intuition is a wonderful thing. Galen told me how after you'd located the bomb, you had it disarmed and then staged a fake explosion in Shepard's office. Now, intuition made me wonder why you did that. And then Galen told me you'd placed that phony call to Shepard so that you could tape any incriminating communication between him and Betworth. Why did you want to lure Betworth here? Why not just call out the Marines and round everyone up?"

"So you're saying you killed Shepard to help me out."

"I didn't kill Shepard or Betworth." He stared directly into Andreas's eyes. "It was Runne. You'll find the bullets came from his rifle. Wonderful shooting, wasn't it?" He smiled. "I couldn't have done better myself."

"I imagine that's true," Andreas said dryly.

"Of course, it was also Runne who answered his phone when Danley called and told him he was ready to take you out. But unfortunately he killed your true-blue CIA man, Danley too. You'll find his body on the bluff. Such a shame. But what can you expect when terrorists like Matanza send in their hired guns? You were lucky Keller was able to discover the plot in time to save the day."

"And what about Runne?"

"Why, didn't Keller track up there and surprise him from behind? I don't know how else Runne could have gotten that broken neck."

Andreas's gaze shifted to Alex. "You were there?"

"I was there."

"And you concur with Morgan's statement?"

She looked at Morgan and then slowly nodded. "The bullets came from Runne's rifle."

"And the two of you were just passing by, I suppose," Andreas said sarcastically. "My God, you look like you've been through a tornado."

"I feel like it." Alex took a step closer to Morgan in silent support. "But I couldn't have gone through it with anyone I'd trust more. You can trust him too, Mr. President."

"He doesn't have to trust me," Morgan said. "He can reel me in any time he decides he needs a patsy. I'll make myself available." He paused. "But not Alex. You clear her and she stays clean. That's the deal."

"You don't make deals for me," Alex said. "When are you going to learn that?"

Morgan ignored her, his gaze focused on Andreas. "I think you can arrange it so that you get what you want for the country. Shepard will have died a martyr's death. The country can always use another hero. Ask Alex." He smiled crookedly. "And you can use me, if you need to do it."

"I thought you were tired of being used," Alex said. "And I'm not letting that happen to you. I don't think he will either. So shut up and let him decide."

"Thank you," Andreas said dryly. "How nice to have a choice."

Alex smiled. "If I didn't trust you, I wouldn't give it to you. Right is right."

"She likes to use that phrase," Galen said. "But it's usually followed by a stubborn attack."

Andreas was silent, his gaze on her face. "It's a very good phrase." He turned to Keller. "You'd better go up to the top of the bluff again and make sure that no evidence is disturbed."

"Again?" Keller repeated.

Andreas nodded. "I have to commend you, Keller. I had no idea you were still fit enough to take down a murderer like Runne. You're quite the hero."

Keller smiled faintly. "I rose to the occasion, sir." He moved toward the path leading up to the bluff. "I'll make sure that everything is as it should be."

"I believe Morgan probably made everything tidy, but the area will receive intense scrutiny." He turned to Morgan. "And you should not be around for some time to come. Out of sight, out of mind."

Morgan nodded. "Whatever you say." He turned away and started up the path. "I left my rifle up there with Runne. I'll

Iris Johansen

just go up and get it and make sure Keller has the scenario right. I'll be right back."

Alex watched him climb. He was moving quickly, his gaze on the top of the bluff.

"It's going to take a little while to clear you, Ms. Graham," Andreas said. "We have to keep the Matanza guilt story in place if we're to keep this conspiracy from the public. Betworth managed to tar you with the same brush. We'll give it a while and then discover evidence of your innocence. But we will do it."

"I don't have any doubt you will. We've already agreed right is right. So you'll clear Morgan too."

Morgan had reached the top of the bluff. He was silhouetted against the sky, and he looked lean and tough and . . . alone.

Sweet Jesus.

"That's more difficult," Andreas said. "His past is considerably more tarnished. But we'll— Where are you going?"

She was streaking up the path after Morgan. "He's not coming back. He lied. He's been stung too many times to believe that— He thinks he's made a deal with you, dammit."

He was out of sight.

"Morgan, you come back," she shouted. "I'm not going to stand for this!"

She reached the top of the bluff. Keller was kneeling beside Runne, but Morgan was nowhere in sight.

"Where is he?" she asked Keller.

He nodded toward the north side of the bluff.

She ran to the edge.

No Morgan.

Her hands clenched at her sides as tears stung her eyes. "Don't you do this to me, Morgan. You son of a bitch, it's not *fair.*"

No answer. No sound.

No Morgan.

Epilogue

Trinidad

Her footsteps made no sound on the soft sand.

Yet she knew he was aware of her presence. He didn't look up from his canvas, but she could see the slight tension in the muscles of his back.

"You shouldn't have come, Alex."

She kept walking toward him. "How did you know it was me?"

"Your smell. I'd never forget your smell. Not if I lived to be a hundred and fifty."

"I'd never forget your smell either." She stopped beside him. "Though I might not be able to detect it from ten feet away."

"How did you find me?"

"Galen. It took him a while, but he finally located you. It would have helped if you hadn't moved around so much."

"You shouldn't have come."

"You said that before."

"It bears repeating. Andreas cleared you. Go on with your life."

"I am. I'm here."

"I may have to stay on this island for a long time. Andreas

has to be very careful about trying to clear me. There might be too many questions. And we've already discussed this isn't the kind of life for you."

"No, it's not. But I don't have a choice right now. It's where you are." Her voice was shaking. "And where you are, there I'll be. Make up your mind to it. You may not love me now, but you will. I'll see to it."

He didn't look away from the painting. "That's not the problem."

She stiffened. "That's the most bullshit statement of commitment I've ever heard. I deserve better."

"I'm not committing. Go home."

"The hell I will." She took his arm and twirled him to face her. "You listen to me. I'm here, and I'm going to stay here. I'm not going away because you think I'd be better off without you. You're stuck with me. I can live on an island. I can live on the run. I can live anywhere as long as I'm with you. If I get bored here, I can always go and help Melis rescue dolphins or something. Now, put down that paintbrush and let's go find somewhere to make love. It's been too long."

He looked down at her. "You won't go away?"

"No."

"Not ever?"

"Forget it. I'm here until hell freezes over. You've had it, Morgan."

A smile lit his face as he threw his paintbrush down. His arms closed around her. "Thank God."